Yanking her against him, ... handcuffs shut on the other wrist. "You're not going anywhere, Willow Tarata."

She pressed herself against Ramirez. The better to distract him.

His body reacted to hers instantly. Unfortunately, her body reacted, too.

His arms tightened on her. Wrapping his hand in her hair, he arched her back until his eyes filled her vision. His energy surrounded her, trying to drug her and pull her under. Focused on her lips, he lowered his head, stopping a breath away. She waited, unable to breathe.

His mouth parted, hovering just above hers. "'You have the right to remain silent.'"

She let a kittenish smile curve her lips. "I'm sure I couldn't be able to keep quiet."

"'Anything you say can and will be used against you in a court of law.'"

"I'd rather you be used against me."

"Stop it." His jaw tightened.

But she noticed he didn't push her away...

RAVES FOR *CHOSEN BY DESIRE*...

"4 Stars! This combo of magic, ancient Chinese scrolls, and dangerous passion adds up to plenty of fun."
—*RT Book Reviews*

"A fast-paced action thriller from the moment that Carrie questions why she is stealing the scrolls and never slows down as a mutual enemy craves what she took. [It is] fun to watch Max's agony of falling in love with a person he considers a lowlife academic crook. The return of the stars from the previous entry enhances an entertaining... taut thriller."

—Midwest Book Review

"Terrific...Another winner by this amazing author... Can't wait for the next in this series now."

—RomanceReviewsMag.com

"Perry not only does it again, but she does it one better... [she] leads her readers through a minefield of danger, passion, red-herring clues, and mystery. Deft at pacing and character development, the story unfolds like an intricate fan."

—BittenByBooks.com

"Very engaging...It's got a unique supernatural twist to it that creates an intense story line...surprisingly funny... I found myself laughing and smiling quite a lot through-out this book...the author develops every character well...I will definitely be checking out the rest of the Guardians of Destiny series."

—BookwormConfessions.com

...AND *MARKED BY PASSION*

"Sexy...[a] breezy writing style and steamy love scenes."

—Publishers Weekly

"Exciting and simply terrific. Original and inventive...[the] story is so exceptional that it can only earn the top rating."

—RomanceReviewsMag.com

"Get ready to stay up late, Kate Perry has written a fabulous blend of urban fantasy and romance...filled with unique mythology, exciting plot twists, and sizzling chemistry between its characters. I will be impatiently waiting for the next Guardians of Destiny novel."

—JEANIENE FROST,
***New York Times* bestselling author**
of *One Foot in the Grave*

"A sexy world of kick-ass action! You'll want to immerse yourself in [this] first in a thrilling new series, complete with a smoldering hero and the toughest, sassiest heroine around."

—VERONICA WOLFF,
author of *Sword of the Highlands*

"A fun, hip, and passionate romp...smart...The tension between the hero and heroine is hawt, hawt, hawt and compelling. Yum!"

—SisterGoldenBlog.com

"An entertaining, witty, and sensuous tale that is guaranteed to have you rolling with laughter and fanning yourself all at once...I found [Perry's] quirky sense of humor seeping through into the characters, making the book both steamy and hilarious."

—BookPleasures.com

"4 Stars! A great premise with an interesting but stubborn protagonist...Keep an eye on this author and series."

—*RT Book Reviews*

BOOKS BY KATE PERRY

Marked by Passion
Chosen by Desire
Tempted by Fate

TEMPTED BY FATE

KATE PERRY

FOREVER

NEW YORK   BOSTON

Copyright © 2010 by Kathia Zolfaghari
All rights reserved. Except as permitted under the U.S. Copyright Act of 1976, no part of this publication may be reproduced, distributed, or transmitted in any form or by any means, or stored in a database or retrieval system, without the prior written permission of the publisher.

Book design by Giorgetta Bell McRee

Forever
Hachette Book Group
237 Park Avenue
New York, NY 10017
Visit our website at www.HachetteBookGroup.com.

Forever is an imprint of Grand Central Publishing. The Forever name and logo is a trademark of Hachette Book Group, Inc.

Printed in the United States of America

First Printing: December 2010

10 9 8 7 6 5 4 3 2 1

ATTENTION CORPORATIONS AND ORGANIZATIONS:
Most HACHETTE BOOK GROUP books are available at quantity discounts with bulk purchase for educational, business, or sales promotional use. For information, please call or write:
Special Markets Department, Hachette Book Group
237 Park Avenue, New York, NY 10017
Telephone: 1-800-222-6747 Fax: 1-800-477-5925

Acknowledgments

Bear with me because I have a fair amount of gratitude to express, not to mention a whole lot of love. I'm warning you now: I may get mushy and sentimental. Brace yourself. If you can't stand it, just start reading the story—it's mush-free. Mostly.

First, the gratitude. A huge round of applause to...

My readers. You guys rock. Thanks for the unwavering support.

Matt, the kung fu cop, for explaining all things homicide to me. (Mistakes and/or embellishments are my own.)

Holly, and Latoya, and all of Team GCP.

Java Beach, both its crew and its patrons, for giving me an awesome workplace.

Now, the love.

For pouring more support, kindness, and affection on me than I knew existed, extra-slobbery smooches to...

Parisa	Veronica and Adam	Katie and Gail
Andre	Clara and Owen	Afra and Diego
Julie	Mom and Dad	Emilio

Phil	Dave and Kristen	Dawn and George
Scott	Malik and Kekoa	Jon and Barbara
Carin	Candace and Jerry	Jen

I'm truly blessed to have you all.

Legacy of the Guardians of Destiny

Centuries ago, in a time before man fought his wars with iron and steel, a group of monks lived in peaceful seclusion in a monastery in Southeast China. They studied nature and its wonders, ever fascinated with the world in which they existed. Joyfully, they welcomed anyone within their fold who showed similar interest and piety.

As time passed, man changed. Instead of coveting knowledge, man coveted power. Instead of revering earth and its bounty, man revered its riches.

For ages, the monks remained untouched by avarice and corruption, but eventually the chaotic world encroached on their tranquil one. Neighboring gangs besieged and battered them, for no reason other than to wreak havoc.

And so to protect their way of life, the holy men developed an art of war. As there were five elements in Chinese cosmology, they created five correlating fighting principles, documented in five scrolls. One scroll for each element: earth, fire, wood, metal, water.

Over time, the monks became so adept at harnessing the elements that they developed other abilities. Each element had its own set of powers, and each secret was recorded in the scrolls for future generations to learn.

Tales of the extraordinary leaked through the provinces, until they reached the ears of one particularly ruthless overlord.

Amazed, he journeyed to the monastery to begin his own study.

The monks were impressed by the man's seemingly pious mien, but one, Wei Lin, saw within the overlord's heart to the truth: the man coveted the sacred scrolls and their ability to unlock the mysteries of nature and man. To possess the scrolls was to possess unlimited potential for power.

To protect the world from the overlord's greed, Wei Lin stole the scrolls from the monastery and left under the cover of night.

For decades, he searched before he found five families worthy enough to guard them. One family for each scroll, led by men so virtuous they could resist the temptation to harness the powers for their own gain.

Wei Lin entrusted them with the scrolls, and blessed each man with a mark. Using the power of the elements, he bound the mark to each family, ensuring that it would be passed down, generation to generation, to the descendant bearing the truest heart—to the one soul worthy of being called Guardian.

Prologue

Twenty years ago, somewhere in New Zealand

A flute shrilled—one sharp note of warning.

Willow looked up from the piece of wood she was carving. Mama's flute. Their danger signal.

Dropping her knife and the half-finished tiger, she ran down the dirt lane, back to the little house they'd been living in for the past few months.

They'd lived there before—a long time ago. Mama said Willow couldn't really remember, that she was too young back then. But she remembered. She remembered it because back then Mama used to cry a lot.

Willow ran faster.

Her mother came out to the porch just as Willow rounded the corner. Mama's white-blond hair flew wildly around her head, and dirt streaked her clothes. Her eyes looked as wild as her hair.

"Come, Willow." Mama grabbed her arm and rushed

her through the garden and around the back of the house. "To the *tarata*."

Willow loved that lemonwood tree. Mama once told her they were found only here in New Zealand, that they were special trees for the Maori, like her. Even though they were called trees, they were really just big bushes, and that always tickled her.

Not today, though. Today all she felt was Mama's fear.

Mama was *never* scared. And that terrified Willow. "What's wrong?"

"The Bad Man is coming."

Willow gasped and stumbled on a rock. Mama said they had to move all the time because the Bad Man wanted them. She said he'd never stop until he found them, and when he did, he'd hurt them. Willow didn't understand why. Mama had said she didn't, either.

"Quick, Willow." Mama shook her arm. "You need to hide. He's almost here."

"How do you know?" She hadn't heard a car or anything.

"I can feel it," her mother said under her breath, like she was distracted.

"Because you're a Guardian?"

She nodded grimly. "And because I'm a woman."

"But—"

"No more questions, Willow. Now isn't the time." Mama stopped abruptly and parted the leafy bush. "Hide in the middle. Don't make a sound, Willow. Do you understand? Not one peep, no matter what you hear."

Willow nodded. She stared at the *tarata*. Usually she loved hiding in it, because when she came out, she smelled lemony like the leaves. Today she didn't want to go in. If she went in, she was afraid she'd never come back out, and she'd never see Mama again.

Her mother crouched down in front of her and held both her arms. "Listen to me, Willow. You need to hide. You're the next Guardian. You need to be protected. And you must protect this." From inside her shirt, her mama pulled out a rolled parchment.

The Book of Wood.

Willow knew all about it. She'd even seen it before. Mama never let her touch it, though.

She looked at her mother. "Let's bury it and run. We've always run before."

"The scroll is powerful. Even buried, it'll attract unwanted attention. And we can't run any longer. He just keeps coming." Her mother got that look she got sometimes, like she was seeing things in her mind. Sad things. "The only way to keep you and the scroll safe is to face him. Once and for all."

Something in her mother's voice scared her. "Can't you hide with me?"

"No, sweetheart. I have to face this." Mama soothed her by running a hand down her pale hair.

Willow noticed that her mother's hand was trembling.

"I need you to protect the scroll, Willow." She took Willow's hand, put the scroll in her palm, and closed her fingers over it.

The mark on her ankle burned for a moment. Willow wanted to scratch it, but her mother held her shoulders tight.

"Listen to me. You're the next Guardian. I've trained you. Everything you need to know is inside you, Willow. Practice, and don't doubt."

She nodded. "Yes, ma'am."

"If anything happens to me—" Her mother looked away for a moment, swallowing audibly. When she met Willow's gaze, her eyes were as fierce as Willow had ever seen them. "If anything happens to me, you know what to do. Just as we've practiced. You know where the papers and money are hidden; go away and hide so even I couldn't find you."

"But, Mama—"

"No." A hard shake, and then Mama pushed her into the bush. "You have everything inside you, Willow. Remember that."

Before Willow could say another word, she felt the swell of her mother's magic. It wrapped around her and the *tarata* that hid her, warm like a nest of blankets. She looked through the leaves. Mama still knelt on the ground, her eyes closed.

The branches creaked and began to shift, creating a solid cage around her. The leaves thickened, slowly blocking Mama from her sight. "*No.*"

Her mother opened her eyes and stared straight at Willow. Through the rustling of the leaves, Willow thought she heard "I love you, sweetheart," but the *rustling* was so loud she couldn't be sure.

"*No.*" Willow sobbed once more, and then pressed her hand to her mouth. Mama had told her to be very quiet. She could do that.

She sat there forever, leaning into the cradle of the branches. She'd just begun to drift off to sleep when she heard her mother scream.

Willow shot up to her knees, her heart pounding, the scroll clenched in her hand.

"Tell me where she is, Lani," the man said calmly, as if he were asking for a cookie. "Tell me where she is and I'll let you go."

"I told you, I sent her away. You can't think I'm that naive." Her mother laughed, but it wasn't like her usual laugh. It was hoarse and faint and there was nothing fun in it.

It scared Willow more than anything.

"No, you aren't naive. You are, however, weak." His voice changed. It sounded dark and evil, like the trolls in the story Mama had read to her once. "All the power you have, and you're still weak. Pathetic."

Mama screamed again.

Willow sat paralyzed. Mama needed her. But if Mama, who was so strong and brave, couldn't handle the Bad Man, then what could *she* do?

Keep the scroll safe.

She nodded. Mama wanted that. As much as she wanted to go kick the Bad Man, she had to do what Mama wanted.

Muffled sounds of struggle pulled her out of her thoughts. She huddled in a ball, trying to block the sounds out, trying not to hear her mother's groan.

The scroll hardened in her hand. Out of nowhere, she felt a jolt, like the time she stuck her finger in the electrical socket. Her mark burned—badly—and she felt like she was going to throw up.

Then it stopped.

And there was silence.

Willow stared at the scroll and knew the battle between her mother and the Bad Man had ended. Tears filled her eyes until she couldn't see anymore. But she could feel her mother's power pulsing inside her. *Mù ch'i.*

Only not her mother's anymore. Hers, now.

She dropped her head to her knees and let the tears fall. She didn't make a noise. She didn't have the energy.

Dark came and went, and the whole time she sat in a ball, afraid that if she moved, he'd find her. Morning crept through the thick leaves, and still she waited.

And waited.

Finally her mother's words came back to her. "*Just as we've practiced.*"

She reached out to the branches. Before she touched them, they parted, as if they knew what she wanted.

They did know, she reminded herself. She was the Guardian of the Book of Wood now. It was her destiny, her mother had told her when Willow was really little. It'd been her bedtime story for as long as she could remember: the tale of the monk who stole five elemental scrolls and marked five people he thought worthy to guard the scrolls against people like the Bad Man. The scrolls infused their Guardians with special powers to help keep them safe.

Her mother had been marked, and so was she. Guarding the Book of Wood was her job now.

Blinking back another round of tears, she crawled out of the bushes.

The house was before her, unnaturally still. She swallowed the urge to call out for her mother, and carefully—quietly—wove her way back to the house.

The door was open. Just like they practiced, she sent her senses out, but she felt nothing human. She slipped through the door.

A pair of legs was splayed on the floor. Her mother's legs.

Willow wanted to turn away, but she couldn't. Heart pounding, she followed the long legs up to the bared tummy. The couch hid her mother's face. It didn't hide the silver blade sticking out of Mama's chest.

She leaned closer. A throwing star, like the one Mama kept hidden in the drawer. A reminder of bad things, she used to say.

Willow swayed, grabbing the door. The wood cushioned her grip and radiated with calm energy. She drew it into herself, thanked it for its generosity, like Mama had taught her, and turned to leave. She had to dig up the getaway fund from its hiding spot.

But then something on the floor caught her eye.

Mama's flute.

Without thought, she hurried to grab it. The wood pulsed in her hand, in a way it never had before. She tucked it into the waist of her pants, comforted by its smooth feel. With one last glance at her mother, she ran.

Chapter One

Present day, San Francisco

It wasn't the black, moonless night. It wasn't the mis-shapen trees. It wasn't even the fog, creeping through the branches. But something *was* off.

"Totally off." Walking up the steep hill, Willow looked around with her senses. With *mù ch'i*. Her powers were more reliable than her eyes. She'd be less likely to be taken in by a setup.

The path through Buena Vista Park wasn't lit. She glanced up, wondering if the lamppost lights had burned out or been taken out.

"One guess for the right answer," she muttered, touching an old cypress tree as she passed. Peace flowed from her fingertips into her body.

She nodded. The oldest trees in San Francisco were right here—eucalyptus, cypress, and pine. They were the reason she picked the park for the meeting. Deep-rooted and full of life, it was perfect for helping her ground herself. Perfect for comfort. At least on most nights they would have been a comfort. Tonight, not even the ebb and flow of the trees' energy soothed her.

She kept her pace slow, alert. "Something's very off."

It was more than just tonight. She'd felt it ever since she arrived in the city last week.

Danger awaited her.

Common sense told her to leave town and avoid it, but what choice did she have? Six months ago, she'd read about a university professor who had been found dead in her office. With that, Willow knew she had to come to San Francisco eventually. He'd be attracted by the story—not because of the unusual death, but because the woman had been a historian who had a special interest in the Scrolls of Destiny.

It took all her willpower not to race to California and wait for the Bad Man to show up. Instead, she'd stayed in Paris and waited for the investigators she'd hired to report on any suspicious activity. She needed to be methodical about this—careful. She couldn't risk rushing it and messing up her chance to finally catch the Bad Man.

"The Bad Man," she said derisively. It galled her that she still hadn't learned who he was, or even his real name. He'd played such an intimate role in her life. He'd shaped her almost as much as her mother had.

Willow slowed her pace and her breathing, to control her heart rate. This was it, she could feel it. He was close—she just had to find him. After twenty years, she'd finally have justice.

It took six months before one of the investigators she'd hired caught a break: he claimed he'd found an informant who had knowledge of the Bad Man. But the informant would only speak with her face-to-face.

A trap set by the Bad Man? Likely. But what else could she do? She had to check it out. So she'd taken the first flight out to the West Coast.

And now here she was, hiking up a pitch-black hill at two in the morning.

"At least it's not the Golden Gate Bridge," she whispered to herself. That was where her informant had wanted to meet. She shuddered. Crossing all that steel would have been a bitch. Anytime she was around too much metal, it became difficult to perform. Metal chops wood, just like a child's Rochambeau.

Willow crested the hill. Ahead of her, two figures sat on a bench.

Her broadsword-shaped birthmark, the mark of a Guardian, stung. An internal warning system. One that had been clanging in alarm ever since she stepped foot in the city.

"At least here there are plenty of weapons." She touched the low branch of a tree and headed to the two shadows. They didn't move or acknowledge her presence.

She stopped. "Something is so wrong," she muttered. She let *mù ch'i* branch out to the two figures. The scroll's energy coursed through her, jagged and uneven.

Her mother had taught her that everything had energy—even plastic and other man-made materials had energy to some degree. Drawing on the energy of trees came naturally to the Guardian of the Book of Wood, but it took skill to read and manipulate energy from other sources. Skill she didn't have, because her mother hadn't been around to help her perfect her technique. Hence, the occasional fitful starts when she used *mù ch'i*.

She was better, though. But she wasn't delusional enough to think she could ever be as good as her mom.

Through the force of her will, *mù ch'i* mellowed into a smooth flow, extending to the figures on the bench.

But she felt nothing, which meant the two bodies ahead were dead. "Damn it."

The faint wail of sirens overrode the soft whisper of the wind in the trees. She paused, listening.

They were headed toward the park.

"Damn it." She hurried to the bodies, yanking her leather gloves on. The one on the right was the man she'd hired. Half his head was bashed in, but there was enough of him intact for her to ID him from the pictures she'd seen.

Always make sure you know who's working for you. She'd found that out the hard way.

She patted him down, while taking in the scene carefully. Staged. Because someone wanted to set her up? If the approaching sirens were any indication, the answer would be yes.

She took his wallet and slipped it into her pocket before turning her attention to the other guy. Presumably, the informant. He was less messy, with a thin line of blood trickling from a small hole in his head. Bullet, 9mm. Professional.

The sirens stopped abruptly.

They were here.

Through the trees, she caught flashes of red and blue lights. They'd probably parked at the top of the hill, at the park's east entrance.

"Which means they'll be on my ass in minutes," she said, transferring everything from the informant's pockets to hers.

A card fluttered to the ground. The wind grabbed hold, but just before it got lost in the night, Willow caught it and stuck it in her already stuffed pockets. Taking in the scene one more time, she turned and strode toward the copse of trees and bushes just beyond the scene. She stepped behind a five-foot-tall bush. Not tall enough to hide her five-ten frame, she let *mù ch'i* reach inside the plant and urge it higher until its branches provided enough coverage without obscuring her view.

She tugged off her gloves and touched her long hair. The white-blond was like a beacon in the night, but she never covered it. It'd become something of a calling card. Plus, it tied her to her mother in one more way. Just to be safe, she encouraged extra foliage to sprout in front of her.

Two cops huffed up the hill a moment later. It seemed they knew exactly where to find the bodies.

"Of course they did," she whispered, shaking her head.

More officers flooded the scene shortly after, including several plainclothes policemen. She watched as they cordoned off the scene with yellow police tape and began methodically recording their findings. It was a process she'd seen before, in different countries all over the world. Slight variations, some forces more inept than others, but pretty much the same procedures. Being in her line of work, it behooved her to be familiar with the way the police operated.

Her mark burned, sharp and insistent. Instinct made her turn her head to the left, just as another man crested the hill.

Her breath caught in her chest, and she had to force it out with a harsh exhale.

He walked to the scene with an air of authority. The officer in charge. Which meant he was Homicide, detective level. He wore a suit, no overcoat despite the bitter San Francisco wind that whipped through the city all year round. Even though it was past midnight, his clothing was immaculate. So was his dark hair, cut short and neat.

Willow couldn't see details, which frustrated her, but something about him was familiar, and for a moment, she was tempted to come out from hiding and walk to him.

"Ridiculous," she said under her breath. Standing at the edge of the scene, he took a small notepad and pen out of his inner suit pocket. He motioned to the first officers to arrive on the scene and asked them questions.

Too low to hear, damn it. She frowned, holding a branch to help calm herself. She knew what he'd be asking. When did they get the call? Had they disturbed the scene? Any witnesses found?

He finished talking to the two patrolmen and ducked under the police tape to inspect the bodies. Suddenly he knelt, laying a palm on the ground.

Willow swallowed a curse. Her boot print on the dirt.

He stood up and scanned the area. Sharp gaze—he probably didn't miss much.

And then he focused on the bush where she hid.

He couldn't see her. She knew he couldn't see her. But somehow she felt his gaze penetrating deeply—all the way to the space inside her that had been closed off for the past twenty years.

She didn't like it. Not one bit.

When he turned around and waved one of his minions over, Willow exhaled.

"Forget the cop," she muttered. "Time to move."

She had to examine what she'd taken and hope it'd lead her to something of value. Not that she was going to hold her breath.

Pulling her mother's wooden flute from her pants pocket, she backed out of the bush, silently so as not to attract any attention. As an extra measure of caution, she had the trees across the way rustle, drawing attention away from her.

She waited until she was a little distance away before she put the flute to her lips and blew a delicate, mournful tune in honor of the dead.

It was the night from hell, and only getting worse.

Homicide Inspector Rick Ramirez glared at the crime scene. Not much to go on so far. East side of Buena Vista Park, two victims, male. No witnesses. No signs of struggle. No ID on the victims.

Why should it be easy?

At least there was a footprint. A woman's shoe, based on the heel.

He crouched down to get a closer look. Women didn't murder just for the hell of it. Homicides with female offenders were typically in the context of domestic abuse, or as an act of desperation. Two men, one shot execution style and the other with a bashed-in skull? A woman wouldn't have been his guess.

Of course, all sorts of unusual things had been happening in the city the past year. Things he'd been hard pressed to explain. This barely rated on that scale.

A bush fifteen feet away rustled, seemingly without cause. Ramirez looked up, frowning. Something wasn't right. Still, to cover the bases, he signaled a couple of his men to investigate.

Odd. He scanned the area, feeling like he was being led astray somehow.

Out of the corner of his eye, he caught a glimpse of a figure. Tall, but obviously a woman. Enveloped in black, like the shadows that clung to her. Except for her hair, which shined a brilliant white even in the dark.

The same woman who made the shoe print? Instinct said yes. He took off at a run, trying to remain as silent as possible so he didn't alert her to the chase.

But as he rounded the bend, she was gone.

How could she be gone? He scowled into the night, looking behind the trees and bushes.

Nothing.

"Damn." He raked a hand through his hair. Cursing again, he headed back to his team. The sooner he wrapped up, the sooner he could go home and get some rest.

As he made it back to the scene, he heard the faint whisper of a tune. Like a flute—soft and sad—carrying on the wind.

Chapter Two

R<small>ICKY</small>."

Ramirez continued tapping the keys on his laptop. Only his partner called him that. But then his partner got shit about his own name—James Taylor—all the time. Ramirez figured Taylor was allowed to have fun at someone else's expense now and then.

Of course that didn't mean he had to respond. No one else dared call him anything other than *Ramirez.* Or the occasional *Rick,* shortened from Ricardo. And he preferred it that way.

Taylor's chair creaked as he spun around to face him. "Ricky, you hear me?"

Rick continued to ignore his partner and pecked at a couple more keys. He'd come back directly to the office, despite the fact that he felt like his eyes were abraded with sandpaper from lack of sleep. Murders that weren't solved in the first forty-eight hours tended to remain unsolved. He didn't have the luxury of downtime. Besides, he'd wanted to note his impression of a tall woman with white-blond hair.

"Ricky, your grandma's on line two."

Groaning, Ramirez leaned back and rubbed the bridge of his nose. "Can't you take a message?"

"You know she's relentless when she wants to talk to you. I don't want to risk a curse." Taylor crossed himself. "With a witchy grandma who practices voodoo, no wonder you're so straitlaced."

"She's a healer, not a witch. And I'm not straitlaced."

Taylor laughed. "My friend, if Houdini had been bound as tight as you, he wouldn't have escaped."

That wasn't true. Yeah, while working, he followed the rules. The rules were rules for a reason. You went by the book or there was chaos, and no one could exist in chaos.

And lately he was all about work. For a Homicide inspector in San Francisco, there was no such thing as downtime. But in the past year, his caseload had been especially heavy—and not with typical cases. They'd been increasingly bizarre and unsolvable, starting with Jesse Byrnes's murder last year, and continuing with the two bodies this morning. He'd include Dr. Leonora Hsu's death in that list, but he'd only consulted on the case because his friend Carrie had found the body, and the cause of death had been ruled natural, anyway. Although, death because one's blood completely solidified didn't fall under "natural" in his estimation.

The Byrnes homicide had a clear resolution, as well—there was irrefutable evidence against the perpetrator, Paul Chin, including weapon and motive. Chin, having fled the country, was still at large. Only Ramirez couldn't shake off the feeling that the crime scene had been off—like something more had happened there than was apparent.

Just like today's scene.

It was a sensation in his gut. His grandmother would call it *el sexto sentido*—the sixth sense. He chalked it up to years of experience in Homicide.

So when his gut told him there was something similar between today's scene and the Byrnes homicide, he listened. Even if it made absolutely no logical sense.

"Hell." He raked his hair back and opened a new e-mail to his contact at the state department to make sure no one by Chin's description had reentered the country. He'd also run a check to see if there were any women wanted with long white hair. A long shot, considering how easily hair could be manipulated.

"Ricky, answer the phone, or I swear I'll make your life hell when your granny gives me hives." Taylor pushed his belly out of the chair. "I'm going home to May. Maybe she'll make me breakfast in bed. Pancakes."

"May?" He snorted in disbelief. In his opinion, May was scarier than his *abuelita*. She ruled his partner with an iron skillet. Though his partner—not to mention his partner's stomach—was happy to be ruled by her.

"She will when I tell her I want to use her body as my plate." He winked and shrugged his suit coat on. "See ya later. Don't forget to answer the phone."

Shaking his head, he reached for the receiver and pressed line two. "Inspector Ramirez."

"*Hijo,* I had a vision."

He groaned. "Lita, can't this wait until I get home? I'm leaving shortly."

"My vision was about you, *hijo.*"

Something in her tone made goose bumps rise on his skin.

Ridiculous. He shook himself. He was just tired. If he'd had a few hours sleep, her pronouncement wouldn't have fazed him. It wasn't as though it was unusual for her to have *visions.* "Lita, I'm coming home now. Maybe you can tell me after I have some sleep."

There was silence on the other end of the line. Then she said, somewhat ominously, "I'll see you when you get home."

Great. He hung up and closed his laptop. Now he not only had two dead bodies to deal with but a portentous Latina grandmother. The bodies had to wait—his *abuelita* wouldn't.

Ramirez was so tired, he drove home with special care. Fortunately, he lived minutes from the station, at the other end of Bryant Street in the Mission.

He'd grown up in the Mission, but back then, it hadn't been the fashionable party district it was now, dotted with hip restaurants and bars. Back then, the Mission had been the city's slum. He and his grandmother had lived in a tiny apartment, with windows that didn't open and carpet that reeked of cat piss. He'd slept on the couch in the living room and Lita had the bedroom, which she also used as her office—her term. When he was a kid, he'd called it the voodoo room.

Not to his *abuelita*'s face, of course, though she probably knew. But the opaque jars of herbs—and other things best left unidentified—looked like something out of a horror movie.

Tools of a *curandera,* she always said.

Some people thought a *curandera* was nothing better than a witch doctor, but as skeptical as he was about everything, Ramirez knew better. Elena Ramirez was a gifted healer of physical ailments. Some people claimed of spiritual ailments, as well.

He wasn't sure he believed in the woo-woo aspect. He was too grounded for that. But he had great respect for his grandmother as a healer. Her knowledge of herbs—and people—was vast.

Vast enough, and sought after enough, to support him as a kid. He'd done what he could to help out, especially once he was old enough to contribute.

There was an open spot on the street a couple houses down from his. He parked and headed home.

Fifteen years ago when he'd bought the house, it'd been a dump. The first thing he'd done was remodel the lower level into an apartment for Lita, complete with a storage room for her herbs, a large sunny bedroom, with windows that opened, and a lush garden out back. He lived in the two stories upstairs, close enough that he could watch over her without stepping on her independent toes. She was spry, but she was in her eighties, and he was a realist.

Lita was in the backyard, shovel in hand, kneeling in a bed of dirt, when he got home. Just where he thought she'd be. Ramirez let himself into the side gate and walked up the stone path he'd laid for her. "Lita, I wish you'd let me hire a gardener for you."

"My plants are my babies," she said without looking up. "I'd no sooner have someone else care for them than I would have hired a babysitter for you."

Plants were different than children, and she was

decades older now, but he knew better than to point out either fact.

"You look tired, *hijo.*"

He smiled faintly as he unbuttoned his coat and sat on a stone bench. "How would you know? You haven't looked at me yet."

She glanced at him for a brief moment, her gaze piercing, before returning to her weeding. "I don't have to look to know, Ricardo."

She only called him by his name when she was worried. Great. She hadn't had a vision about him in a long time, but the last time she'd made him wear a sachet with some foul-smelling herbs around his neck. She'd insisted that it was going to save his life. The guys at the station hadn't let him live that one down for months.

The sachet *had* saved his life, however. In apprehending a homicide suspect, the man pulled out a knife. Ramirez would have been stabbed in the heart; except as he moved, the herb pack flew out and hit the perp in the eye, throwing off his aim. Ramirez had ended up with only a scratch along his ribs.

But that was just a fluke.

He sighed, wondering what he was going to have to wear this time. He hoped whatever it was, it wouldn't make him reek. Or smell girly. "Aren't you going to tell me about your vision? It had to have been important for you to call me at work."

Lita said nothing. The *schtck-schtck* of her spade scraping against hard dirt resonated between them.

Closing his eyes, he waited. There was no rushing her, even when he hadn't had sleep in over thirty hours.

"The white witch is coming."

He reopened his eyes.

"The white witch is coming," she repeated. "In her heart is darkness."

For some reason, *white witch* made him think of the woman skulking away from the murder scene last night. He pictured her tall form and long, billowing hair, and he tensed.

"Terrible darkness and sorrow." Lita's eyes filled with tears, as if she felt this so-called witch's pain. "But you have to trust that she is good."

Good? In his gut, he knew she had something to do with the two deaths.

"She *is* good, underneath," Lita said, as if she had heard his thoughts. She stared at him with searing intensity, her knuckles white around the spade's handle. "Promise you'll have faith in her."

Faith. That wasn't something he'd ever subscribed to. It implied that you trusted something intangible— something that didn't exist. Elena believed in God. Ramirez had been raised Catholic, too, but he'd only ever seen religion as a means for people on power trips to control the weak.

His grandmother knew it, too. It'd been a contentious topic between them for as long as he could remember. But when it came to her visions, she believed implicitly. She pointed the tool at him. "You must trust fate, Ricardo—"

"Fate is what we make it."

"—because your fates are entwined."

That he could believe. "Because she's tied to my current case."

"Because she's tied to your soul."

He scrubbed a hand over his eyes. "Lita, I'm tired. Can this wait until later?"

She grumbled under her breath in Spanish. She always reverted to her native language when she was upset. Then she shook her head and tried to get up. "This cannot wait. This is life or death. If you don't have faith in her, your heart will be lost. *You'll* be lost."

He stood and helped her up by the elbow. He'd be lost if he didn't solve another case. The captain was breathing down his neck about the number of unsolved murders on his plate. But the only thing he needed right now was his bed, not a debate. "I'll take it under consideration, Lita."

"So stubborn." She clutched his arm, her grip surprisingly strong. "I worry, *hijo*. You see only black and white, but sometimes the two mix and form shades of gray. Not everything is clear-cut, especially your white witch."

"She isn't *my* white witch." Yet. "But I promise to think about what you said."

His grandmother watched him with that gaze that saw everything. "Thinking is not the same as believing. In this, you need to believe."

He believed, all right—that the white-haired woman was knee-deep in murder.

Lita threw her hands in the air. "*Ay, por Dios.*" Shaking her head, she wandered into her apartment, muttering to herself.

Ramirez waited until she was inside before ascending the back stairs. He loved his grandmother with his whole heart. There was nothing he wouldn't do for her. But when she got one of her ideas in her head, his frustration knew no bounds.

He let himself into his house. The back door opened to

the light, airy kitchen. The first level also had a large living room, his media room, and a bathroom. Upstairs was the master suite and a spare bedroom and bath.

Ramirez locked the door and trudged up to his room. He'd done much of the remodeling himself, which meant it'd taken him forever. Usually when he came home, he felt a sense of peace and cleanliness. Today he felt nothing but fatigue.

Undressing, he only put his clothing away by force of habit. He took a moment to brush his teeth—another habit—and splashed water on his face. His limbs heavy, he pulled the heavy drapes, which he'd bought specifically for the times when he didn't get to sleep before dawn, and climbed into bed.

It took him longer than he expected to fall asleep, Lita's white witch prominent in his thoughts. But finally he dozed off, the sad strains from a flute echoing in his mind.

Chapter Three

Swirling the cognac in the tumbler, he eyed the liquor. One-hundred-forty-year-old Louis XIII—one of the finest cognacs in the world. But he couldn't enjoy it, because it reminded him of Lani's eyes.

Frustration gnawed at him, dark and roiling, just like it always did when he thought of her. Ungrateful bitch. He'd offered her the world—*his* world. All he'd asked for was that she share hers. But she'd thrown it back in his face. She'd withheld the most important part of herself from him: the powerful part. The Guardian part.

Then she ran away. Bad enough, made worse when he found out she was pregnant.

His child. His daughter.

Not for the first time in thirty years since he'd discovered her existence, he wondered about her. He had reports, the occasional blurry photo, but it wasn't the same as knowing her. Lani took that away from him.

He threw the crystal across the room. The sound of it shattering should have brought some satisfaction but didn't.

"Really, Edward. I know you have more money than God, but Baccarat crystal is fine enough for respect even from you. Not to mention that I'm sure the hotel will take exception to destruction of their property, no matter how much you're paying for this suite."

He glanced at Deidre. "A glass is easily replaced."

"Are you insinuating that I'm disposable, too, darling?" She stirred from where he left her limp on the couch, stretching her alabaster limbs with a feline purr. "It certainly didn't seem that way half an hour ago."

He gazed down her naked body, at the bite marks he'd left. "You have your uses."

She laughed. "My connections or my charms? Or perhaps both?"

It was through Deidre's connections that he was able to track Willow. It galled him to know he'd spent twenty years pursuing her with no results. But it made him proud, too—his daughter obviously had something of him in her if she could successfully evade him for two decades.

Yes, Deidre had proven to be useful in more ways than one. He stared at her now. "Come here."

A knowing smile curved her mouth as she ran her hand down the center of her torso and between her legs. "Is this what you want?"

"No."

She arched her brow, but made no move to get up. "You're thinking about your plan, aren't you? You took care of her investigator and the mole, didn't you?"

"Of course."

"Then it's all in motion. It's only a matter of time until you catch her."

Yes. He just had to be patient a little while longer.

"It's a brilliant plan, darling." Deidre slithered over to him and knelt in front of him.

"Don't you mean *your* plan was brilliant?"

Smiling, Deidre rewarded him by wrapping her hand around him and squeezing. "I *did* come up with it, didn't I?"

Yes, she did. It annoyed him, but he only cared that it was successful. At this point, he'd use any means possible to bring Willow to his side.

He'd recognized that Deidre was good for a lot more than her sexual talents as soon as he'd met her at a mutual acquaintance's soirée in Milan. Her connections alone made tolerating her worthwhile.

And so far, Deidre's scheme seemed to be working. Willow had been lured by the prospect of information on him. The next step was to set her up so she was wanted by the police. Then he'd isolate her from everything she held dear, cut off so severely from everything and everyone that she'd have no choice but to turn to him for help.

"I just wish I understood what this woman means to you, darling." Deidre studied him. "Any other woman would be perturbed by the competition."

"But you're not any other woman, are you?" He was surprised Deidre hadn't bluntly asked who Willow was. It wasn't like her to beat around the bush. However, she was smart—she knew how important catching Willow was to him. She wouldn't jeopardize her position with something like jealousy. Deidre fancied herself the next Mrs. Rodgers-Dynes. He had no problem encouraging that—for as long as she proved helpful to him. If her plan worked, he might even reward her.

If it didn't...

She eyed him as if she could read his thoughts. She sat up, reaching for another glass and the decanter on the side table next to him. She poured him a generous finger of liquor and put it in his hand. "Relax, darling. I'll take care of you."

Closing his eyes, he took a sip and relaxed back against the chair, picturing the look in Lani's eyes as he drained the life from her body. He had taken her life, and soon he'd take her daughter.

Chapter Four

Willow woke up, feeling the pull of cypress trees. They resonated differently than other trees, like the ancient sequoias up north or the lemonwood hedges back home. Resilient and flexible, willing to adapt.

Even though it was still dark outside, she rolled out of bed and pulled on her running clothes. She took a moment to hold her scroll like she did every morning, to feel its familiar power flow through her. In it, she could feel echoes of her mother.

Walking out of her rent-by-the-week motel room, she let her senses stretch into the shadows. Nothing waited for her, but she knew better than to relax. She wasn't in the worst neighborhood in San Francisco, but Broadway Street catered to a certain type of male clientele. A lone woman on the street could be taken as fair game, and she didn't need that kind of trouble.

Slowly she began to jog, letting her body warm up. She wasn't entirely familiar with the city, but she knew exactly where to find the trees.

She headed there. Around the Marina and through the Presidio.

She ran along the bluffs, aware of the small groups of homeless people camped in the sparse copse of trees, until she found a secluded spot. She let *mù ch'i* reach out to the trees and, feeling welcomed, sat cross-legged between two large cypresses.

Setting her hands on the ground, Willow felt the roots beneath her, grounded and bracing. She closed her eyes and let her energy flow out.

The trees accepted her. She breathed deeply, trying to let herself meld into the ebb and flow of their energy, the way her mother had shown her. But, like always, she didn't feel the total connection—not the way she had when her mother guided her.

Focusing her will, she tried harder, but the trees resisted. Distantly she heard the shudder of leaves. And then she was pushed out of the flow of their life force.

She exhaled in anger, opening her eyes. Instead of feeling infused with fresh energy, she felt like she'd gone ten rounds with a Samoan.

Frustrating. She wished she were more complete in her training. She remembered the smoothness with which her mother practiced her art.

She wanted that for herself.

As it was, it felt like part of her was missing. And if that wasn't aggravating enough, she could sense the missing part just beyond her reach—like if she just tried harder, she could grasp it. Only no matter how hard she tried, it still remained out of reach.

She pulled the flute out and began a slow, peaceful tune her mother used to play to calm her down. Today it made her feel more sad than settled. She felt like she was letting her mom down, in more ways than one.

Sighing, she put the flute away and unwound her legs to make her way back to the motel.

Motel was overstating it. It was a dump. Calling her room threadbare was generous. But it was cheap, and the other tenants kept to themselves.

Mostly. Except for the woman two doors down who always wanted to chat.

Willow shook her head. She wasn't a chatterer. Most people got the message, eventually, but the woman two doors down was relentless.

Willow took care to walk noiselessly down the hall to her room. She slipped the key into the lock and twisted.

The tumbler made a soft click as it unlocked.

"Shit." She hurried to open the door and duck inside.

Behind her, a door opened. "You're up and at 'em early this morning."

Too late. She dropped her head, wanting to just slip inside and shut the door behind her. But for some reason, she couldn't ignore the woman. Latent manners rising to the surface? Whatever it was, it was damn annoying.

"I thought I heard you go out, but you sneaked out quicker than I could get out of bed and pull my robe on."

Sighing, Willow turned around.

"Oh, you went for a run." The woman leaned on her cane in the doorway. She looked rough, like she'd had a hard life accented by alcohol and drugs. Her hair stood on end, the bleached strands brash against the dark roots. She looked close to sixty, but she could easily have been thirty. "I used to run, but now I've got a bum leg."

Willow glanced at the cane but said nothing.

"You can't tell now, but I used to dance, too. I loved to dance." Her eyes went dreamy, probably remembering a better time.

Willow could relate, and that made her feel uncomfortable. "I need to clean up."

The woman came back to herself, her smile slipping a little. "Of course. Silly me, keeping you here when you're probably getting cold."

Willow felt like she'd kicked a puppy, but she wasn't here to socialize—she was here to find the Bad Man. She retreated inside her room, said "Good-bye," and closed the door before the woman could make a peep.

Stripping out of her clothes, she showered, got dressed, and put on a modicum of makeup. She straightened her room, dumped everything she'd poached from the two bodies on the bed, and went through it. Again.

Her cell phone rang. She picked it up and looked at the screen. It was Morgan, her business partner since they met almost eleven years ago, although Morgan often claimed they were more like sisters, having gone through so much time together over the years. Willow had no idea what having a sister was like, but if they were at turns irritating and endearing, then, yes, Morgan would be hers.

Willow already knew the background on the man she'd hired, but Morgan would have answers about the other guy. She answered the phone. "What have you got?"

"I miss you, too. It's delightful hearing your voice after all this time."

The sarcasm in Morgan's voice was so familiar, Willow instantly felt better. Not that she'd tell Morgan that. "Are you going to tell me what you found, or do we have to have tea and crumpets first?"

"You're so uncivilized. Good thing I love you." The light tapping of her fingers on the keyboard filtered through the line. "I ran the driver's license number you e-mailed me last night."

"And?"

"Joel Rocco. Six feet, one hundred ninety pounds, rents an apartment in Daly City. Average amount of credit card debt, drives a late-model Buick. One ex-wife, pays her a pittance in alimony. No children. He works as a bouncer for several clubs in San Francisco. Pretty typical, really."

A typical guy didn't get executed. "No criminal record?"

"He's clean. And before you ask, yeah, I checked everything, even my underground sources."

"He was killed. He can't be completely clean."

Morgan cleared her throat. "I hesitate to mention this, but did it occur to you that he was killed because of you?"

"Of course that occurred to me." In fact, it was more than likely. She was being manipulated—she was certain of that. There was more going on than she knew. That drove her mad, but if she wanted to catch the Bad Man, she had to play his game. She just had to make sure she played it smarter than he did.

"Jesus Christ. And you're not worried?" Morgan asked. "Because, I've got to tell you, I'm pretty freaked out over here. I have a bad feeling about this. I think you should come home."

By home, she meant Paris, where they first met and were still based. But Willow shook her head. "You know I can't."

"Well, will you promise to be extra careful?" She

sighed. "What am I saying? Of course you won't be careful. You'll take crazy risks and then rely on me to bail you out when things go bad."

"I'm not going to take risks." Willow picked up the business card. Black, with glossy red script: *Bohemia.* She'd looked it up—it was a club somewhere off Market Street. She bet Rocco worked there.

What were the chances the club had anything to do with the Bad Man? Miniscule. Most likely, Rocco was only after the cash she was offering for information. A lot of people came forward with *information,* but no one had actually given her anything that checked out. She was as clueless about the Bad Man's identity as she'd ever been.

But this was the closest thing to a lead she had, and she wasn't going to rule anything out until she'd checked. She flicked the card with her fingertip. "Morgan, I think I feel like going dancing tonight. There's a club in town that is killer."

"Only someone who's seen you in action would know how scary that statement truly was. Send me the club's name and I'll get you information."

"Thank you."

"I just want to state, for the record, that this reeks of a trap."

Yes, it did. "What choice do I have?"

"Plenty, you just refuse to see them. Look for my e-mail."

Ending the call, Willow gathered everything from her bed and returned it to the rickety dresser drawer that served as her filing cabinet. She rested her mother's flute next to the scroll.

It rolled forward, over the photo she'd tucked away in front. She withdrew it and held it up.

She'd found the picture among some paperwork hidden with her mother's getaway fund. In it was a man she'd never seen before. He had dark hair and piercing gray eyes that had made her skin crawl.

"The Bad Man." She didn't know it for sure, but inside she was positive.

If only she could ID him, but he was like a phantom. No one recognized him. No one knew who he was. Not even Morgan could dig up any intelligence on the man, and Morgan could move mountains with her computers.

Willow returned the picture back to its spot. She'd find him. She had to find him. He had to be brought to justice, and she wanted to be the one to do it.

Which meant she was going clubbing tonight. To Bohemia. Because as of right now, that was the only clue she had, as meager as it was.

Willow sauntered down the street, wearing tight black pants, a black halter top, and high-heeled boots to fade into the crowd while at Bohemia.

No one had to know that it'd been over a year since she'd been in a club. The last time, she'd gotten her man, of course. She hoped she'd be equally successful this time and find something that'd lead her to more information about her quarry.

She checked the time. Eleven, on the dot—the perfect time for reconnaissance at a club. Before eleven, there weren't enough bodies to provide coverage, and after, people were too drunk to provide any answers.

Tonight she was determined to get answers.

The queue outside the door was long, held back with a velvet rope. Without regard for it, she strode up to the bouncer.

He looked much like Rocco, muscle-bound and bald—only alive. As he looked her up and down, a smile curved his lips. "You want in, baby?"

She tipped her head and offered him a coy smile in return. The less she said, the less memorable she'd be.

That was the trick—being forgettable. Look good enough to fit in, but not so good you stand out. Which is why she wore all black. A person wore black to be invisible in a city. She'd pulled her hair back into a ponytail high on her head, sleek and tight.

"I want in, too," he said as he unhooked the rope. "Maybe later?"

Maybe not. But she let her smile heat up—just a little—and sashayed past him, into the club.

The relentless beat of music pounded her the moment she stepped in. She stopped next to the coat check to take inventory.

The DJ booth sat elevated to the left beyond the bar. A bank of occupied booths lined the right wall. One packed dance floor in the middle, three bartenders, half a dozen waitresses taking and delivering drink orders, and four discreetly located bouncers hugging the corners of the room. The hallway in the back had a steady stream of traffic, probably to the restrooms.

She headed to the bar, which was always the best place to gather information. A barstool cleared and she slipped onto it.

A moment later, one of the bartenders leaned in front of her. "What can I offer you, sexy?"

Not what you want to offer me. Willow smiled demurely. "Gin and tonic."

"Got it," he said, visibly disappointed.

The bartenders were all handsome by most women's standards, with pretty-boy looks. They had to be used to getting any woman they wanted.

But she wasn't most women. Pretty looks didn't do it for her. She liked dark. And rugged. And forbidden.

Like the cop at the crime scene.

She frowned. Why did he come to mind? Even if she were in a different line of work, cops couldn't be trusted. They were supposed to be the good guys, but in her experience, the ones who weren't in league with criminals were only concerned about where their next donut was coming from.

But the cop at the crime scene was different. There'd been something about him. The crime scene had been bustling, but he'd stalked on the periphery, separate from everyone else. She felt a pang. It was how she lived her life: on the periphery.

Flipping her ponytail over her shoulder, she pushed the thought away. As if she'd ever have any kinship with a cop. Nor would she get involved with one. Not in this lifetime. Not with her past.

"Here ya go." The bartender handed her the drink, letting his fingers touch hers. "On the house."

She raised her eyebrows, resisting the urge to wipe her hand on her pants. She pretended to take a sip. "Nice."

"I am." His grin was all wolf. "I haven't seen you in here before."

"It's my first time."

"A virgin. You came to the right guy for your first

time." He leaned on his elbows, his necklace dangling out from his shirt. "I'll be gentle, but only if you want me to be."

Willow barely resisted rolling her eyes. But she wanted information, and this idiot wanted her. Using him was a no-brainer. "A friend of mine works here and told me to check it out. He thought I'd like it."

"Who's your friend?"

"Joel Rocco," she said, watching him covertly for his reaction.

"Rocco's your friend?" His gaze became speculative, dipping to the deep vee of her halter. She didn't have to be a Guardian to read the sexual thoughts zooming through his head. "Why didn't you say so?"

He didn't know Rocco was dead yet. If he'd known, he wouldn't be thinking sex. Deciding to play along, she leaned forward—just a little—to improve his view. "Would it have made a difference if I had?"

"Yeah. I would have taken you straight back." He smiled, oily and lascivious. "If you wait for my break, I can take you then. Technically, employees aren't supposed to fraternize with the patrons, but I know a dark corner."

She was sure he did. Instead of telling him to shove it, she smiled encouragingly. She had no idea what he was talking about, but she knew it was significant. And if she couldn't go *straight back* on her own—wherever the hell that was—she needed him.

But first... "Is Rocco around?" she asked, fully aware that he couldn't be.

"He was supposed to be on, but I heard he didn't show up." The pretty boy ran a finger down her arm. "His loss, my gain."

"When is your break?"

"Half an hour."

"I'll wait for you. Over there." She nodded to the other end of the bar, next to where the waitresses picked up their drinks. The better to overhear gossip. It was a good place to watch everything that was happening.

Which wasn't much.

Twenty minutes into her watch, she spied a tall man talking to one of the waitresses. He was thin but muscular, shown off by a sheer white shirt, unbuttoned halfway down his hairless chest. His pants were tight, leaving nothing to the imagination. A Rolex glinted on one wrist, and a thick gold bracelet shackled the other.

Rich and entitled. It was in the way he moved—in the way he talked to the waitress. The owner? Probably.

The waitress scurried away and he surveyed the crowd. Willow eased back into the shadows and pretended to take another sip. She was going to talk to him. But not yet. *Not before I find out what* straight back *means,* she thought.

Hopefully, it wasn't just the storeroom where the staff got it on with patrons.

She didn't think so. It felt bigger. It felt like where she needed to be to get answers.

The proprietor glanced at his watch and strode to a side entrance she knew was locked. He pulled out a set of keys, unlocked it, and went through.

It took him ten minutes to come back. With him was a man in a long black coat. Average height. Dark hair, probably brown. Expensive clothes—obviously custom-made, noticeable even in the darkness of the club. The two of them headed to the long hallway.

The owner was no one important, but this new dark-haired man made her edgy. He seemed familiar and foreign at the same time. She reached out with *mù ch'i,* hoping to place him and settle her muddled feelings.

Suddenly the man stopped. He turned around slowly, looking around the club.

The Bad Man.

Her breath caught in her chest, and she pressed back into the shadows, as deeply as she could go. His features were distorted in the alternating flashing lights and darkness. She could be wrong. She could be projecting. She wanted him so badly.

She shook her head. She wasn't. It was him.

He looked around the club one more time before the tall man gestured to the back. Nodding, he continued to follow the proprietor.

She had to get back there. She looked at the time. Ten more minutes before the bartender's break. She was tempted to go back there on her own, but she didn't want to blow her chance of getting in.

He'd felt her probing. How could that be? She stared at the spot where he'd stood, trying to understand who he was. She'd never considered it, but maybe he had some sort of power. He'd killed her mother, after all. Her mother had been strong, both physically and as a Guardian. Was he stronger?

It didn't matter. She narrowed her eyes. She was going to exact justice, even if it meant her own destruction. Failure wasn't an option.

"Ready, sexy?"

She turned as the bartender slipped his arm around her

waist. She stood up and started to move, which caused his arm to drop. "Let's go."

"Eager, huh?" He hurried to keep up with her. "I like that."

Eager to see what the Bad Man was up to. She let the bartender lead her down the hallway, like this was his idea. The restrooms were to the right. Several other doors lined either side. At the end of the hall was another door. A burly man in a black suit stood guard outside it.

Bingo.

"Is this the only way in and out?" she asked the bartender, her tone casual.

"No, there's a street entrance, too. Most people use that one."

She let her hand trail down his arm. "Who was the flashy guy? Your boss?"

"Yeah. Quentin owns the club." A frown lined his forehead and he stopped in his tracks.

Shit. She'd offended him. His thoughts weren't hard to read—his face was like an open book. "Don't worry, baby," she cooed, wrapping herself around him. "He's not my type."

His face cleared up. "What's your type?"

The cop's face flashed in her mind. "Blond and beefy."

"Then you've come to the right place."

She again resisted rolling her eyes. "Take me back there."

He grabbed her hand and yanked her along like an eager puppy. He stopped in front of the bouncer. "Hey, Clancy. I'm supposed to show her to the back."

The bouncer nodded at her escort before looking her over. "She on the list?"

"She's in with Rocco."

Willow gazed directly at the bouncer. Hopefully, he didn't know Rocco was on a slab in the morgue.

He didn't. At Rocco's name, the bouncer smirked and moved aside, unlocking the door. "Have fun," he said suggestively as they entered.

"Rocco's the big man on campus, huh?" she asked once the door closed behind them. A heavy velvet curtain blocked their path, a red glow seeping through the edges. From beyond the curtains, she heard the slow beat of sexy music rather than the frenetic dance music in the main club.

"Well, yeah, since he works directly for Quentin. Come on." He pushed aside the curtain.

"So who was the guy with your boss?"

The bartender glanced at her, pouting again. "What guy with Quentin?"

"The one who looked rich and old. He didn't look like he belonged."

He shrugged. "Maybe he was an investor. We've had a few walk through lately. Or maybe he was just coming back to the Easy. A lot of rich business guys come here."

Before she could ask what the Easy was, he pulled her straight into hell. Or as close as you could get on earth.

The front was like a typical club: lively and brash. But the Easy pulsed to a different beat. More decadent, more covert. An echo of the front space, only smaller and seething with some darker energy.

Willow searched the room for the Bad Man, first with her eyes and then *mù ch'i*. Nothing.

How could that be? They just walked in here. Frowning, she looked around again—and then did a double take.

People were having sex on the dance floor.

Bump and grind—sure, expected in a club. But literally? Yes, some couples and groups were only engaged in foreplay, but the vast majority were getting freaky, as Morgan would say.

A sex club. Willow knew they existed, but she hadn't expected to find herself in one.

How was she going to find the Bad Man in this orgy?

"This way." The bartender took her elbow and led her past the dance floor. "I'm not supposed to be back here, but I know a place where no one will notice."

She let him lead her, taking the opportunity to check out the booths. Sure enough, there were people in all states of undress, doing all manner of things.

But no Bad Man. Where could he have disappeared to?

In the back, doors lined a wide hallway. People milled, holding drinks, watching the other people, who were pushed up against the walls and in dark corners. She sought them out with *mù ch'i,* but the Bad Man wasn't there.

"Wait." The bartender opened a door and peeked inside. He looked over his shoulder at her, grinning. "All clear. Come on."

She walked into the room. There was a velvet love seat in the middle. One wall was all glass—a window. Though on closer inspection, she realized it was a two-way mirror.

On the other side of the glass was a bedroom with a

man tied to the four-post bed. A woman sat on him, rocking herself against him.

As jaded as Willow believed herself to be, she felt her eyes widen as another man joined them, covering the woman's back.

"Kind of cool, isn't it?" The bartender settled on the couch, spreading his arms along the back. "Come have a seat."

She leaned against the glass, hoping it was clean. "Are all the rooms outside like this one?"

"Yeah, but in other flavors, depending on what you're into." He eyed her eagerly. "You into other things? Because I could try other things."

Not even in his dreams. But she'd let him think whatever he wanted, to search the other rooms. She smiled coyly. "Maybe. How long is your break?"

"Not long enough." He devoured her body with his eyes.

Gross. She was taking a long, hot shower to disinfect when she got back to the motel. "Think you can get me a drink?" She could see it was on the tip of his tongue to protest, so she said, "I'm looser when I'm a little more relaxed."

"Okay." He rushed to his feet. "Be back right away."

He tried to kiss her as he left, but she turned her head, pretending to watch the trio in the room next door. The door clicked shut, and she counted to ten before opening it and looking out.

No sign of him or the club owner.

Short of opening all the doors and looking in, she didn't know how she could discover if they were in one of the rooms. She couldn't do that without getting kicked out, and getting kicked out wasn't an option.

The bartender came back, drinks in hand.

"Shit," she muttered, retreating into the shadows of the hallway. She stilled her energy to the point where she'd go unnoticed. He walked right by her, into the room, only to emerge a moment later, a confused look on his face. He looked around for her for only a moment before he got distracted by the other patrons.

Willow waited until he left; then she began a round of the place. She found the corner that promised the best view of the club and posted there. A friendly waitress walked by, and she flagged her.

"What can I get you?" the woman asked, balancing a tray away from her body. They were probably schooled to do that so as not to obstruct the view.

"Gin and tonic."

The waitress nodded and walked away. She returned quickly.

Willow exchanged a twenty for the drink. "I was looking for a friend, but I don't see him."

"Who's your friend?"

"Rocco."

The woman pursed her lips. "I haven't seen him tonight, but he's usually with the boss."

"I just saw Quentin, but Rocco wasn't with him." She frowned as if piqued. "Is there someplace I can look for him?"

"Quentin's office, only no one's allowed up there except the high rollers. But you can watch for him." She pointed to a set of stairs to the left. At the top, another hulk guarded the passage.

Willow stretched her senses to see if she could feel

the Bad Man, but all the steel in the building blocked her ability.

"Anything else?" the waitress asked, shifting on her feet.

"No thanks."

She nodded and walked away.

Willow sat there and watched. Her impatience was tempered only with the knowledge that she was close—closer than she'd ever been.

An hour later, the owner emerged, sauntering down the stairs like a king overseeing his kingdom, one of his army of bouncers at his back. No sign of the Bad Man.

"Damn." Willow looked at the closing door upstairs. Was he still up there, sequestered in a private room?

The owner headed out the door that connected the Easy to Bohemia. *Follow the owner or try to breach the citadel?* She looked up at the office and the guard manning the door.

Follow the owner. She had no idea if her quarry was up there. For all she knew, Quentin was heading to meet him again.

She waited for a count of ten after he'd disappeared behind the curtain to go after him. She peeked through the door, wincing when she saw him talking to her bartender suitor. She consoled herself with the fact that the bartender didn't know anything about her.

Their conversation was brief. She waited until the bartender returned to work, then reentered Bohemia to follow Quentin.

Another one of his minions stopped to talk to him, pointing to the front. Quentin nodded and headed for the entrance.

To meet the Bad Man? Holding her breath, Willow tracked the owner.

But it wasn't the Bad Man whom Quentin met. Instead, it was a tall, well-built Latino who had sharp eyes that missed nothing.

Chapter Five

The cop.

Willow watched him pause inside the entrance to the club and look around. Even though he was speaking with Quentin, she felt a brief spike of fear he'd come looking for her.

Irrational—completely irrational. He couldn't know she was here. Morgan would have called her paranoid. Morgan would have said that *Willow* was the one who wanted him to find her.

Okay, maybe that was the case, at least a little bit. Who could blame her? He was not only handsome but totally intriguing. Of course she was going to feel affected by him—particularly after that scene in the club. Of course she'd imagined him kissing his way up her neck, to the especially sensitive spot below her ear. Of course she'd wondered how his hands would hold her—softly with care, or greedy and insistent.

She didn't think she'd mind either.

She frowned. Now wasn't the time to fantasize

about a man she could never have, no matter how he intrigued her.

As he scanned the crowd, everything in her stilled. She withdrew her energy, ducking into the shadows for good measure. She just had to stay invisible long enough for him to go away so she could sneak out the side door.

She watched him take in the club. Did he know about the world behind the door at her back? She found herself oddly curious as to what he'd think about it.

He had a notepad and pen out, and he was obviously asking Quentin questions about Rocco, if she had to guess. Except the cop's gaze kept flickering to the dark corner where she hid.

She held her breath, feeling like she was cowering in the *tarata* all over again. She hated that feeling. She was strong and capable—no longer a victim.

Needing to be active, she checked her shields and inched closer to hear what they were saying.

She caught up to them in time to hear the owner say, "You know, one of my bartenders saw a woman by that description. Long white-blond hair and a smokin' body."

The cop studied Quentin sharply. If she didn't know better, she would have said he looked annoyed. "Did your employee talk with this woman at all?" the cop asked.

"He said she asked him questions about me. Why? Do you think some chick took out Rocco?" Tugging his sleeves down, Quentin smirked. Then he nodded at one of his bouncers who signaled him from across the room. "I'm being paged. If you'll excuse me, Inspector. Feel free to check out the club."

"I trust you'll be available for further questioning," the cop said.

"Of course. Anything to catch whoever did this to Rocco." The owner's smile reeked of insincerity.

Willow was certain the cop had to have noted that, but he simply nodded politely. Surveying the club one more time, he headed to the bar, presumably to talk to the bartender.

This was her opportunity to get the hell out of there. She started toward the exit.

Only he turned around, as if he sensed her. His hawk-like gaze zeroed in on where she stood.

Leave. She couldn't control minds, but she had a strong talent for planting thoughts to influence people's deci-sions. She'd discovered the aptitude over ten years ago, the same night Morgan had become her responsibility.

Now wasn't the time to think about that night. Instead, she focused on the cop, imagining the thought as a seed in his mind, urging it to take root and to grow. Watching him frown, she waited for him to turn around and walk out.

He took a step closer.

"It didn't work?" She blinked, taken aback, and then turned up the intensity. But the more she tried to dig the thought into the ground of his mind, the harder the dirt became, until it was impossible to penetrate.

"What the hell?" Was it the metal around her? The distance shouldn't have mattered.

As she started to creep closer, keeping the hallway wall to her back, she felt something behind her. She turned right as the door to the sex club opened and one of the waitresses bumped into her.

Distracted, she did something she hadn't done since she was nine years old—she let her shield slip.

Willow knew the moment the cop saw her. She felt it

all the way into her soul. She turned around and met his eyes. Dark and focused.

She shivered.

She couldn't be caught. The Bad Man had been here once—he'd be back again. This club was the last piece of the puzzle. Twenty years of searching led here. She was so close to her goal, and nothing—*nothing*—would stop her from achieving it.

So she did the only thing she could do: she ran.

Cutting through the crowd on the dance floor would get her closer to the side exit, but it'd also give her a chance to resettle *mù ch'i* around her, to block the two men from seeing her escape. "Dance floor it is."

The moment she stepped onto the floor, a guy grabbed her by the hips and gyrated behind her. Normally, having some random person wiggle his crotch against her ass would have pissed her off, but dancing with him gave her the opportunity to refocus herself.

Drawing her energy around her, she pulled it in. She stepped away from the guy, who exclaimed in confusion behind her. Carefully she pushed her way through the crowd to the other side.

The exit was five feet away, and no one stood between it and her.

She headed right to it, reaching for the handle. But just as her hand touched it, another hand closed over hers.

"Inspector Rick Ramirez, SFPD Homicide Unit."

A faint lemony scent teased her nostrils. *Tarata.* For a moment, she felt transported back to New Zealand and running free through the bushes.

Willow shook herself. She had to concentrate here. She focused her attention to the cop.

"I have some questions to ask you," Ramirez said.

Virile types responded to sex, so she unleashed a smile guaranteed to distract him from work. She ran a finger down the front of his dress shirt, stopping midway to toy with one of the buttons. "You look like you're the type of man who already has all the answers."

He looked down at her hand, and his eyes narrowed. "There was a double homicide last night in Buena Vista Park. A woman fitting your description was seen leaving the scene."

Damn it—who'd seen her? There had been no one about. He couldn't have seen her as she'd walked away. She'd taken care to mask herself. She hid her concern with a flirtatious tilt of her head and asked, "What's my description?"

His gaze was like a caress up and down her body—long and thorough. "Five-ten, thin, long blond hair."

"Tall, thin, and blond?" She chuckled, low and sexy, even though she was freaking out on the inside. "That could be anyone."

"Your hair color is distinctive. White blond."

Her hand started to go up to her ponytail, but she caught herself and curled it into a fist at her side. She was supposed to be disrupting his composure, not the other way around. Eyes narrowed, she turned up the heat. "Oh, I was at a scene a couple nights ago, honey, but the man with me was very much alive when I left him the next morning. Although he *did* say he died and went to heaven."

The cop's jaw tightened visibly. "You're claiming you weren't near Buena Vista Park yesterday?"

She felt a measure of satisfaction. Suppressing a

smirk, she pressed her body to his. "I'm not much of a nature girl, but I'd make an exception for you."

He glared at her. "I'll need your partner's information so I can verify your alibi."

"I'd rather have your information." She pulled Ramirez closer. The cold button of his suit coat brushed her bared belly, and goose bumps rose on her skin.

The smell of *tarata* wrapped around her again, making her feel off balance, like she was in a different, happier world.

A delusion. She'd never be happy as long as the Bad Man was running loose. The sooner she got away from the cop, the sooner she could return to figure out how the club owner knew her nemesis.

She shook off the feeling and channeled her determination into a sultry smile. "Actually, I'd rather have you."

Willow leaned in and kissed him.

The kiss started out as candy sweet and empty, just enough lip to distract him. But he just stood there and let her kiss him, no reaction on his part. That annoyed her, so she gave a little more.

It backfired.

Yes, Ramirez responded, but his reaction drew a startling one from her. Suddenly she was pressed against the door, his body flush against hers. He was perfect—in her heels, they were the same height. His hands gripped her sides, firm and masterful.

It made her uncomfortable. It made her hot. It made her want him.

No—*she* didn't want him. She had to keep that clear in her head. Her body wanted him, but her body wasn't in charge here.

As if to prove her wrong, her leg slipped between his. The ridge of his growing erection pressed into her thigh. She resisted—barely—the urge to let her hand trail over it. But she couldn't resist rubbing it with her leg.

He growled into her mouth, and his hands tightened on her.

And then he let go and stepped back.

Not far enough. She could still feel his energy surging at her. It made her woozy, like she was going to sway back into his arms. Only she wasn't the type of woman to sway. So she slipped back into the role of femme fatale.

Leaning against the door, she crossed her arms and smirked at him. She glanced right—the bartender had moved past them. Time to get out. "Not bad. But not good enough for a next time."

She reached for the door, but he caught her arm. "It didn't escape my notice that you never gave me your name."

Of course it hadn't—he was entirely too observant. She frowned, dropping the sexpot act and going for bitchy hauteur. "Am I being detained?"

"Not yet, but if you don't cooperate, I'll take you in on obstruction of justice."

Her eyes narrowed. "I believe I've been cooperative."

"Is that what you'd call this?"

She tugged her arm, testing his grip. "I didn't hear you complaining."

His face went stony. "Your name."

"Sophie Mitchell," she lied smoothly, using one of her aliases. She peeled his hand off her and stepped around him. "Now if you'll excuse me."

He blocked her exit, pulling out a small black notepad

and pen from his inner coat pocket. "I'll need your contact information, too."

She gave him a chilly smile. "I'm in the book."

His attention wavered for a moment as he flipped open his notebook. Willow took the opportunity to dart out the door, pulling her energy inward to become invisible.

She heard his vehement oath as he followed her outside. He stopped and searched for her. She forced herself to breathe and keep moving, even though his gaze seemed to track her.

But that was impossible. He couldn't sense her if she didn't allow it. If he were another Guardian, maybe. Only he wasn't. Her mother told her she would have sensed another Guardian. Not that she expected to ever run into one. Four others in the whole world? Unlikely.

He raked his hair, clearly frustrated.

Despite herself, she remembered his hand grazing her. It'd been strong and capable. Forceful but gentle. Exciting. She remembered how hard he'd been, just from one kiss, and shivered.

"Walk away before you do something stupid," she mumbled to herself. She turned and strode into the night, back to her threadbare motel room.

Chapter Six

Where the hell was she? She'd been right there a moment ago.

Ramirez focused on the space ahead of him. He could almost see the outline of her, a ghostlike silhouette walking away. It must have been his grandmother's woo-woo talk getting to him. He shook his head to clear his thoughts and went south, down the alley. There was more transportation in that direction, and parking was available if she'd driven. Not to mention the club's entrance, which he didn't put past her to go back into.

Any doubts he had about her involvement in the crime were wiped away after her little scene inside. He knew she was hiding something.

He focused on locating her, but her words kept playing in his mind. *"I'd rather have you."* Completely insincere, but damn it if it didn't grab him low and hard, nevertheless.

Hard was right, and everything about her had contributed to that state. Her lips, her hands, her body—all alarmingly right. But because he hadn't had sex in a while, or because they'd just felt right? He wanted to rationalize it with his celibacy, but he couldn't lie to himself.

Only she didn't read true. Not the way she was dressed, or the way she acted. Even her name sounded false. Sophie Mitchell? Yeah, right.

Not seeing her, Ramirez looked left, toward the long line waiting to get into the regular club. Nothing. Looking over his shoulder, he caught a glimpse of her bright head turning a corner.

"Shit," he said as he took off after her. He didn't care what she claimed, his gut said she was involved in the murders, one way or another. And his gut feelings were never wrong. He'd had these same feelings with Gabrielle Sansouci Chin. He still believed she was complicit in a couple of murders, but he'd never been able to prove it. He wasn't letting this one get away.

He saw her walking down the street with complete confidence, her stride long-legged and sure, even in the idiotic heels she wore. A woman as tall as she was, with legs so long, didn't need to wear heels like that. She would have been perfect barefoot.

He frowned. Thinking about any part of her being bare wasn't a good idea. He needed to keep this professional. Personal feelings had no place in a case.

He ran after her, concentrating on keeping his footsteps stealthy. He knew the moment she sensed him—her back stiffened and she looked over her shoulder at him.

Suddenly the outline of her body wavered, as if his vision was going blurry. What the hell? He blinked, confused, but it still didn't clear.

Acting on instinct, he lunged and grabbed her arms. The moment their skin touched, the wavering stopped. He whirled her around and pressed her against the building next to them. "I don't think we've finished our talk, Ms. *Mitchell*."

She glared at him, and he had the impression it was the first real emotion she'd shown all night.

"You know I could call you on police brutality," she said angrily. "You can't detain me unless you're willing to take me into the station."

He arched an eyebrow. "How do you know police procedure so well?"

"Reruns of *NYPD Blue*," she said with the haughtiness of a queen.

A lithe Elvin queen. He looked into her mysterious light gray eyes, noticing her sharp cheekbones and determined chin, and pictured her with that pale blond hair streaming around her as she lay naked on a forest floor, the surrounding trees raining leaves on her body.

Ridiculous. He steeled himself against the fantasy and glared back at her. "We both know you aren't who you say you are."

"Who do you think I am, then?"

The White Witch. He forced the thought from his mind.

"I don't know, but I'm going to find out," he replied, conscious of the proximity of her. A strand of her hair had come loose and teased his neck.

She smirked. "You do that."

He had this insane urge to smell her skin and hold her close to keep her safe. He leaned in, conscious of the fact that he was crossing the professional line but unable to help himself.

Hell—he'd crossed the line already, with that kiss, and that infuriated him even more. He had always prided himself on his professionalism and the ability to keep his cool. Losing it was unacceptable and difficult. His body wanted her badly. He didn't have an active imagination, but apparently he didn't need one to picture her legs hitched around his hips.

He reined himself back. The investigation was his top priority. Maybe if he told himself that, another several dozen times, his dick would believe it, too. "I find it hard to believe you have no ties to either of the two homicide victims."

She leaned back against the building, casually and at ease, humor flirting with her lips. "And why is that, Starsky?"

At least she hadn't called him Ponch. That always pissed him off. "What other reason would you have to be at Bohemia if you had nothing to do with either victim?" he asked.

"Maybe I like to get my groove on."

He knew that wasn't the reason, but he could picture the scene all too well—her body undulating, loose, limber, and graceful. Only not to the music, but to a lover's hands, and he felt himself harden again.

Focus, he ordered himself, putting a wall around his unruly reaction to her. "Or maybe you know Joel Rocco."

She shrugged, that mocking hint of a smile fixed in place.

He wanted to kiss it off her face. *No,* he didn't, damn it. Scowling, hoping to intimidate her, he asked, "Was Rocco your lover?"

Amusement lit her eyes. "Don't tell me you're jealous, Starsky."

Hell, if that wasn't what he was. His jaw tightened. "Answer the question."

"Or what? You'll cuff me?" She pushed off the wall and stepped into him. "Maybe I'd like that."

She didn't touch him, but his body lit on fire like she'd reached into his pants and taken hold, as if she'd wrapped him in a sexual web.

He exhaled, trying to focus, trying to regain his professional demeanor, but all he could see was her cuffed to his bed, open and inviting and wet for him. He cleared his throat. "Maybe I should take you to the station."

"Or you could just take me here," she retorted, her breath soft on his neck.

He wanted to—desperately. He glanced at her lips, curled in mockery of his obvious dilemma, and it pushed him over the edge. Before he could talk himself out of it, he hauled her flush to his body and took what she was offering.

The moment his mouth touched hers, all thoughts of the investigation left his mind. He slipped his hands under her nonexistent top. He'd never felt skin so soft. If her back was this silky, what would the inside of her thighs feel like? Something shifted. She breathed a low moan into his mouth and melted into him.

Something elemental howled in triumph inside him at her surrender. He drew her in closer—as close as they could get fully clothed. He inhaled her faint evergreen scent, clean and pure, and knew *this* was who she really was.

Her hands ran up his shoulders. Tangling her fingers in his hair, she drew herself up into him, and he groaned as her hip brushed his erection.

Just as quickly as she gave in to him, she pulled back, her eyes wide with passion and surprise. Good. He hated to think he was the only one affected. He raked his hair back, his scalp tingling from where her nails had scraped, and tried to regain his composure.

She stepped back, her hand touching her mouth as she stared at his. And then she ran. Again.

Chapter Seven

The kiss was the most powerful thing she'd ever felt—in some ways more profound than *mù ch'i*. Not knowing what to do, Willow listened to her intuition and got out of there as quickly as she could. She tried to come up with different reasons for her flight, but she knew there was only one excuse: she was too blown away by his kiss to attempt to draw on *mù ch'i*.

She'd never been kissed like that before. It'd felt like a tornado had suddenly swooped down, uprooting her, and shaking her branches to the point of snapping. The thought of it was encompassing and overwhelming.

His hands were warm and rough and forceful. How did a pencil pusher get hands like that? They took unapologetically.

And she'd wanted to give.

She tripped, almost falling to the ground. "Damn it," she said, peeking over her shoulder as she caught her balance.

He was still behind her, keeping up with her fast pace

with ease. Frowning, she added a burst of speed. She rounded a corner and then made a sharp turn down an alley. She looked behind her and saw that he was gone.

She slowed to a walk and took a deep breath in, holding it before releasing it through her mouth. She needed to calm down and think. She took the street to her left, hoping to loop around, unseen, to make it back to the motel.

Down the block, a man stood on the corner. She scanned him quickly as she headed in his direction. Contrary to popular belief, most people minded their own business. In Willow's experience, only drug addicts were unpredictable and prone to sudden violence, and by the way this man was dressed, he didn't seem like a street-corner addict. Dismissing him as a threat, she bowed her head and walked past him.

There was a change in the air—a sudden increase in intensity. Willow turned around, just in time to block the first punch thrown. Without thought, she followed up with a strike to his throat and a high knee to his sternum.

He grunted, losing his breath as she connected with his neck, but he blocked her knee—and the left hook she followed up with.

They stood, facing each other.

If only she'd brought her wooden dirks with her. That taught her to be unprepared. At least he was as surprised as she was. She grinned without humor, stepping out of his punching range. "Not as easy as I look, am I?"

As he reached into his pocket and pulled out a switchblade, he scanned her up and down in that smarmy way some men had. "That remains to be seen, love."

Willow kept her face impassive, but she cringed on the

inside. Metal chopped wood. It was her kryptonite. Her powers wouldn't prevent her from being cut, and she still had scars from previous run-ins involving sharp metals to prove it.

"What?" Hunched into a fighter's stance, the man tossed his knife from hand to hand. "Not so tough in the face of a little blade?"

She angled her body to give him less of a target and concentrated on the matter at hand—finding out who he was.

Based on his accent, he was obviously British. Was he a bouncer from the club? His black clothing would suggest so, but a bouncer would have no reason to come after her. Plus, he felt more exclusive than a regular bouncer, more like a private bodyguard. The question was, who was he guarding?

"You can't be so hard up you need to take a woman at knifepoint," Willow taunted.

"Careful, love," he said, swiping at her. "I was told to bring you in alive, but I doubt anyone would care if you were roughed up a little."

She edged backward. "Who's paying you? I could offer you more."

He chuckled, a sinister sound. "I'm sure you could, love."

"At least tell me what this is about."

"You must have crossed the wrong people." He lunged, knife straight out.

She arced a crescent kick, catching his wrist.

Crying out, he shook his hand, but he still held on to the knife in his fist. Murder darkened his gaze.

"So much for taking me in alive, huh?" she taunted.

"You only have to be breathing." He glared, transferring the weapon into his unharmed hand as he advanced. "Barely."

"You know, I have a small problem with that." She noticed the tree behind him. Its leaves were wispy, but the branches were low enough to be of use. All she needed was for him to back up, which was a challenge, when he was so intent on advancing toward her.

He brandished the knife, flipping it back and forth in his grip. "You're assuming I care, love."

"You're assuming I'm going to cooperate."

He sneered. "Your cooperation isn't required."

"Oh, good. Then you won't mind if I do this." She spun around and delivered a right roundhouse.

She caught him off guard, but not off guard enough. He clumsily jumped back, so her foot only grazed him. He slashed with the knife but missed.

She rounded to his right, and he followed. *Just a little closer to the tree.* "You know," she said conversationally, "switchblades are illegal in California."

"You're not going to be telling anyone, now, are you?" He lunged at her again, but she saw it coming by the way he swelled into action, and she was ready. Planting a compulsion in his brain, she urged him to drop the knife.

His hand opened and it pinged to the ground.

As he looked down in confusion, she did a double block, cupping his arm and spinning both of them around so his back was to the tree. Before he could react, she punched him in the nose. With a gurgled moan, he staggered backward. Blood began to spurt almost instantly. "You'll pay for that," he said in a low growl, not even bothering to wipe away the blood.

She shook her head. "You just don't get it, do you?"

"You're the one who's going to get it." He shifted his weight, ready to pounce.

She focused *mù ch'i* and felt the tree's energy. It was distant, its energy faint. She pushed toward it, but it resisted.

Gritting her teeth, conscious that he was a second away from attacking, she shoved *mù ch'i* toward the tree. It shuddered physically, the leaves rustling so violently, her attacker looked back.

Willow concentrated her energy on a branch, willing it to whip forward. It hit the man's arm, and his knife went flying. "That was your first mistake."

His head whipped around and he growled at her. "Bitch."

"And that was your last one." With another surge of *mù ch'i,* she had the tree limb smack the man on the side of the head. His eyes rolled up and he dropped like a rock.

"Bastard," she muttered. She retracted her energy from the tree, but something stuck and it snapped back at her. Gasping, she staggered backward.

Straight into Ramirez's arms.

For someone as levelheaded as he prided himself on being, he'd seen some crazy things in his life.

Like what just happened here.

He held Sophie—or whatever the hell her name was—in his arms; then he looked at the thug on the ground. He'd seen him attack her and, inexplicably, Ramirez's heart had almost stopped. But she'd dispatched him efficiently, using a tree as backup after he conveniently dropped his knife.

She looked at Ramirez with her eyes wide. Some of her hair had come loose and clung to her bare shoulders. Her face was pale, and she breathed heavily.

Ramirez frowned. "Are you okay?"

She blinked at him as if she didn't comprehend.

He shook her lightly, fighting the need to cradle her. "Are you okay? Did he cut you?"

Another blink, and she shook her head. He thought she was just clearing her mind, but then she said, "Let go. I'm fine."

He released her, only because he needed to see if she'd killed the man. If he was dead, she'd be able to get off on self-defense, but he'd still have to take her in. His teeth clenched at the thought of locking her up, but what choice did he have?

Ramirez leaned down and checked the man. He was still breathing. Ramirez exhaled, oddly relieved. "You're in luck. He's just knocked out."

He stood to face her, only she was no longer there.

Chapter Eight

Ramirez stood on the street, futilely searching for a woman who had disappeared into thin air. Twice.

He tugged his sleeves down and muttered. This was why cops turned to alcohol.

He needed a soundboard to process what he'd witnessed. Not his grandmother—Lita would only go on about fate and facing destiny. He couldn't go to his partner, because Taylor would make him visit the department shrink.

Carrie Prescott. He could talk to Carrie.

He pulled out his cell phone and called her.

She answered on the first ring. "Do my eyes deceive me? It looks like my old friend Rick Ramirez is calling me, but that can't be."

Hearing her light, sweet tone, he felt his mood lift. He could tell she wasn't alone, the faint buzz of other people talking crackled over the line. "Why not?"

"Because my old friend Rick Ramirez has been MIA for weeks, and to call me after midnight is uncharacteristic. Unless he suspects me of offing someone."

Smart-ass. "I need to talk to you."

"I figured. Max is out tonight, so I'm at the Pour House hanging out with Gabe. Come meet me here."

"Be there in ten." He shut his phone, walked back to his car, and headed to the Pour House, a bar in the Mission, located a few blocks from his house. Not that he was in the habit of hanging out in bars, since he didn't drink often. He'd seen too many of his colleagues destroy themselves with alcohol.

The first time he'd stepped foot into the Pour House was during an investigation regarding a body found in an alleyway a few blocks away. He'd met Gabrielle Sansouci that day and had known instantly that she was hiding something.

In the end, her brother, Paul Chin, had been implicated in that murder, as well as the murder of her ex-boyfriend. Ramirez didn't know how Gabrielle was involved, but he had no doubt she was. Something was off about the crime scene, and she'd acted strangely. Her actions were similar to *Sophie's*.

It stuck in his craw that he hadn't even been able to bring in Gabrielle's brother. According to sources, Paul Chin had fled to South America. Damn rich people. They thought money could buy their way out of anything. But one day he'd bring Chin in and make sure he was tucked away in prison, where he belonged, money or not.

His gut told him Gabrielle was the key to bringing her brother in. Chin had to contact her eventually, and Ramirez would be there, ready, when Paul did. Ramirez had gotten in the habit of checking in at the bar. At first, it'd been solely to wait for Chin, but over time he'd developed a friendship with one of the other bartenders, Carrie

Woods. Ironically, Carrie was Gabrielle's best friend and had been involved in a strange death six months ago, as well. That death had been ruled natural.

Ramirez grunted as he pulled into a parking spot. As if a woman's blood solidifying in her body could be called natural. If he'd been in charge of the investigation, he wouldn't have been so quick to rule out foul play, but it'd been out of his jurisdiction. Despite that, he trusted Carrie. He had the feeling he could tell her about the strange things he'd seen and she wouldn't check his forehead for fever. Something told him she wasn't a stranger to inexplicable occurrences.

He walked into the bar's mellow scene. A couple sat at a table, a trio of young men played pool on the worn table in the back, and there was an older man alone at one end of the bar. At the other end sat a familiar reddish-blond curly head, leaning on her elbows. She'd just married an incredibly rich and powerful man, but she wore her usual jeans and sneakers, although he could tell they were finer than what she used to wear.

He walked to her and sat on the stool next to her, stealing a glance at the beverage in front of her. It was made to look like a gin and tonic, but it was probably soda water and lime. Even before she was pregnant Carrie hardly ever drank. "Sure you can handle that?"

"Hey, stranger." Turning her bright smile on him, she hopped up and hugged him.

He unbuttoned his coat. "Your husband driving you to drink already? You've been married, what? Two days?"

"Two weeks. And, no, Max is perfect."

Ramirez felt a pang of envy. Not that he'd ever expected to be in a relationship. With his hours, the danger, the stress...definitely not conducive to long-term relationships. "I think Max is the lucky one."

"Well, duh." She laughed and knocked his arm. "Where have you been? I know my husband is territorial and jealous, but he won't hassle you too badly for visiting me."

Her husband, Maximillian Prescott, was actually a solid guy. He seemed stable and clearly worshiped the ground Carrie walked on. Ramirez had to like anyone who took care of his own as carefully as Prescott did. "My caseload has been heavy."

Carrie got serious, putting a hand on his arm. "Are you okay? It's not getting to you, is it? You know, if you need a vacation, Max has a great house in Santa Monica. I'm sure he wouldn't mind it if you used it. Actually, he has houses all over the world. Pick one. I'll have Max loan you his plane, too."

Houses all over the world. A private plane. Ramirez shook his head. "Your reality is so skewed."

"I know." She laughed. "Isn't it great?"

He felt the air shift behind him. He turned right as Gabrielle ducked under the bar top.

She had her hands full of empty bottles, but that didn't stop her from glaring at him. "Aren't you supposed to hang out in donut shops?"

"Why, when you have such a sweet disposition?" he asked blandly.

Carrie snorted.

Gabrielle flashed a glare at her friend and then dumped all the bottles into a bin. Without a word, she pulled a bottle of Patrón from the top shelf and poured him a shot. She shoved it across the bar at him and, with another evil look, went to engage another customer in conversation.

Ramirez picked up his shot glass. "She grows more charming each time I see her."

"Can you blame her? You're out to lynch her brother." Carrie clinked her glass to his. "They may have World War Two–type history between them, and she says he deserves what he gets, but deep down she cares. Gabe is very sensitive on the inside."

He raised his eyebrows but said nothing.

"She is." Carrie grinned. "I don't get why you guys hate each other so much. You're like oil and water. And to think, at one time, I thought you were interested in her."

His moral code forbade him from being interested in a woman who was on the other side of the law, and he was fairly certain Gabrielle Sansouci Chin crossed the line whenever it suited her. So did *Sophie Mitchell*—he had no doubt about that, either.

His frown deepened. Watching her take out that man had been exciting. She was so tough, and then she'd surrendered to him so sweetly. So passionately.

He could still taste her on his lips.

He shook his head and shot back the rest of his tequila.

"Hmm." Carrie leaned back and looked at him speculatively. "Do I detect woman issues?"

He pushed the glass away from him. "You should leave the detecting to the professionals."

"So are you going to tell me why you called me in the middle of the night?"

"How did your professor actually die?"

She froze, her glass raised halfway to her lips. After a moment, she set it down with a *thunk*. "Not this again."

"Wait." He held her arm when she started to retract from him.

"No." She tugged away from him. "If I knew you were going to beat this dead horse, I wouldn't have agreed to meet with you."

"That's not what I mean."

"Well, then, what *do* you mean?"

His jaw clenched tight. Everything in him fought saying the words, but it had to be done. "Have you noticed that there's something going on?"

Carrie rolled her eyes. "You'll have to be more specific than that."

"Strange things." He tugged at his collar. "Unexplainable things."

She stilled. "What sort of unexplainable things?"

"The kind where a person's blood freezes in her body." He looked her in the eye. "The kind where a tree limb whips down and knocks a man out."

"What tree? There was no tree with Leonora. Max—" She snapped her mouth shut.

Ramirez studied her closely. "Max what?"

"Nothing. Don't expect me to betray my husband's confidence."

Gabrielle chose that moment to return. "Everything okay here?" she asked, looking at her friend.

Carrie nodded, smiling weakly. "We're fine. Rick might need another drink, though."

Gabrielle's expression turned on him, her hostility more than obvious. "Do you? It's last call."

"No."

She pointed at Carrie. "Refill?"

"No thanks." She patted Gabrielle's hand.

That seemed to reassure the woman somewhat, but it didn't stop her from pointing her finger at him and saying, "I'm watching you. You do something to upset her and you're toast."

They both watched Gabrielle slip under the bar again and begin to clean up. Ramirez glanced at his watch. So much had happened, it seemed like it should have been later than it was.

"Sorry about Gabe. Ever since I told her I was knocked up, she's been superprotective." Carrie shook her head. "Between her and Max, I'm going insane. Max actually insisted on bathing me the other day."

Ramirez cocked an eyebrow. "Did he?"

Her face flushed red, and she slapped his arm. "Stop."

"You're the one who said it."

"I just meant he's being overly protective."

"Understandable. I'd do the same." Not that he'd ever believe he'd have kids—not when he couldn't even sustain a relationship. Ramirez glanced at her stomach, trying to picture himself in Prescott's shoes. Yes, he'd be every bit as protective, offering to wash her long, pale hair.

He frowned. Where the hell did that thought come from?

"Uh-oh. You're thinking about her again."

"Have you become a mind reader since you've gotten pregnant?"

"Nah, I'm just attuned." She looked sideways at him. "So what's her name?"

"I don't know." He picked up his shot glass, forgetting it was empty, and set it back down in disgust.

Carrie wrinkled her nose. "You don't know? You haven't talked to her?"

"I have."

"Unless you want to be here all night, you better just tell me everything. And I don't think you want to be up all night. You look tired."

He gave her a flat look. "Is that a subtle way of saying I look like shit?"

"Pretty much." She propped her elbow on the counter and rested her chin in her hand. "I'm waiting."

What did he say about her? He searched for the right words. He surprised himself by saying, "She's like a lone wolf."

Carrie nodded. "Takes one to know one."

"What does that mean?"

"You aren't exactly a social creature. Don't look at me like that. You know you're a loner. When was the last time you went out?"

"Where?"

"See." She rolled her eyes. "You never go out, much less socialize. I don't even know if you have friends."

Other than the guys on the force, he didn't, but he wasn't about to admit that to her.

"How long has it been since you've gone on a date?" she asked.

He blinked. "A date?"

"Where you partake in refreshments, discuss topical matters, and exchange bodily fluids. Not necessarily in that order."

He'd had a short affair with that attractive prosecutor a year ago. She'd been going through a divorce and he'd been happy to be her rebound fling. He hadn't been near anyone's body fluids since... well, not until tonight. "My caseload has been busy."

"Uh-huh." She rolled her eyes. "So you're saying if a

woman threw herself at you, you'd be too busy to get it on with her?"

He pictured the way *Sophie*—he really hated that name—pulled him to her. The way she kissed him, with cold precision. He could still feel her shock the moment the calculation gave way to desire—honest desire. He could still feel *his* shock at the satisfaction he felt getting past her barriers to the real woman below.

That real woman intrigued him, more than he was comfortable with.

"Your loner threw herself at you?" Carrie squeaked a little too loudly.

He was conscious of other people's gazes on them, especially Gabrielle's. He frowned. "You find it hard to believe a woman would want me?"

"Heck, no." Her curls bounced around her face as she vehemently shook her head. "You're hot. Totally hot. I can't think of a woman who wouldn't want you. Except Gabe, of course."

"Of course."

"Forget other women. I want to know about your loner." She leaned in, grabbing his lapel and tugging him closer. "What did she do?"

She'd turned his world upside down with the mere touch of her soft lips. "She lied to me."

"That's not what I meant and you know it." Carrie's round eyes filled his vision. "Did you kiss her?"

"No." Not a lie—*Sophie* had kissed him.

Carrie wilted. "Aw, man. I was hoping for some juicy details."

"Aren't you a newlywed? Don't you have juicy details of your own?"

"I do, but it's not as titillating as other people's juicy details." She shook off her disappointment. "So what's she like?"

Tall. Sassy. Sexy. Really sexy. "I can't tell."

"*You* can't tell?" She pointed a finger at him. "The cop who's trained to evaluate people? The master of ferreting out people's dark sides?"

He shot his so-called friend a sharp look. "She's not who she says she is."

"Who is she?"

"I don't know." He held the glass in his hands, turning it around and watching the light reflect off it.

"And that bothers you, because you're all about truth." Carrie nodded. "You really don't know her name?"

"She said it was Sophie Mitchell."

"And you don't believe her." Carrie's forehead furrowed. "But you want her."

"I never said that."

"You didn't *not* say it, either. I'm pregnant, not blind. If the tension in your body is any indication, you want her with the intensity of a thousand suns."

He cocked his brow.

Grinning, she shrugged. "It was in an old Chinese text I just translated. I've been waiting for days to use it in conversation. But let's get back to your loner."

"She's not *my* loner." That thought made him grit his teeth. If he didn't know better, he'd say it was from frustration.

"But you want her to be yours." She said it as a statement of fact.

"She can't be mine. She's involved in a case I'm investigating now."

"Hmm." Carrie rubbed the tip of her nose in thought.

"It'd be a conflict of interest. Aside from that, I don't trust her. She has something to do with this case. Not to mention the strange thing I saw."

"Couldn't that have been a coincidence? The wind could have kicked up and moved the tree. Stranger things have happened."

"Like a woman's blood freezing to a solid state in her body?"

Her lips pursed. "You're going to have to let that go."

He couldn't, just like he couldn't let go of what he saw *Sophie* do, and he was positive she was the one responsible. "A person who lies about her name has things to hide."

"Well, maybe it's not what you think." She put her hand over his, her gaze uncharacteristically serious. "I have a feeling about this. You see things in black and white, but sometimes there are areas of gray."

"You sound like my grandmother."

"Your grandmother must be a very wise woman." She squeezed his hand. "I'd just hate it if she's The One, and you blew it because of your ethics."

He felt the corner of his mouth quirk. "Those damn ethics, always getting in the way."

"Seriously." She punched his arm. "Don't judge her, even when you find out what she's hiding. Not without talking to her first."

He was definitely going to talk to her because he was determined to find out what *Sophie* was up to. First thing in the morning, he was doing a background check.

He stood up, straightening his coat. "Come on. It's past pregnant women's bedtimes. I'll give you a ride home."

She shook her head but stood up anyway. "It's out of your way. You only live a few blocks from here."

He tugged a curl. "You're lucky I'm taking the long way home tonight."

"You always say that." Grinning, she slipped her arm around his waist and gave him a half hug. "You're really great, you know that?"

"Don't sound so surprised."

"I'm not. I'm just not sure you realize it." She gave him a sidelong look as she put on her coat. "When do I get to meet her?"

"She could be a suspect in a murder."

"I like to live on the wild side." Calling out a good-bye to Gabrielle, she took his arm. "You know," she said as she let him lead her out of the bar, "I'm having a small dinner party soon. If I invited you, would you come?"

"I didn't realize you cooked."

She flashed her incandescent grin. "I don't. Max has taught me that's what caterers are for."

"Useful guy."

"In more ways than one. So would you come?" Her grip on his arm tightened in excitement. "It's my first dinner party ever, believe it or not. It'd be totally casual. And you could bring your loner."

"No," he said, emphatically and without hesitation.

He felt bad when Carrie wilted before his eyes. "You won't come?"

"Of course I'll come if you want me there. But I'm not bringing Sophie." Damn, it galled him to call her that. She didn't seem like a *Sophie* by any stretch of the imagination.

Carrie pouted. "But I wanted to check her out."

"*No.*" He narrowed his eyes at her. "And if you get any ideas about meddling, I'll tell your husband."

"Oh, that's low, but admittedly brilliant." Carrie stopped walking and looked around. Then she shuddered violently.

Alerted, Ramirez searched the street and saw nothing out of the ordinary, but Carrie had good instincts, and something had obviously set her off. "What's wrong?"

"I don't know." She scanned the area.

He followed her gaze, but he didn't see anything—or anyone—there. "Are you okay?"

She shook her entire body, like she was trying to get something loose. Then she turned to him with a tentative smile. "I'm fine. Just a goose walking over my grave."

It was more than some imaginary sensation. He surveyed the street, more carefully this time.

"It was nothing." She tugged his arm. "Come on. Let's go."

He gave the surroundings a last cursory look and then quickly led her to his car, just in case.

Chapter Nine

Willow watched Ramirez put his arm around the pretty blonde. Their body language spoke volumes. They were close—comfortable with each other.

Women didn't let men they didn't trust touch them that way.

She gritted her teeth. She wanted to kill him. Or her. Or both of them.

No, just him.

No—that was too strong. She hadn't known him long enough to warrant that kind of emotion.

Rather, she wanted him to sting the way she did right now. How could he have kissed her that way when he had a woman? Yes, they'd only shared a couple kisses, but as much as she wanted to deny it, those kisses had done something to her.

He obviously didn't feel that way. Not with the way he smiled now at that blonde. The way he tugged on her hair. Willow had gone to school for a short time once, and there'd been a boy who pulled her hair like that.

Mama had told her it was how boys showed they liked a girl.

She glared at the cop. Bastard. That woman looked sweet and innocent. He deserved to be shot for toying with her. No—not shot. That was too quick and easy. If she had her way, she'd hoist him into a tree and hang him from the limbs. Then she'd shoot slivers of wood at him, one tiny piece at a time, until he writhed from the pain. *Mù ch'i* stirred, a faint urge to act on her desire.

When she'd first inherited her powers, the compulsions had been stronger. But her mother had prepared her for that, describing the feelings in great detail. As a kid, Willow hadn't appreciated the mental training, certainly not as much as learning to fight, but she'd been thankful for it later. Using her mother's advice, combined with self-discipline and practice, she'd taught herself to control the impulses rather than let them control her.

Those years meant shit right now. To say she was tempted to let herself slip was an understatement.

The blonde shivered and looked around.

Frowning, Willow stilled. The woman wouldn't be able to see her—she wasn't worried about that. But there was a light taint to her energy, as if she'd been in contact with an element. Upwind, Willow sniffed the air and found more than one element, but the traces were ever so subtle, except for the tang of sea salt, which clung heavier to her. Was it a Guardian?

No. She'd never met another Guardian aside from her mother, who used to say being a Guardian was a solitary responsibility, but that she'd know if she met one. Carrie figured there would be a spike in the energy she felt around the person. Most people had a simple energy field, open or closed depending on their personality and experiences. When she looked at herself, she had another layer overlapping that. The woman felt more connected and brighter, but she didn't have the extra signature.

Then who was she?

Average height, reddish-blond hair, average build. Casual but expensive clothes. Messenger bag slung across her chest. Wedding ring on her finger.

Willow glared at Ramirez. Reaching into her jacket, she pulled out her cell phone. Without looking, she selected the only number in her contact list.

Morgan answered on the first ring just like she always did, regardless of the time of day. But she'd had trouble sleeping for as long as Willow knew her. "Talk to me."

"I need you to do a background check on someone."

"Shoot." The tapping of Morgan's fingers on her keyboard was faint and rapid. "I feel compelled to tell you I don't mean that literally, because we all know how literal-minded you are. Just that I'm ready for you to go ahead."

Willow waited a couple beats before she asked, "Are you done?"

"Yes. Ready."

Looking at the couple as they got into a car, Willow said, "I need any info you can get on Rick Ramirez."

"I'm good at what I do, Willow, but *Rick Ramirez* isn't exactly an uncommon name. Do you have anything else I can use to narrow down my search?"

Willow rattled off the license plate number.

"Got it. Call you back in a few."

Willow snapped the phone closed and watched the couple drive away. She wanted to follow them, badly; instead, she headed toward the bar they'd come out of.

The Pour House.

She knew many cops tended to be alcoholics; she'd used that to her advantage in the past. But the idea that Ramirez fit the stereotype didn't sit right with her. Ramirez hadn't seemed like a drinker. He was too sharp, both in his demeanor and his dress. And her impressions of people were never off.

Although, she never let anyone get to her the way he had, either.

Feigning casualness she was far from feeling, she strolled into the bar even though it was obviously closing. Out of habit, she reached out with *mù ch'i* and marked the exits and pinpointed all the people inside. Someone was in a back room.

Willow turned subtly and pretended to look around; yet her focus was on the door behind her. It must have been the bartender, except something made her feel twitchy. She ran a hand down her pants. If only she had her wooden dirks on her.

A woman stepped out of the back room, a guarded smile on her lips. She was long and lanky, with a similar build to her own, except with black hair streaked with various blues. Her sharp cheekbones and almond-shaped blue eyes told of a mixed ancestry. Perhaps part Asian? Her energy was overlapped with a matching force. The deep, musty scent of earth reached Willow, and she froze.

So did the bartender.

Their gazes locked, and Willow knew, instinctively and without doubt, that the woman was the Guardian of the Book of Earth. The Earth Guardian must have recognized her for who she was, as well, because the bottle of liquor in her hand fell to the ground and shattered.

The strong link between them—the recognition—pulled Willow. Even from across the room, their energies snapped and crackled, willing them closer even as it pushed them apart.

"Oh, my God," the bartender muttered. Somehow it echoed in the space of the room despite the background music.

A tremor quivered through the ground. The bottles behind Willow began to shake, softly at first and then with more intensity. She glared at the Earth Guardian, not sure whether this was posturing or a threat.

Life had taught her, when in doubt, expect the worst. So, keeping a close eye on Earth, she pictured herself as a tree with roots going deep into the ground, cutting through its porous surface. The bartender gasped, clutching her chest as she staggered back. Taking the opening, Willow rushed through the bar.

"Shit," Earth muttered before she reached out her hand, still holding her chest. "Wait."

Like hell Willow was going to wait. She got out of there as fast as she could in her spiked heels. Luck was on her side. As soon as she stepped outside, an unoccupied cab passed. Flagging it down, she hopped in, ignoring the ripple of discomfort from the surrounding metal of the car. "Broadway and Montgomery," she said, slamming the door.

The driver looked in the rearview mirror. "Really?"

She frowned at him. "Yes, really. Go."

For a second, she didn't expect him to listen to her, but then he drove despite his reluctant expression. She was conscious of the occasional glances he shot her in the mirror, but she closed her eyes and tried to figure out what had just happened, and what it all meant. She was also curious as to how Ramirez figured into it.

It wasn't a coincidence that Ramirez was at that bar. Did he know that bartender? He had to. But that didn't mean he knew she was a Guardian. It was a tenet that you didn't reveal your Guardianship. Then there was the blonde with the taint of scroll to her.

Damn it, why hadn't Morgan called back yet? She yanked her cell out of the tight pocket. It was several rings before Morgan answered. "Give a girl some time to work magic," her friend and partner complained.

"I don't need magic. I just need answers."

Morgan mumbled as she typed furiously.

Checking a street sign to make sure the cabbie wasn't ripping her off, Willow said, "I'll pretend you didn't call me an impatient brat and just reiterate my desire for answers."

"Jesus Christ, Willow. You could have told me he was a cop. I almost got flagged when I did my initial search. I had to bail and start all over. If I had known, I would have taken extra precautions." More tapping. "Make me feel better and tell me you didn't know he was a cop."

Willow kept quiet. Morgan always got around to the point eventually. Engaging with her usually meant waiting longer.

"I'm onto you, you know," Morgan grumbled. "Your silent treatment doesn't work on me anymore."

Willow just waited.

Her partner sighed. "Fine. He's a cop, which I'm sure you already know. He's in Homicide, which makes me wonder what you've been up to, since you've apparently made his acquaintance. Inspector level, promoted three years ago. Hot damn, he's hot. Kind of like Benjamin Bratt and Enrique Iglesias rolled into one. *Yum.* I'd totally do him. God, he must have—"

"Morgan?" Willow broke into the monologue.

"Hmm?"

"Focus."

"I *am* focused. I'm just commenting on his obvious good looks. Jesus." She paused, her pout loud and clear in the silence, but she continued. "His partner, James Taylor, has been in Homicide eleven years. He's lived with a woman named May Dahler for fifteen years."

May. The blonde *would* have a name as sweet as she looked. "She must have started living with him when she was fifteen. She barely looks old enough to get into a bar."

"May Dahler? Based on the birth date on her Social, she's going to be fifty-five next January. It appears she fudges her age by a couple years on other paperwork."

"Fifty-five." Willow frowned. "Do you have a physical on her?"

"Five feet seven, one hundred fifty pounds, brown hair, brown eyes."

"That's not the woman he was with."

"Inspector James Taylor?"

"No, Ramirez."

"I wasn't talking about Ramirez," Morgan said with barely concealed impatience. "I was telling you about his partner."

Willow clamped her mouth shut and concentrated on calming herself. With her luck tonight, she'd scare the driver and he'd crash. "I wanted to know information about Ramirez."

"I was getting there."

She mentally sighed at the sadness in Morgan's tone. "You know how important this is to me. The sooner I take care of it, the sooner I'll be back to taking freelance assignments."

"Promises, promises," Morgan said, but she didn't hold out. "Inspector Ricardo Ramirez is one of the youngest people to ever be promoted to inspector. He lives at 2586 Bryant Street with his grandmother, or rather his grandmother lives with him."

"His grandmother?" She would have mocked him for being a mama's boy, only she couldn't. Not after those kisses. She knew he was all man.

"Yeah. Elena Ramirez. Looks like she raised him. Minor scuffle with the law when he was a kid. The record is sealed, but I can hack it if you want."

"Not necessary."

"Never been married. Never lived with anyone that I can tell. He's pretty much a golden boy."

Willow exhaled a breath she didn't know she was holding. For some reason, hearing he wasn't married was a huge relief. But then who was the woman? "He was with a blonde. I need to know who she is."

"That really narrows it down for me, Will. Thanks for making my job easier."

The sarcasm was par for the course. Willow just ignored it, like usual. "They met at a bar in the Mission area called the Pour House. For that matter, do a check on the bartenders there. I also want to know everything you can possibly find out about a woman in her late twenties, early thirties, black hair, mixed Asian ancestry."

Morgan complained some more under her breath, but

Willow could tell she was noting everything. Morgan was nothing if not thorough. "I'll get you the information as soon as I find it."

"Good." She looked at the street signs. "I've got to go."

"You okay, Will? You seem...I don't know, distracted or something. In the ten years I've known you, I would never have used *distracted* to describe you."

"I'm fine. Just get me the information. Fast." She closed her phone and tapped on the passenger seat in front of her. "Pull over here."

"Here?" He frowned over his shoulder. "You sure?"

"Yes."

He glanced at her top, and his frown deepened. "You're going to have trouble dressed like that."

She pulled a bill from the tight pocket of her pants. "I'll manage."

He started to say something else, but she opened the door and slid out before he could lecture her further. Slamming the door, she strode around the corner to the motel.

She let herself in and went down the hall to her room. As she unlocked the door, the older woman's door opened. "You're out late again. And don't you look scandalous."

Hell. Willow closed her eyes and centered before turning around.

"I used to wear shoes like that," the woman said, pointing with her cane. "Destroyed my arches."

"I'll keep that in mind."

The woman's lipstick-stained mouth pursed. "You out looking for a man?"

Willow's mouth quirked. "You could say that."

"You be sure to pick a nice man. I liked bad boys

myself, which is why I ended up like this. You heed my words and find someone decent. Exciting ain't all it's cracked up to be."

"I'll keep that in mind, too. Good night." She stepped inside and closed the door before the woman could continue.

As she kicked off her shoes, she couldn't help but think about the woman's words. A decent man. She snorted. As if they existed anymore. And then she thought of one man who lived with his grandmother. Ramirez's face appeared in her mind, his eyes heavy-lidded, right before he took her mouth.

She shook her head. She wasn't looking for a decent man. She was looking for the very bad one who killed her mother. Period. And no one was getting in the way of that, no matter how much her body wanted him.

She undressed, neatly stowing the clothes away, and climbed into bed after washing her face. Tomorrow she'd pay another visit to the club, and this time she'd talk to the owner. This time she wouldn't let anyone get in her way.

Chapter Ten

The woman was bound with leather cuffs, naked except for red heels and a blindfold. The man ran a crop across his palm, and the woman shuddered at the hissing sound.

Edward could care less. As he sat in his private room in the Easy, he glanced at his watch. Collins was late.

Deidre shifted next to him on the couch. He knew the tableau titillated her by the avid way she watched. It irritated him, that she could be so detached when the stakes were so high.

Where the hell was Collins?

He'd left orders not to be disturbed, unless it was someone bringing news of his daughter's return. The door behind them opened. A thrill of anticipation shot through him.

Then he became aware of the stench of defeat that drifted in with his employee, and knew he wouldn't be meeting his daughter today.

Edward kept his gaze on the scene in front of him, riding the cold tide of rage that swept through him. He could feel Collins's discomfort behind him.

Good. Let the incompetent bastard squirm. "It took you longer than I expected."

"I didn't..." His employee cleared his throat. "She got away, sir."

Fucking incompetence. "Explain."

"I had her. At least I thought I had her. And then something hit me from behind and knocked me out." Collins shifted, his discomfort audible. "It felt like a club, but I didn't hear anyone come up behind me."

Her power. It had to be.

A feeling of pride spread through him. Ironic, since that had annoyed him to no end in Lani.

Although Lani hadn't always annoyed him. When he'd met her, he'd been captivated by her light. It'd drawn him in, like he was a damned cliché.

True, her light had drawn him in, but it was her power that seduced him. He'd noticed it right away—she'd worn it like a cloak, pulled tight around her. He'd wanted to know where it stemmed from. He'd wanted to know the extent of its strength.

He'd wanted to possess it.

At first, she'd resisted him, but it wasn't long before he'd won her over. A few sappy gifts, some pretty words, and she was his. He'd been almost disappointed by how easy it had been.

Once they were married, there was nothing easy about Lani. She closed herself to him completely. He'd found out completely by accident about the scroll that gave her mystical powers. It'd infuriated him that she'd kept it hidden from him. She was *his wife*—everything she was belonged to him.

And then she had the nerve to turn her powers on him instead of sharing them.

He didn't tolerate betrayal. He'd pursued her with cold purpose. It had taken him years to figure out metal weakened her, and once he found her, he had been prepared.

Not prepared, however, to discover he had a daughter he didn't know about.

A daughter he still didn't know. He had to forcibly unclench his jaw to speak to Collins. "I'm not pleased."

The bodyguard swallowed.

Deidre slipped her hand over his, lightly gripping his fingers as if to offer comfort.

He didn't want comfort—he wanted his daughter. Lani had kept her away from him for too long. He'd thought he could make Willow need him, that she would stand by his side. That if he killed his wife, it would resolve their rift. But it had only deepened the gulf. "I trusted you to handle this. I don't employ you for failure."

"No, sir, you don't."

"Tell me you at least followed her."

His silence was answer enough, but then he said, "I got knocked out. When I came to, she was gone."

"Leave," he said to Collins. He'd get what he deserved later.

Deidre crossed her legs and waited until Collins left before she spoke. "An unfortunate setback."

"She'll come back here," he said tightly. "She saw me. She won't be able to resist coming back."

"Whoever she is, she's a worthy opponent."

Yes, Willow was worthy. Another reason to feel proud. It made the game that much more interesting.

"Let me take care of this."

He glanced at Deidre.

She returned his gaze steadily. "I'm serious. Let me handle this. I'll send several of my men after her."

"What can your men do that mine haven't?"

"She can't possibly evade four men at once, could she?"

He felt a grudging admiration for Deidre. Not even his men had the balls to stand up to him this way. "You're willing to help?"

"I've been helping from the beginning, darling."

Her presumption irritated him. The slut hadn't *helped* him—he'd used her.

But she was oblivious of the distinction and his thoughts. She curled her legs under her and faced him. "What does this woman want?"

That was easy. His daughter wanted *him*. He studied Deidre, trying to decipher her motives. "Why?"

"Maybe it's time to dangle it in front of her. To lure her into a trap." She caressed his fingers. "What do you think?"

He pulled his hand away. "I won't allow her to escape again." In actuality, it was a good idea, although he'd never admit that to her. It'd bring Willow right into his grasp.

"Then let me help." Deidre took Edward's hand again and, locking eyes with him, drew his finger into her mouth.

It did nothing for him. Willow had stolen his focus. Nothing else mattered now—nothing else would matter until Willow was at his side, once and for all. Until he had access to Willow's powers, the way Lani had denied him.

With her gifts, there wasn't anything they couldn't

accomplish—nothing they couldn't procure. Unlimited power was the end result. He'd rule the world.

He eyed the woman by his side. Perhaps he could use her just a bit more. So he nodded. "Do it."

Deidre tilted her head. "Consider it done."

Chapter Eleven

Nine o'clock in the morning, Gabe Sansouci was pacing back and forth in front of her three-person audience. She was trying to figure out how to tell them what she knew without freaking anyone out, which seemed totally impossible, given how freaked out *she* was. Being direct was the only way.

Agitated by the energy zipping between them like lightning, she studied the two other Guardians: her boyfriend Rhys Llewellyn, Guardian of the Book of Fire, and Max Prescott, who held Metal. It was bad enough with three Guardians—their powers were intensified and harder to control when they gathered together. How crazy would it be with four? She could only imagine that the outcome would be bad. Hands on her hips, she said, "So last night this Guardian walked into the bar."

Max stared at her flatly. "Please tell me you didn't barge into my home and drag me out of bed to tell me bad jokes. Because I could have still been snuggling with my naked wife."

"*Max.*" Blushing, Gabrielle's best friend Carrie smacked her husband with a pretty solid left.

Rhys arched his eyebrow. "As much as it pains me, I'd have to agree with Max, love."

Usually she melted whenever he called her *love* in his crisp British accent. But right now, after the incident last night and the ensuing lack of sleep, she wasn't inclined to being soothed. "This isn't a joke. When have you known me to willingly wake up before noon?"

Rhys nodded at Max. "She has a point."

"Damn right I have a point." She started pacing again. She could still feel the residual aftershocks from the surge of her power last night. It vibrated inside her, making her feel volatile. "Last night before closing, a woman walked in—"

"But I was there before closing last night," Carrie interrupted.

"She came after you and Ramirez left."

"How do you know she was a Guardian?" Max asked.

Gabrielle rolled her eyes. "The zap I felt when she walked into the room was pretty telling—a definite disturbance in the Force if I ever felt one."

"She?" Frowning, Carrie turned to her husband. "Didn't Francesca deliver the Book of Water to a guy?"

"Yes."

"She was the Wood Guardian." Gabe wrinkled her nose. "I thought I smelled fresh-cut wood when I got close to her."

"Why was the Guardian of the Book of Wood in the Pour House?" Max asked, a puzzled look on his face.

"Hey, don't look at me like that. It's not my fault she

walked into the bar." She glared at him. "I've never seen her before."

"Why don't you just tell us what happened, love?" her boyfriend said in that aggravatingly reasonable voice of his.

She threw her hands in the air. "That's what I was trying to do."

Carrie reached up and patted her arm. "We're listening, Gabe."

"The short of it is, she was sitting at the bar when I walked out of the storeroom. We saw each other, I lost it, broke a few bottles, and then she hit me with the Force and ran out." Gabe rubbed the spot on her chest. It felt like something had thrust into her and split her in two. It still ached, and she had a huge bruise, too. She'd had to hide it from Rhys that morning because he overreacted to things like that.

Rhys stood with the quick grace of a striking rattlesnake and held her by her arms. "Why didn't you tell me? Did she hurt you?"

See? That's what she was talking about. She smoothed the superfine wool of his suit. "I'm fine. Really."

He didn't look like he believed her, but he eased down a little. He took her hand and pulled her down next to him on the couch, keeping hold of her.

"You know what?" Carrie said slowly. Her gaze distant, the same look she got when she was contemplating the complexities of ancient Chinese texts. "I felt something weird last night as Rick and I were headed to his car."

Max went on instant alert. "What?"

"Easy, big boy." She patted her husband's leg. "I just felt a strange sensation. Kind of like a ripple in a pond."

Gabe stared at her friend, the klepto, who'd stolen the Book of Water from a monastery in China because she wanted to make a splash in her academic world. Carrie had lucked out. Except for the occasional rippling twinge, she'd emerged from her time with the Book of Water unscathed. She could have been killed, or worse, for what she had done. She'd also managed to find true love in the process.

"I think I must have felt her," Carrie continued. "I wouldn't have felt the zap you guys apparently feel when you're in the same room, but I'm still a little sensitive to your energies."

"The question is what she wanted," Max said, slipping a protective arm around his wife's shoulders.

"The question is what the hell is she doing here," Gabe corrected. "It's against the commandments."

Max raised his brow. "Commandments?"

Amusement lit Rhys's eyes. "Gabrielle was taught several rules where the scrolls are concerned."

Gabe raised a finger. "One, the Guardian who protects the scroll possesses its power. Two, the Guardian must keep his scroll hidden—"

"I think I know the basic tenets of being a Guardian," Max said dryly. "I've had the job a few years."

She shrugged. She couldn't help it. She'd only come into hers last year. The other Guardians had had their scrolls forever. They'd learned the ins and outs of being a Guardian from a master, right at the source of it all in China.

What she did know was that the scrolls were *not* meant to be united, because it harbored way too much concentrated power. It was the reason they were separated in the first place. "Doesn't it bother anyone that four out of five Guardians are all in San Francisco right at this moment? Isn't that frickin' bizarre? It's not supposed to be that way."

Rhys lifted her hand and kissed the inside of her wrist. "Gabrielle is concerned about the fate of the world."

Max grunted. "She should be. I've seen her in action."

Rhys's lips quirked, but to his credit he held his smile back.

"Sure, laugh it up, you two." She wanted Max and Rhys to get over their animosity, just not at her expense. They hadn't recaptured the closeness they'd once had, but at least they didn't go for each other's throats anymore. "When the world gets blown to bits, don't look at me."

"I don't think the world is going to self-destruct."

They all looked at Carrie.

Looking thoughtful, she ran a hand over the small mound of her belly. "If you guys weren't supposed to be in the same space, Wei Lin would have made sure that couldn't happen. He would have set those parameters when he stole the scrolls, found the five people worthy of protecting them from the rest of mankind's misuse, and marked them."

Gabe shook her head. "Maybe he trusted the Guardians to know to do that on their own."

Carrie shook her head. "I don't believe that. If it were so taboo, he would have done something about it. I should know. I stole his journal."

Like any of them needed to be reminded of that. Carrie's sudden bout of thievery resulted in all of them almost being outed as Guardians just a few months ago.

They needed to keep their identities concealed for fear
of being discovered, and having the world after their
powers.

"I'll look into it," Carrie announced with her usual
enthusiastic perkiness.

"No!" Gabe and Max exclaimed together.

Rhys addressed her calmly. "No need, darling. I'm
sure among the three of us, we can suss out what this
other Guardian wants."

"What, you're going to storm her house with swords
and torches?" Carrie rolled her eyes. "In case you guys
forgot, I'm a scholar. I'm an expert at research. Let me
look into the potential hazards of having the Guardians
amassed in one place."

Max shook his head. "You—"

His wife covered his mouth with her hand. "I promise
I won't do anything crazy or put myself in any danger.
I'm just going to do a little reading."

"The last time you did a little reading, you almost got
skewered by your thesis advisor," Gabe pointed out.

Her best friend shot her an exasperated look. "Thanks
for bringing that up. Like Max isn't protective enough."

"I'm willing to let Carrie do her research," Rhys said.
"As long as she doesn't put herself in danger."

"I won't," she promised. At Max's snort, she squeezed
his thigh. "I swear I won't."

Max leveled a look at Rhys. "You'll check from your
end."

Rhys smiled, that killer shark smile Gabe had seen
him flash just before he decimated one of his business
opponents. "Of course."

Gabe sat back, cuddling into his side. She didn't feel

sunny and light, but she did feel a little better for having the other three on it, too. Despite the challenges of the three Guardians being in one place, they (and Carrie) made a pretty great team. If only they could keep from killing each other, and everyone else in the world.

Chapter Twelve

Martin Weinberg, from the Computer Forensics Unit, slapped a manila folder onto Ramirez's desk. "This chick is like the wind."

Ramirez looked up from his laptop. "What does that mean?"

The kid was practically frothing at the mouth. He snagged the chair next to the desk, flipped it around, and straddled it. "She totally doesn't exist. I'd stake my rep on it."

As young as Weinberg was, his rep was solid. All the detectives used him when they needed more than the usual information. Weinberg had been a famous hacker before he was recruited out of the schoolroom to join the force. Ramirez knew the kid wanted more fieldwork, which made him eager to help with any case.

"What makes you say that?" he asked even though he didn't have a single doubt that *Sophie Mitchell* was fabricated.

The kid leaned forward, his gaze bright. "Dude, don't

get me wrong. The cover is brilliantly done. I mean, *brilliant*. I couldn't have made up an identity better than this."

A cover. Ramirez leaned back in his chair and straightened his tie. It wasn't like he didn't know she'd been lying. He hesitated, torn between needing to know who she was and not wanting to, at the same time. "What did you find?"

"The alias is perfect. There's an existing birth certificate, credit cards, passport, apartment, the works. And the records all go back in time."

"If it's so perfect, what makes you think it's fake?"

"Because I'm a supergenius." He recoiled in affront. "Duh."

Ramirez nodded, ignoring the smirk Taylor shot him. "I don't know how I could have forgotten."

"Damn straight. Anyway, before you rudely doubted my abilities, I was going to tell you that most credit reports only extend seven years into the past. No one ever researches beyond that, given there's a valid driver's license and birth document. But I, of course, always check further back." Weinberg leaned in again, his momentary pique forgotten in his excitement. "There's no paperwork before ten years ago."

It was on the tip of Ramirez's tongue to ask if he was sure, but he didn't want to insult the kid any further.

"So I dug deeper. You told me to go all the way, right?"

Ramirez nodded. "I did."

The kid widened his eyes, trying to look innocent. "Even if it meant tapping into networks I shouldn't have been in?"

"Stop." Ramirez rubbed his face. "Don't tell me. I just want to know what you found out about her."

"All of it?"

"Of course."

The kid pulled out another manila folder and smacked that on top of the previous one. "Willow Tarata. Age unknown. Kiwi, though some might call her a citizen of the world, given all the countries she'd lived in. She doesn't travel under her own identity, but under several different ones, including Sophie Mitchell."

Willow Tarata. *Willow. That* name suited her. Tall and reedy. Sad. Grounded. Vibrant with life.

He straightened in his chair. What the hell was coming over him? She was a suspected criminal. If Taylor knew the direction his thoughts were going, Ramirez would never hear the end of it. He picked up the folder and stared at it. "Go on."

Weinberg leaned in. "The most interesting part is that she has plenty of money, but she's never been employed. It looks like she receives a modest deposit each month. I'd need more time to find out where the deposits come from, they're so wrapped up in red tape."

Interesting wasn't the word he'd use. "Does her address in New York check out?"

The kid shook his head. "Totally bogus, dude. That building is condemned and about to be gutted."

Ramirez glared at the dossier, anger blurring his vision. Why he was so furious, he had no idea. He'd known she'd lied to him—it wasn't as though this was a surprise. Yet, that didn't seem to make a difference.

The kid drummed his fingers on the chair's metal back. "I tried tracking where she was now, but she hasn't left any kind of trail. She's like a ghost. Whoever is masking her trail is a fricking artist."

"Anything else?"

"All in the report, boss." He blinked eagerly. "Brilliant work, if I say so myself. Aren't you going to read it?"

"Yes, I am. Thanks for this."

"Because there's this one part where—"

Taylor leaned over from his cubicle. "I think that means you're dismissed, kid."

"Aw, man. Already?" He stood reluctantly. "I thought I could wait to see if you had questions. Or to see if I could help you when you go after this *bee-yatch*."

Ramirez frowned. "Don't be disrespectful."

The kid sighed in defeat. "Call me if you need more. Or if you want to go to the range sometime. I've been practicing and I—"

"Out," Ramirez ordered.

With a regretful sigh, Weinberg stood and scampered away. His expression made Ramirez regret being harsh, but he needed to read the report, and he didn't want an audience.

"Annoying kid, but he knows his stuff." Taylor nodded at the file. "What's that about?"

He hadn't told his partner about Willow. He'd had no choice. He couldn't exactly say he saw a woman at the scene of the crime who had disappeared into thin air, leaving behind the breathy harmony of a flute. He'd be laughed straight out of the station and into a mental hospital. "At Bohemia I noticed a woman who seemed suspicious."

"Seems like your gut was right once again. I swear you've got some kind of freaky ESP, just like your grammie. My big gut is only useful for packing in more of May's good food." He patted his round belly. "I assume you think she's connected to the case."

Without a doubt. Only he was reluctant to admit that to his partner, and that disturbed him. "She doesn't fit the profile."

"But you must think she's involved. Otherwise, you wouldn't have asked the wonder kid to dig into her background."

"He's a supergenius, not a wonder kid," Ramirez said mildly.

Taylor waved his massive paw. "Whatever. I'm saying you've caught a scent and are hot on her tail."

Ramirez laughed without amusement. "That would be an accurate assessment."

His partner stood. "They finally got me an address where the PI lived. It was like he didn't want to be found. I'm off to check it out."

"Do you need backup?"

"Nah. It should be routine, right?" Taylor said as he pulled on his wrinkled suit coat.

Ramirez shook his head at the yellow stain on his partner's shirt. Taylor tended to wear as much food as he ate. "Mustard?"

"Curry. Went to an all-you-can-eat Indian restaurant with Meeks for lunch."

"Does May know you're going out with pretty coworkers?"

"Heck, no. But she knows I'd never step out on her. She keeps me in line with her meat loaf. That dish would make an atheist believe in God." He grinned. "You think Meeks is pretty?"

Compared to the other Homicide inspectors, Meeks was a goddess. He used to think she was very pretty, but that was before he'd met a certain tall blonde. "She's prettier than you."

"That's not saying much." Taylor's grin turned conniving. "Want me to set you up with her? You know she's new in town and could use a friend."

"I'll keep that in mind. You going sometime today?"

"Yeah." He gave a two-finger salute. "See ya tomorrow."

Hand on the file, Ramirez waited until his partner was gone to open it. The first several pages were details about Sophie Mitchell, confirming everything Weinberg said—where she lived, details on her business, her passport information, and the list of dates she left and reentered the country, etc. It looked legit, unless you were suspicious by nature. Plus, it looked too perfect, just as the kid said. He had to give it to Weinberg for having good instincts.

Ramirez flipped through a few more pages until he got to the real information about Willow Tarata. Looking closer, Willow seemed to come into existence twenty years before. There wasn't much on her there, either, beyond a well-used passport record. He saw no credit cards, no bank accounts. Over the past ten years, Willow's activity had waned, which was directly opposite to Sophie's, probably by design.

Was *Willow* another fabricated identity?

Probably, at least a little. But deep down, he suspected *Willow* was closer to the truth of who the woman was than *Sophie*. *Sophie* didn't ring true at all.

He turned the page, read Weinberg's barely legible handwritten notes, and stopped. Skimming slowly through the page, he ignored the notes to focus on the facts. Then he read the kid's notes again:

> *I was dicking around, doing random searches on events and stuff, and I noticed a pattern between this chick's activity and certain unexplainable deaths all over the world. Coincidence or hit man? You decide.*

After reading Weinberg's notes half a dozen times, Ramirez looked into Sophie Mitchell's profile. Sure enough, Sophie's travels abroad coincided with questionable events. Weinberg included a brief report on each victim.

Jaw tight, Ramirez read through the profiles. Most of the men were criminals, or linked to questionable activity. Some people would say the world was better off without them, that whoever took them out did everyone a service. But to him, murder was murder. Being justified didn't make it right. He scrubbed his face. No one but the courts had a right to decide another person's fate. There was a reason there were rules. Without rules everyone would be running around like half-cocked vigilantes.

His gaze settled on the bland passport picture clipped to the front of the folder. Her features were all familiar— the high cheekbones, full lips, and long, straight hair. But she looked flat. Lifeless. Empty.

He shouldn't have felt like he knew who she was. She'd faked everything the few times they'd been together— except when he'd kissed her. That alone was evidence that she wasn't empty, and she definitely wasn't lifeless. Inside, something was driving her.

To commit murder?

He frowned at the report. The words *hit man* rang in his head, loud and clanging.

He'd have to find out. And if she was some kind of assassin, he'd have to find a way stop her, even if he didn't like it.

Chapter Thirteen

Willow managed to get out of the motel under the radar, meaning she didn't have to engage with the woman down the hall. Instead of running along the coastline, she decided to run to the Mission and back. To check out Ramirez's house.

She ran by it once, taking in all the details. Unlike some of the other gaudy houses in the neighborhood, it was clean and simple—light blue with white trim, recently painted and kept in good condition. *Homey,* she decided, surprised.

The garden in front was lush but also trimmed neatly. She had a hard time seeing him doing gardening, but she didn't have a hard time seeing him shirtless in the sun, sweat gleaming on his chest.

She cleared the lust from her throat and ran to Cesar Chavez Street before she turned around and headed back. She'd gone a block when her phone vibrated. Taking it out, she checked the caller ID. Morgan. She answered the call.

Before she could say a word, Morgan said, "Someone breached my walls."

"That's a euphemism you've never used before."

"Willow, I'm serious. Someone breached my walls."

Willow stopped running. Morgan never sounded serious like that, unless she was really freaking out. "Tell me what happened. What walls?"

"The walls I've built around your identities. Someone's torn them down and pissed all over my territory."

She automatically wondered if it was Ramirez, but as soon as she had the thought, she dismissed it. He wasn't the usual corrupt law officer; she'd dealt with enough to know the type. Ramirez radiated integrity. Besides, she doubted he had the skills to break through all Morgan's defenses. "Who do you think it was?"

"I don't know. Whoever it was covered his ass really well. I can't trace him." A loud crash sounded, followed by the *plink* of broken plastic. "I've *never* not been able to trace someone."

"That means Sophie Mitchell is compromised?"

"All the aliases are compromised. Ten goddamn years of work, down the drain with one stroke of the keyboard. The only thing they haven't gotten to is the corporation, but even that is only a matter of time at this point." Another crash.

Willow considered planting calm thoughts in Morgan's head, but she knew her friend well enough to know she would have hated having her thoughts tampered with, almost as much as she hated her computer systems messed with. "It's hardly worth destroying your office over. This was bound to happen eventually. We'll create a new corporation. Our clients will still know how to find us."

"No, it wasn't. You don't understand this, do you?"

"Explain it to me."

"Forget the company. Your identities are compromised," Morgan said slowly, as if she were talking to a four-year-old. "The bastard got into all the files, including Willow Tarata's."

Willow stopped cold. "Shit."

"That's what I'm saying."

"And you don't know who?"

"No, but hell if I won't find out. This kind of talent only works for the government and the rich. Have you pissed anyone off that I don't know about?"

"Other than the local police?"

Morgan growled with frustration. "This isn't the moment to find a sense of humor."

Willow didn't bother to explain she wasn't joking. "Let me know when you find something out."

She ended the call and began running again. She needed to think. Ramirez had to be eager to uncover her secrets, but did the San Francisco police have that kind of talent? Probably not. Plus, Morgan was beyond meticulous where her work was concerned. If someone cracked her security measures, they would have had to go beyond what the law allowed.

Could it have been the Bad Man? Maybe.

"Most likely," she added under her breath. She'd felt him breathing down her neck for years, searching for her the same way he'd searched for her mother. If she had a commission for every bounty he'd taken out on her over the years, she and Morgan would never have to work again. Maybe he was closing in on her, just as she was closing in on him.

She slowed to a walk the block before and took her time as she walked by Ramirez's house a second time. It looked like there was a separate residence downstairs. Did he live there, or did his grandmother? As she was counting the number of windows, an older woman came out onto the porch. It had to be his grandmother Elena Ramirez. She had a proud bearing, with milky coffee skin, hair that was salt, sprinkled with specks of pepper, and piercing dark eyes. Just like Ramirez. Willow expected the woman to do something—begin gardening or retrieve her mail—but she just stood there watching her.

A shiver went down Willow's spine as the sharp gaze focused on her. Willow nodded politely and began to stroll to keep the woman from becoming suspicious.

Elena waved her over.

Willow stopped, uncertain what to do, but the woman waved more insistently. Willow told herself to go, since this was a good opportunity to get more information on Ramirez. Besides, she was curious about the woman, so she opened the gate and went up the short walkway.

Ramirez's grandmother waited for her patiently, her gaze never wavering. Willow had the strange sensation that the older woman was peeling away all her layers, down to the naked center of her soul, dark stains and all.

She fought the urge to turn and run, instead taking the scrutiny head-on and striding up the porch steps. She suddenly felt extremely uncomfortable. No one had looked at her with such clarity since her mother had died.

The woman nodded, like she'd come to a decision. "Come in." She turned around and walked into the house.

Intrigued and confused, Willow trailed obediently after the woman. She stepped into a warm, colorful entryway.

To the right was an equally warm living area, lined with picture frames on the walls and other surfaces.

Fighting the urge to stop and look, Willow walked past it to the next room, the kitchen.

Elena Ramirez stood at the stove, stirring a pot of soup, which smelled delicious. "Sit. I'll make you tea." The woman looked over her shoulder and frowned. "And my *posole* is almost ready. You need food. Wash and then sit."

Willow could only stare, completely at a loss for words. She was positive she didn't need to eat, but she wasn't sure she could tell this woman that. Not without serious repercussions. This was all new to her—she'd never had a grandmother. She had no idea how to deal with one. "Please don't go to any trouble. I still have to run back, and I'm not hungry, anyway."

Elena filled a kettle with water and set it on a burner. "There are many kinds of hunger, *mijita.*"

She didn't like the endearment, but she didn't know how she could explain why without sounding like a madwoman. So she stuck to the basics as she washed her hands. "Your home is nice, and the neighborhood seems friendly. Have you lived here long?"

"Long, and yet it seems like only yesterday that we moved in."

"We?" she asked as casually as she could, drying her hands as she sat down.

Elena turned around, an eyebrow raised. "Me and my grandson, Ricardo, of course."

Willow saw Ramirez in the woman's expression, and it made her feel something curious in her chest. "It must be nice living with your grandson."

She humphed, taking down a set of opaque canisters from the shelves and carefully measuring the tea leaves into an old china teapot. Replacing the canisters, labels out, she took a bowl and filled it with whatever she was cooking. Turning, she set it and a spoon in front of Willow.

It was on the tip of Willow's tongue to refuse, but the aroma of cumin and a hint of herby sweetness, mixed with clove, wrapped around her and teased her senses. Without thought she dipped the spoon in and took a tentative taste.

The soup was warm and rich and basic, reminding her of the childhood she had spent with her mother. She lifted another spoon and stopped halfway to her mouth, taking in the earthy tang of running through the trees. For an instant, she felt the warmth of the New Zealand sun shining down on her. Unbidden, tears sprang into her eyes. She froze, mortified by her own reaction. She hadn't cried since the day the Bad Man had found them. She certainly didn't want to cry now, especially not in front of this strong woman. And definitely not on Ramirez's turf.

Elena handed her a napkin. "Good food touches the soul. You haven't had that in a long while."

Willow blanched at the statement. How did she know? The crazy part: she didn't doubt that Elena knew precisely how long it'd been. She narrowed her eyes, letting *mù ch'i* flow out into the space between them, like the soft branches of a *tarata*. Her energy surrounded the woman, and Elena began to shine brightly, the aura around her radiating warmth. Yet in a blink of an eye, the glow disappeared.

Willow stared at the woman, who gazed back at her

calmly. Willow couldn't have been more surprised when Elena asked, "Do you believe in fate?"

Not sure how to answer, Willow busied herself with another spoonful of soup. After she swallowed, she said, "Most people wouldn't invite strangers into their house, much less feed them."

Amusement sparked in Elena's eyes. "We're not most people, are we?"

"You don't even know my name."

"Names are elusive, taken and given at will. It's what is rooted beneath that matters." Her direct gaze dared Willow to argue that, but she couldn't. Willow knew better than anyone how flimsy names were.

"You didn't answer my question," Elena said. "Do you believe in fate?"

Wiping her mouth, Willow shrugged. "Fate is what we make it."

The old woman chuckled. "Why did I know you would say that?"

She had no idea, and she was sure she didn't want to know. She devoured the last bit of soup and pushed the bowl away from her. "That was delicious. Thank you."

"I wonder when you're going to ask about my grandson."

Willow choked on her spit. "Who?"

Elena got up and brought her a glass of water. "Ricardo. We both know he's the reason you're here."

She mentally flailed. "I'm not sure what you mean."

"Aren't you?"

Starting to stand, Willow tried to deflect what felt like an inquisition. "I appreciate the food, but I should get going. I've already infringed on your time enough."

"He's looking for you."

She plopped back onto the seat. Had he told his grandmother something? She didn't picture him as the type to divulge work details. "I'm—"

"Don't tell me you don't know what I mean," Elena said sharply. "You insult my intelligence, not to mention everything your mother taught you."

Willow's breath caught in her chest, and she almost choked. As it was, it took a minute before she could speak. "You knew my mom?"

"Personally, no."

Willow shook her head. "Then how do you know what she taught me?"

"I know. Some people are connected in unexplainable ways." Elena leaned forward, her expression fierce. "You have powerful gifts and the ability to help people. Your mother saw to it. Don't build something unworthy on that foundation."

Willow didn't know whether to ask more about her mother or trash the kitchen in her anger.

"Anger isn't your natural way. It doesn't belong to you. The anger, as well as the hate and revenge, have grown like weeds around your heart." Elena's face softened with something that was dreadfully close to pity. "They've overtaken the ground you need for your own growth. It's time to cull them. You need to allow love to bloom in their place."

Her identities had been compromised, but none of her files, not even the ones on *Willow Tarata,* included information on her mother. How did Elena know? "What could you possibly know of what I need?"

The woman smiled softly. "I've seen it. You're not the only white witch in the world."

Shaking her head, Willow pushed back from the table. "I don't know what Ramirez told you, but you have no idea what you're talking about."

His grandmother tipped her head. "Don't I?"

"No, you don't." Willow headed for the door.

"You didn't finish asking me about my grandson," Elena called after her.

Frozen in the kitchen doorway, Willow looked back at Ramirez's grandmother.

A placid smile wreathed the sly woman's face. "Perhaps next time."

"There won't be a next time," Willow declared as she stormed out. But even as she said it, she knew it was a lie. She needed to figure out what game Ramirez was playing. She needed to make sure he wouldn't interfere in her pursuit of the Bad Man.

"Have faith in your goodness," Elena called out as Willow walked out the door.

"*Faith*," she mumbled in derision as she stomped down the porch steps. In her experience, faith was a concept for fools who needed justification for the bad things that happened. But sometimes there was no justification beyond the will of an evil man.

Chapter Fourteen

His grandmother had taught him long ago to heed his intuition. So when Ramirez got a niggling feeling that he needed to go home at midday, he didn't question it. He arrived in time to see Willow Tarata jog down his walkway.

What the hell was she doing here? How did she find out where he lived?

Pulling over sharply, he watched her look both ways down the street, her eyebrows drawn, mouth set. Something had upset her. Before he could puzzle that out, she turned and ran toward downtown. He sat mesmerized by the elegant curve of her backside and the long, swishing length of her hair.

He glanced at the house. A curtain in his grandmother's apartment fluttered. He saw Lita's face in the window, watching Willow run away. Then she turned and looked directly at him, her eyebrow raised as if to say, *What are you waiting for?*

"Hell," he muttered, getting out of the car. Grabbing his suit coat, he shrugged into it as he took off after her.

Willow's pace was easy, but she ate up distance with her long legs. As she reached Duboce Street, her shoulders tensed. Noticing her wariness, he ducked into a doorway right as she stopped and turned around. He waited for what seemed like minutes before peering around the corner.

She was on the move again.

Careful to maintain enough distance so she wouldn't sense him, he continued following her all the way to Yerba Buena Gardens. He didn't know whether to be thankful or to curse. Yerba Buena teemed with all sorts of people, from children and their mothers visiting the play park, to tourists, to businessmen attending conferences at the Moscone Center. With all the people, it'd be easier to stay undercover. With all the people, it would also be easier to lose her.

Except Willow surprised him by settling herself under the shade of a tree.

He sat on a bench a good distance behind her and to the left. She closed her eyes. In that space, something fell away from her face—a tightness, a suspiciousness. He wouldn't say she looked peaceful, but it was the closest he'd ever seen to stillness on her. Then she radiated with energy, a glow that lit her from below her skin and shined outward. She looked absolutely beautiful.

Her true self, he realized. He had the irrepressible urge to touch her. To run his fingers across her face, to bask in that light. He caught himself standing up, about to go to her.

Damn it, focus, he thought, forcing himself to sit down again.

She set her hands on the ground, a caressing motion

that made him ridiculously jealous. The tree next to her shook, a gentle shudder, before two long twigs dropped. She reached up, opened her hand, and caught them at the right moment before they had the chance to hit her on the head.

What the hell? He looked at her sharply, trying to understand what it was he was seeing. Her eyes were still closed, but she brought the twigs to her chest and held them against her. Then she bowed her head, as if giving thanks, and opened her eyes. Still holding the branches, she gracefully rose to her feet and sauntered away.

If he didn't know better, he would have thought the tree handed her those twigs because she asked for them. But he knew better.

Right?

There was before, though, when that other tree had conveniently swayed right into her attacker. But he'd imagined that, too.

His grandmother would say there was much in this world that defied conventional definition; sometimes the right answer didn't suit, because our worldviews were too narrow. Certainly, some of the things he'd seen her do defied explanation.

Lita had called Willow a *white witch*. What did that mean?

Knowing his grandmother, it could mean anything. She could be a healer, for all he knew. But why would a healer need twigs?

He shook his head and followed her all the way to a motel on Broadway, next to a particularly sleazy strip club. He watched her walk inside and up to the second floor. He slipped through the door before it closed, in time to see her clear the top of the stairs, her hair giving a saucy flick as she turned left.

Waiting until he heard a door close on the floor above, he jogged up the steps and took stock of the motel. If he had to describe it in one word, he'd call it *seedy*. Ramirez frowned. He could see her staying in some swank, modern motel, where the furniture was metal and leather, like Max's apartment. He could even see her staying in a warm cabin, surrounded by trees.

He couldn't see her staying in this dump.

A door opened five feet away and Ramirez braced himself. He'd expected to see Willow lean in the open doorway, with that sassy tilt of her head and caustic attitude. Instead, a prematurely aged woman with matted hair peeked her head out. Her bloodshot eyes narrowed. "Are you here to arrest Darryl? Because he cut out of town yesterday."

He wasn't surprised that she pegged him for a cop. Most people with questionable pasts could, and she looked like she'd covered some mileage. "No."

Understanding dawned in her eyes. "You're here for *her.*"

He didn't have to ask who she meant. "Why do you think that?"

"You're talking to me, but your attention is on her door." She jerked her chin across the hall.

Bingo. He wanted to ask questions about Willow but didn't think the woman would be receptive. Instead, he noted her room number as he nodded his thanks.

"You better not be here to hurt her." She lifted her cane and waved it at him. "She's more delicate than she lets on. You'd have to make it through me first."

How did a badass like Willow inspire loyalty and caring from this type of woman? "I just want to talk to her."

Her eyes tracked him, clearly not believing a word he said. She started to say something else, but then she just shook her head and ducked back inside.

Time for answers. He walked over to Willow's door and knocked.

Someone was at the door.

Willow dropped the whittling knife and picked up one of the dirks she'd just carved. Unfortunately, her room didn't have an escape route, since the window was barred on the outside, but chances were that it was just the woman from two doors down. Willow had managed to sneak in without talking to her. The woman had probably realized it and wanted to say hi. Still, she gripped the dirk so it was hidden against her forearm and opened the door.

Her heart stopped, then started again, beating hard against her chest cavity.

Ramirez.

She searched his gaze, wanting to ask why the hell he was there. But she knew it'd drive him crazy if she played it casual, so she leaned in the doorway, crossing her ankles. "Didn't get enough, Starsky?"

He remained cool and analytical, like the detective he was. Damn him. "I could ask the same of you," he said.

There was an underlying accusation to his statement. She studied him, trying to figure it out. Had his grandmother told him she'd been to his house?

It didn't matter now. Whatever had happened, he'd

managed to find his way to her motel . . . which could only mean that he'd followed her. She'd known she was being tailed. Even if she couldn't see him, she'd sensed it with *mù ch'i*. She should have known it was Ramirez by the way her mark had prickled. "Impressive, Starsky. If you ever decide to retire from the force, you could become a private investigator. But that doesn't explain how you found which room I was in."

Slight movement over his shoulder caught her attention. The nosy woman's head poked out from behind the door. Her eyes widened as Willow stared her down, and she shut the door soundly.

"I guess that answers that." Willow turned back to Ramirez. "What I still don't know is what you're doing here."

He took a step toward her, forcing her to retreat into her room. It was either that or have him pressed up against her, and that didn't seem like a good idea. At all. Not with the way her body betrayed her whenever they touched.

Ramirez closed the door behind him and surveyed the room. His sharp gaze fell on her bed. "A hobby?" he asked, reaching for her whittling knife.

She took the knife out of his hand and gathered the dirks before he could question her any further. Opening a dresser drawer, she deposited everything inside, then turned to face him. "I'm still waiting for an answer to my question."

He regarded her steadily, seemingly at ease. "Why don't you tell me why you think I'm here?"

She leaned her hips against the dresser and crossed her arms. "I think you're here because you can't get enough of me."

Ramirez's gaze traveled down her body. "Most people would assume when a Homicide inspector visits, it's about a murder."

She felt like tinder under a flame. "I'm not most people, Starsky. Besides, I didn't do anything to warrant your interest. Not yet, anyway," she said, unable to control her eyes from roaming the contours of his body.

He flushed, the slightest tinge of pink under his tan skin. What kind of man blushes these days?

The same kind who lives with his grandmother, she silently answered. Any other guy and she would have thought him a total wuss and, therefore, not worth the time. But Ramirez was a 100 percent virile, masculine man.

"Why shouldn't I suspect you of being involved in the murders?" he asked, all business again. He was, obviously, a man with a mission. She wasn't sure what she preferred, the staid cop or the hot guy. Certainly, the cop was less discomfiting.

"Because I told you I didn't do it."

"But you aren't denying you were involved in some way."

Willow sighed, suddenly exhausted. "Can't you let this go?"

"You take a polygraph test and I'll let it go."

Time to change tactics. She pushed off the dresser and walked up to him. "I don't think you want to let it go. In fact, I think you want to grab it and hold on with both hands."

His body tensed. "The only thing I want from you is answers."

She glanced down at his crotch. "Why don't I believe that?"

"Stop," he ordered.

"I'm tempted to ask if you're going to make me, but I have the feeling you'd just take that as a challenge." Although she continued to tell herself this was all an act, she couldn't deny the moisture that began to form between her thighs. She suddenly realized how much she enjoyed having him this close.

"The only challenge here is you." He reached out and took her by her biceps. "Why were you at my house?"

"I was out jogging." To her own ears, she sounded breathless. It was because his hands felt so delicious. Despite herself, she wanted them all over her body.

"Up the walkway to my house?" He tangled his hand in her ponytail and lifted her gaze to meet his. "Why were you there?"

"Maybe I wanted a look at the inner sanctum of an SFPD Homicide inspector." She lifted her hand to toy with one of the buttons of his shirt. "Want to give me a peek?"

Really, he looked like he wanted to give her a swat, which made it that much more surprising when he hauled her up on her toes and kissed the breath out of her.

The next thing she knew, her arms were around his neck and her legs hugging his hips. His hands supported her under her bottom. He swung her around, and they toppled backward so they landed on the bed, him on top.

He nibbled down her neck, each nipping bite as devastating as a lick of fire. She arched, giving him room to work his magic. His hands slipped under her top, skimming up her rib cage to cup her breasts.

She gasped as his fingers strummed her nipples. Then she gasped again when he lifted away from her.

She blinked, staring up at him, stunned by the sudden sense of loss.

Frowning, he shook his head. "What am I doing?"

Before she could frame a properly sarcastic retort, he got off the bed and straightened his clothing. "This cannot happen. You're a suspect, and I'm the lead officer in the investigation. I'm a *cop*."

With a last, hot glance at her, he strode from the room, the door shutting swiftly behind him.

And just like that, he was gone. She stared at where he'd been standing. She should have been happy, or relieved. But all she felt was like something was missing. Inhaling deeply, she caught a whiff of his masculine lemony scent.

"Damn it." She kicked the dresser.

The drawer fell open, and her scroll rolled to the front.

The Book of Wood. It wasn't safe here any longer—not since Ramirez knew where she was. He wouldn't break in to investigate—he was too by-the-book for that—but she didn't put it past him to get a warrant. She needed to hide the scroll, and she knew just the spot.

Grabbing it, she jogged out of the building, down to the Embarcadero and up to the Presidio. She passed the Palace of the Legion of Honor, but before she got to the Sutro Baths ruins, she found a secluded spot and picked the tallest cypress there.

A quick survey of the area revealed no one, so she climbed to the top, a feeling of peace and ease blanketing her with each foot that she ascended. Perching on the most solid branch, Willow sifted through the leaves until she found a crook where she could nestle the scroll securely. She stroked the parchment one last time, before securing it. Usually, at times like this, holding her scroll banished her loneliness.

Not today.

Today she realized that she hadn't felt the customary loneliness at all when Ramirez had been in her room. And that only made her feel lonelier now.

Chapter Fifteen

Willow leaned against the brick facade of a building down the block from Bohemia as she watched the club. Just like the other night, there was a line of people waiting for entry.

Unlike the other night, she was aware of the discreet traffic through the other entrance—the one that led into the sex club. Where she was headed tonight.

She just had to make sure it was safe first. The past two hours hadn't revealed anything abnormal. Still, she couldn't help being wary. The effects of having the scroll away from her left her vaguely queasy. But she also couldn't shake the feeling that Ramirez was on her tail. And, damn it, she hated to admit it, but she *wanted* him on her.

After she'd hidden the scroll, she'd gone back to her room, stripped, and gotten into bed. Only she couldn't go to sleep—not with the feeling of his hands on her, his body pressed against hers. She'd taken a hot shower, trying to wash him off, but that'd only turned her on more.

Pathetic.

She shook her head, feeling her face burn as she remembered masturbating. Not even bringing herself to climax was enough to get rid of the itch he'd ignited in her. Morgan would tell her she needed to chill, and Morgan would have been right. She rolled her shoulders and stretched her neck. She couldn't afford to lose her cool now, not when she was so close to pinning down the Bad Man.

She knew the answers were inside that club, with the owner. She'd talk with him tonight, and nothing was standing in her way. Not even a hard, intense cop, with a great mouth and lethal hands. She told herself he wouldn't be here tonight. He had no reason to be. As hard as he tried to prove otherwise, there was nothing to tie her to the murders. He had no evidence on her.

She pushed off the wall behind her and strode toward the main door of Bohemia. The bouncer from the other night was at the door again. He gave her an appreciative once-over and unhooked the gate for her as she sauntered toward him. "You're out to kill tonight, baby."

Yes, she was, although she was sure he didn't mean it the same way she did—ready with her new set of wooden dirks strapped to the inside of her thighs. Tonight she'd dressed to be noticed, in hopes of attracting the owner's attention. Her red leather skirt and red lace top ensured that. The top was partially see-through, and she wore nothing underneath. Perhaps a mistake, given the way the fabric abraded her nipples, making her think about the cop's touch.

Focus. Tonight was the night she'd discover the Bad Man's identity. She couldn't afford to be distracted. She gave the bouncer a sultry smile as she strutted past him, aware of his gaze following her.

Inside, she checked to see if the eager bartender was on duty, but he was absent. Good. That was one less thing to worry about.

She scanned the room with *mù ch'i.* Clear. She searched the crowd on the dance floor for the owner's tall, thin form, but he wasn't there, either. Not that she expected him to be. Based on her previous excursion, she figured he'd either be in his office or at the Easy. His office seemed the logical choice. She could check out the sex club on the way there.

Heading to the threshold, she planted a distraction in the mind of the man standing guard and walked through the door and the curtains into hell. She looked around casually. No owner in here, either. She glanced up at the top of the stairs that led to his office. The bouncer who manned the entrance didn't look like he'd be swayed by a pretty face. Not that it mattered.

Willow walked up to him, letting her mind stretch. She pictured her mind and his as trees, their thoughts branches. When the image was strong, she let her branches tangle with his, until she was completely obscured from his thoughts. Certain that he couldn't see her, she walked past him and opened the door enough to slip through. Because her thoughts were mixed with his, she heard the bouncer's awareness of the door opening and closing. Planting reassurances that nothing was amiss, she strode down the short hall to the door that said *Office.*

Standing outside, she closed her eyes and let her senses search the room on the other side. She felt an absence of energy—like a black hole.

Death.

Frowning, she focused *mù ch'i* to discern who it might be. Not Ramirez, she realized right away. The residual echo of energy didn't feel like his. But why had he come to mind first? She had no reason to be thinking of him. He wouldn't have been there, anyway.

Who would have been there?

The Bad Man. Or Quentin.

It wasn't the Bad Man—she believed she would have recognized his acrid feel, and she wasn't familiar enough with Quentin to identify him for sure. There was only one way to find out.

Opening the door, she slipped inside and quietly closed it. The room was sleek and opulent, full of chrome and leather. A painting dominated one wall—an incomprehensible modern piece. The wall ahead of her was floor-to-ceiling glass, looking out on the club below.

Willow walked to the chair, the feeling of unease increasing with each step. She touched the back of the chair and spun it around. The owner's dead body slouched to one side as the chair came to a stop.

"Damn it." She shoved her hair over her shoulder, frustrated. Then she froze, seeing the gleaming silver protruding from Quentin's forehead.

A throwing star. *His* calling card.

The Bad Man was sending her a message. He was toying with her, leaking enough information to lure her out into the open. It'd be a new tactic for him, offering himself as bait to trap her. Smart on his part, because she'd willingly risk the danger to have a shot at him.

She focused on the desk.

Is finding a labeled picture of the Bad Man too much

to hope for? She pushed the chair away to clear space in front of the desk and tried the first file drawer. Locked.

She stared at it, considering her options. She could pick the lock, but she'd never been good at that, no matter how hard Morgan had tried to help her refine that skill. It was probably because of the metal. If she'd been the Guardian of the Book of Metal, she would have been set; she was sure of that. Or she could look for the key, which the owner probably had in a pocket.

She turned to the body and patted him down for keys. Finding them in his left pants pocket, she knelt in front of the file cabinet and began trying each one. If the number of keys was an indication of importance, this man was God.

She was on the fourth key, when the office door opened. She began to draw on *mù ch'i* to provide her cover, but the moment she saw the familiar silhouette in the doorway, she lost her concentration and faltered.

Ramirez.

She was caught. Damn his timing. She set the keys on the desk and sat back on her heels. "Never would've expected to see you hanging out in a sex club."

"I'm here on business." His gaze was cold as it raked over her. It stalled on where her skirt was hiked up on her thighs.

"Of course you are, Starsky."

He ignored her snarky comment. "I came to talk to Quentin, but it appears you got to him first."

"Appearances aren't everything." She stood up, taking her time before tugging down the skirt. "Like what you see?"

Despite her attempt at seduction, she knew, by the way

his face hardened, the second that he noticed the body in the chair. "I can't say that I do," he said, reaching into his pocket.

Her internal alarms sounded, loud and insistent. She needed to get out of there, if she didn't want to spend the next couple days explaining why she'd been found in a dead man's office, sitting next to the corpse and going through his stuff. She edged around the desk and drew *mù ch'i* around her. "A pleasure to see you as always, Inspector, but if you'll excuse me."

Ramirez lunged forward just as Willow began to fade out. The cold snap of steel on her wrist made *mù ch'i* falter, and she blinked. "What the hell?"

Yanking her against him, he leveraged her arms behind her and clicked the handcuffs shut on the other wrist. "You're not going anywhere, Willow Tarata."

The chilled metal burned against her skin. She tested the hold and realized she was stuck, but at least now she knew it was Ramirez, and not the Bad Man, who'd cracked her identity. She was surprised to find herself relieved, which pissed her off. She didn't enjoy feeling like she could trust him. Trust led to disappointment at best, and death at worst. Yet that was exactly how she felt. She narrowed her eyes. "You've been busy."

"So have you." He glanced at the owner.

Hoping to distract him, she pressed herself against Ramirez. "Not as busy as I'd like to get. The cuffs are kinky, but I'm willing."

His body reacted to hers instantly. She felt him stirring against her thigh, and she slipped a leg between his, rubbing him to encourage his response.

Unfortunately, her body reacted, too. She tried to

ignore the rush of warmth between her legs and the tightness of her nipples.

His arms tightened around her. Wrapping his hand in her hair, he arched her back until his eyes filled her vision. His energy surrounded her, trying to drug her and pull her under. She fought to distance herself, but she kept getting caught in her own spell. Her plan had backfired.

Focused on her lips, he lowered his head, stopping a breath away. She waited, unable to breathe, not sure which was worse: being kissed by him again, or not having the pleasure of feeling his lips against hers.

His mouth parted, hovering just above hers. "'You have the right to remain silent.'"

Always the cop. She wanted to be annoyed, but she couldn't help but be impressed. "I'm sure I wouldn't be able to keep quiet."

"'Anything you say can and will be used against you in a court of law.'"

"I'd rather *you* be used against me." She'd meant it teasingly, but it sounded entirely too sincere to her ears. She rubbed herself against him, because she wanted to, and not because she needed to distract him. Her motives were so screwed up.

"Stop it." His jaw tightened.

But he didn't push her away, and that thrilled her. Talk about being screwed up. "I don't think you want me to stop."

"What I want doesn't matter here."

"Doesn't it?" She grazed his neck with her lips.

His teeth were gritted, but his hands tightened as if not wanting to let go. "If what I wanted mattered, I wouldn't have found you standing over another dead body."

"I was kneeling, and it's the only dead body you've found me with."

He cocked his brow.

"You can't prove I was at the park." She nuzzled the skin right above his collar, below his jaw.

"We'll see about that."

"I'd rather see about you." She smelled his skin, and warmth spread through her. He smelled like home.

What was she thinking? She couldn't let herself be drawn to him. The feelings made her too soft, too vulnerable. She couldn't be soft, so she made it about pure animal attraction, instead. "Unbutton your shirt for me."

He tugged on her hair so she had no choice but to lift her head. "Why did you kill him?"

"I didn't." She smiled wryly. "Not that I expect you to believe that."

He studied her, silently and thoroughly. She wondered what he saw when he looked at her, and was almost tempted to ask, when he said, "If you didn't do it, you have nothing to worry about."

She gave him an ironic smile. "Because the police deal in justice?"

"Yes."

She snorted. "If that were true, we wouldn't be standing here."

His brow furrowed, but right as he was going to speak, she threw herself forward into him.

"*Willow.*" Ramirez grabbed her as he lost his balance.

She immediately kneed him—high in the thigh rather than the groin. Groaning, he doubled over and grabbed his leg. Before he regained his balance, she kicked his leg to take him down, being careful not to do any damage, an unprecedented show of mercy. She vaguely wondered what Morgan would say about that.

She shook her head. She needed to get out of there before he recovered. She stepped over him and walked to the door. Arching backward, she awkwardly grabbed the doorknob with her cuffed hands and let herself out. Being cuffed was a serious inconvenience. Morgan was going to cackle herself to tears when she found out.

Worse than the inconvenience, the metal scrambled her energy. She tried to cloak herself with *mù ch'i,* but she couldn't connect.

"I'm going to regret not knocking him out and searching for the key," she muttered, striding down the hall. Except the thought of hurting him didn't sit well with her. Shaking her head, she used her hip to push open the door. She'd just have to improvise.

The guard outside the door frowned at her when she walked through. She shrugged. "It was fun, but the bastard lost the key. You wouldn't be able to pick it or something, would you?"

He blinked. "Uh, no."

"Oh, well. Maybe someone below will have a key that works. At the very least, maybe I can get a little more action." She winked at him and sauntered down the stairs. Ignoring the few intrigued looks she got, she pushed through the crowd to the bar and out the side door.

The moment she was outside, she dropped the blithe attitude. "Damn, damn, *damn.*"

Not only was she in this predicament, but she hadn't managed to glean any information on the Bad Man, except for the fact that he knew she was close. Screw Ramirez and his interference.

She winced, thinking of him writhing on the floor. He was going to be pissed. *Really* pissed. Not to mention that he wanted her for murder now. She'd have to take extra care to avoid him.

Willow rounded the corner and walked into a solid mass. As strong, relentless hands closed on her arms, she looked up. Ramirez's dark, furious eyes glared at her.

Chapter Sixteen

Ramirez stared down into Willow's stunned eyes and felt anger rise like a dark tide from the center of his being. He wasn't sure if he felt admiration or fury at being taken so easily by her, but he knew it wasn't going to happen again. He twirled them around so he bracketed her against a building wall, gently, so her arms wouldn't be scraped by the concrete.

God, he was a fool. As much as he wanted to believe she wouldn't have given him the same consideration, he realized that wasn't true. He'd seen her fight, and he knew she could have done damage back at the office. She hadn't, and that didn't compute.

He didn't like not understanding. "Why?"

"You didn't seriously think I was going to hang around and wait for you to arrest me, did you?"

"That's not what I was asking."

"I should think you'd be happy I didn't feed you your balls," she said, looking away.

He lifted her head with a finger under her chin. She

met his intense brown eyes head-on with her usual bravado, but he looked past it and saw vulnerability. He
cursed mentally. Was she manipulating him again?

Wrapping his hand around the nape of her neck, he
held her in place and leaned closer. "I'm not happy at all.
Do you want to know why?"

"Do I really have a choice?"

He ignored her sarcasm. "I don't know who you are
and what you're doing here. First, I see you walking away
from the scene of a double murder—"

"That's pure conjecture," she interrupted.

"—where I also found the imprint of a woman's shoe,
size eight. What size do you wear, Willow?"

She clamped her lips shut and glared at him.

"Then I find you lurking around the place of employ-
ment of one of the victims. And if that wasn't bad
enough, tonight I find you leaning over another body.
What do you have to say about that?"

"I never lurk."

Anger coursed through him. "I'm trying to understand
so I can help you out. I need you to cooperate."

She laughed mirthlessly. "So you can lock me up
instead of looking for the real culprit? Please. Don't think
I don't know how your type works."

"My type?" he said through gritted teeth.

"The officious, black-and-white type who only sees
what he wants to." She lifted her head as if defying him
to deny it. "You want your cases wrapped up in a pretty
bow, solved and filed away so you can eat your donuts
in peace. Well, sometimes it's not black and white.
Sometimes there's murky gray, where nothing is what it
seems."

She sounded just like Carrie and his *abuelita*. That wasn't necessarily a good thing. "Gray is just black and white overlapped. It only needs to be sorted out."

"Sometimes it can't be," she said louder, as if he were having trouble hearing her.

"It can if you'd cooperate."

"If I cooperated, I'd be in prison."

"You'll be in prison if you don't cooperate." He exhaled to calm himself. "I could book you for murder right now, with the suspicion of two others."

She scowled at him.

He could feel her gathering herself to attack. Refusing to be taken off guard again, he prepared himself for her to strike out. He wasn't letting her get away this time, until he got some answers out of her.

When she launched herself at him, he was ready. He grabbed her around the waist, setting his weight to keep from losing his balance. The thing he wasn't ready for was the way she pressed her mouth to his and kissed him.

Her arms were bound behind her back, but he still felt like she had him in a vise. He wanted to resist. He needed to take her to the station and proceed by the book so he wouldn't screw up the investigation. But she parted her lips and touched his with a flick of her tongue, and any thoughts of following procedure flew out the window.

A shock of heat shot through him. His arms tightened around her, hands tangling in her hair. He should let go—he needed to let go—but he opened his mouth to hers and let her in.

Her right leg lifted to hook on his hip, and she rubbed herself against him. Groaning, he lowered his hand to her ass and hitched her closer. Her skirt had ridden up, and his fingers brushed the smoothness of her bottom. She moaned as he slipped his hand under the leather skirt and gripped her firm, bare skin.

He shifted his hand and groaned when he felt her soft, hardly-there thong. He touched the moist fabric. It wouldn't take much to slide a finger under it. She'd be slick and hot. He could feel her heat already. He'd touch her, inside and out. He was dying to touch her.

He edged a finger just under the elastic. Just as he'd thought, she was hot. Damp. Silky smooth. He groaned. Years ago, he'd dated a woman who'd gotten rid of the hair down there, and he'd liked it a lot.

He ran a finger along the puffy outer lip of her sex and felt her leg clench him tighter. His cock surged. It was right against the front of her panties, with only his pants and underwear as barriers. One zip and they'd be skin to skin. God, he wanted that.

She squirmed against him, trying to get closer. Her leg lowered, anchoring around his knee. And then, once again, he was on his ass. Stunned and wincing at the pain radiating from his tailbone, he looked up to find Willow sprinting away from him, awkwardly swaying, side to side, to compensate for her cuffed hands.

Pain shot up and down his backside as he got to his feet, and he growled. He was going to strangle her when he caught up to her.

That wasn't a thought a Homicide inspector had lightly.

She headed back toward the club. He considered taking a shortcut and heading her off, but he didn't trust her not to trick him again, so he kept after her. It didn't escape his notice that he was always chasing her, and that made him even angrier. He sped up when he saw her turn a corner. How the hell did she run in those shoes?

He turned right, and stopped abruptly when he saw her standing still, huffing to catch her breath. He looked past her and saw three large men dressed all in black. They had earpieces that he associated with Secret Service men. He didn't recognize any of them—they looked to be a higher caliber of guard than those at Bohemia. As he reached into his pocket to pull out his badge, the first man attacked Willow with a club.

"*Hey*," Ramirez yelled, running toward them. His blood pounded, and he realized it was with fear for her life. He should have uncuffed her. He wasn't going to get to her in time, and it was his fault that she was going to be hurt.

To his surprise, Willow sprang forward before he could de-escalate the situation. His heart stopped, and he shouted out again.

She blocked the club with a kick to his wrist, followed by two lightning-fast front kicks, low to the man's chest and then high to his face.

Ramirez stopped to admire her form, and then he shook his head. There had to be something wrong with him that he was getting turned on by a woman whipping another man's ass.

The man's head snapped backward as he teetered on his heels, off balance, and then toppled to the ground.

The second man reached into his suit coat.

Shit. Ramirez went for his gun, thinking the worse, only vaguely relieved when he saw the man withdrew a Taser. Still, a Taser could be lethal, and the thought of Willow being hurt in any way infuriated him.

Willow looked at the attacker and laughed mockingly. "Is that all you've got?"

The guy's expression became determined as he aimed at her.

Ramirez ran straight for him and tackled him at the waist. As the guy staggered, Ramirez let loose a left hook, catching the perp behind the jaw. The man rocked backward, his eyes rolling to the back of his head before he fell over.

Ramirez turned around, looking for Willow. She was busy with the last one, who looked determined to run away. Smart man. Even with her arms tied behind her back, she was a force to be reckoned with, which is what the guy must have decided, because as she let loose another kick to his head, he just turned and ran.

"Coward," she yelled after him, staring at his retreating form.

Jesus. And he'd thought leaving her cuffed was going to impede her ability to protect herself.

As if she'd heard his thought, she turned her sights on him. "I was perfectly capable of handling them on my own."

He tugged his coat down and straightened his tie. "I was more concerned about the men."

Her eyes narrowed, and she took a step toward him. His heart kicked up a beat, not out of fear but anticipation. He couldn't deny his disappointment when she casually turned and walked away.

He glanced at the men strewn on the ground. He should have called to have them picked up, but what was he going to say? That he'd taken one out protecting a murder suspect?

Willow was complicating his life. He glanced at the

men one last time, decided they'd be fine, and took off after her. He saw her duck into a small side street, but by the time he got there, she was gone.

"Impossible, stubborn..." He raked his hair back, resisting the urge to punch the concrete building. He paced until he realized it wasn't going to help get his temper under control. The only thing he could think of that might help was paddling her sweet ass.

He knew she'd head back to her motel room, so he'd pick her up there. On the way back to his car, his cell rang. He glanced at the caller ID before picking it up. "Taylor, I'm—"

"Ricky, we've got a call on another body, and guess what?"

A bad feeling clawed his belly. "What?"

"It's at the bar where the other vic worked, that you checked out the other day. Bohemia."

"The caller didn't say who he or she was?" he asked, wondering how likely it'd been that anyone noticed him there. Not having called in the crime put him in a precarious situation.

"No, but get this. He gave us a tip on the perp. You were right. He's a she, and our mystery caller gave us the address to the motel where she's staying. The team and I just arrived at the motel. I'll get things going here and then meet you at Bohemia."

Willow. He started to jog toward his car. "Can you handle it on your own?"

Silence stretched over the line before Taylor finally said, "You okay, Ricky?"

"Fine." He jammed his key into the lock, hopped in, and started the car.

"Because you've never not checked out a crime scene. You say you like to form your own impressions. What's going on?"

"I'm in the middle of something."

"A woman?"

Not in the way his partner meant, but he wasn't going to elaborate. He had to cut off Willow before she stumbled on his team raiding her motel room. "I'll call you later."

Before Taylor could ask anything more, Ramirez hung up.

Gunning it, he raced to the motel, where his team was currently located, and exactly where Willow was headed.

The idea of his men putting their hands on her, even to arrest her, drove him insane. She was his, and he'd be the one to bring her in.

He broke every law on his way there. He parked on a narrow, one-way street a couple blocks away and jogged to the motel. The Crime Scene Unit was there in full force. They'd be inside, going through her things, gathering evidence. He was torn between wanting them to find something incriminating and not finding anything at all. If she really was innocent...

How could she be? He frowned. He'd seen her searching the desk of a man who'd obviously just been killed. Not to mention that he'd placed her at another crime scene.

Careful to steer clear of anyone on his team, he hid behind a Dumpster by a restaurant across the street. Willow pulled up in a taxi ten minutes later. He watched her, still inside the cab, awkwardly paying the driver with her hands behind her back. Trying not to imagine where she'd hidden money in that skimpy outfit, Ramirez hurried to her.

He opened the car door for her, oddly satisfied at the startled look she gave him. Without a word, he took her arm and pulled her out of the cab. He registered the taxi tearing off into the night, but really his entire focus centered on her.

She watched him with grave caution, as if *he* were the one who was wildly unpredictable. Careful to keep her hidden from his team, he hustled her away from the motel to where his car was parked.

She let him drag her for several feet before she said, "I guess your grandmother didn't teach you that it's polite to call before dropping by to visit."

"I'm surprised that wasn't something you two discussed."

"I guess we were too busy talking about your favorite foods. Although I'm not sure Cap'n Crunch counts as food, but whatever."

He glanced at her as he opened the car door. She avoided his gaze, so he couldn't tell what she was really thinking. She started to get in, but he stopped her. She threw a questioning look at him.

"First." He pressed her against the car and ran his hands down the sides of her torso. He tried not to notice the slight arching of her back as his hands brushed her breasts, or the way her breath quickened. He chose not to look down because he didn't trust himself. He knew without a doubt that he would see her nipples hard under that poor excuse for a shirt, their rosiness visible through the lace.

"Searching for hidden goods, Starsky?" she asked, her voice husky. "You should look lower."

He ignored the innuendo, but his cock didn't. "That's where I'm headed." He got to his knees in front of her. "Spread your feet."

"Isn't there a law against doing this in public?"

He ran his hands up her legs, lifting her skirt. Along the inside of one thigh, he found two thin stilettos attached with a garter-type thing. On the other, she had a small cell phone strapped.

"It's set to vibrate, of course," she said.

He unhooked the weapons. Made of hand-carved wood, he realized they were what she'd been working on that night he'd surprised her at the motel. He slipped them into his inside pocket, rose to his feet, and opened the car door. "Get in."

"Isn't that what I'm supposed to say to you?" she said, but she got in without resistance. Then he saw the goose bumps raised on her arms. Of course she was chilled—she was barely wearing anything.

Rounding the car, he got in, turned it on, and cranked up the heater. "You could have told me you were cold."

She shrugged.

Stubborn woman. He took off his coat and wrapped it around her. It only hit her midthigh, but it was better than nothing. Truthfully, part of him didn't mind that her legs were still bare. They were magnificent, long and lean and lightly tanned.

"Careful. You're drooling," she said, her gaze on flashing red and blue lights reflecting off the building wall next to them.

"Are you always this difficult?" he asked as he resettled in the driver's seat.

"You've caught me at my best."

"If this is your best, I'd hate to see your worst."

She nodded. "Me too."

Watching for her reaction, he asked, "Did you kill the men?"

Her lips thinned, her nostrils flaring delicately. He couldn't tell if she was angry that he accused her, or that she'd been caught. But then her expression relaxed into blankness. "You already think you know what happened, and you've got the men in there going through my stuff to prove it. Why bother asking?"

"Willow," he said, holding her face so she had to look at him. "I'm asking because I want to know the truth."

"Why did you help me back there?" she asked, her gaze direct and unflinching.

Because he couldn't bear the thought of those thugs hurting her. Just like the thought of his team rifling through her intimate things bothered the hell out of him. "I asked you first."

She rolled her eyes. "Real mature there, Starsky."

"Is it so hard to trust me?"

"Yes," she said without hesitation.

He felt a pang of sympathy despite himself. He wanted to force her to tell him what happened to her. He wanted to make it right, and he didn't like that at all. He shouldn't have felt any kind of sympathy for a murder suspect. He should have taken her straight to the station and booked her. But he couldn't.

She jerked her chin out of his grip. Then she spoke, so softly he almost didn't hear. "The man who killed Quentin also killed my mother."

"What?" He scowled at her. "How do you know?"

"He's setting me up. I don't have proof of that, so don't

bother to ask. It's just a feeling." She gave him a sidelong glance. "You wouldn't believe in something as esoteric as that."

"I was raised by a medicine woman."

"Yes, but you're pragmatic and logical. You wouldn't believe anything supernatural even if it bit you on the ass."

"You know me that well?"

"Your grandmother was very forthcoming. I had to stop her from showing me pictures of you in your Underoos."

He considered telling her he refused to wear underwear as a child because he hated the elastic, but he thought better of it. "I guess you're right. I'm trying to tell myself it was just good timing that the tree helped you take out that man the other night. Am I wrong?"

She stilled, so motionless that he didn't think she even breathed in that moment. Then she turned to face him, shifting to accommodate her bound hands. "It was dumb luck that the wind kicked up when it did."

"I wish I could believe that."

"Maybe you shouldn't drink so much."

"I don't drink."

"Then what were you doing at that bar with the blonde?" Her eyes widened, and she looked like she wanted to take the words right back.

He smiled slowly. The thought that she was jealous was satisfying. Foolishly so, but satisfying nonetheless. He fingered a long strand of her hair. "*Carrie* is just a friend."

Willow snorted and yanked her head away to free her hair from his touch. "You don't owe me anything, much less an explanation of your social life."

"Tell me why you think your mother's murder and the one at Bohemia are related."

"His calling card. He left that star." She looked him in the eye. "You have to admit not many people use throwing stars to take someone out."

He extracted his notebook and made a note to check for identifying marks on the murder weapon. "When was your mother killed?"

"Twenty years ago. I've been tracking him since, but he's always one step ahead." She studied him, her gaze somber. "Did you sic your team on my room?"

"No."

"Then the Bad Man did." She exhaled as she watched one of the guys cart out a box, presumably with her things in it. "I think he's setting me up to take the fall for that murder, and the murder of the other two men, one of whom worked for me, by the way. He must have somehow found out where I lived and called it in."

The anonymous tip. Her theory was plausible, but he wasn't ready to admit that. "If he knows where you're staying, why wouldn't he come after you himself?"

"Because this is the kind of game he likes to play."

Ramirez made no comment. She seemed to believe what she was saying, and God knew he'd run into his share of sick bastards in his line of business.

"After they catalogue what I have in my room, you're not going to believe me," she said matter-of-factly. She turned to him, her eyes shining fervently. "I have a proposition for you."

He went on alert. "What sort of proposition?"

"Don't get your shorts in a wad." She rolled her eyes. "I'm not going to trade my body to you for my freedom."

Choosing to ignore her trademark sarcasm, he waited to hear what she had to say.

"If you help me, I'll lead you to the man responsible for the murders." She leaned forward, her entire being behind her words. "He wants me. I don't know why, but he'll do anything to take me down. All you have to do is help me, and I'll hand him to you."

Something about that last sentence didn't ring true, but he couldn't put a finger on it. "How do I know you're not really the killer? How do I know you won't just run?"

"You don't. You'll have to trust me." She looked at him directly, her eyes clear gray and full of honesty. "I'll have to trust you, too, and that's going to be just as hard for me. We're in this boat together."

He weighed the pros and cons. Strangely, he believed what she said—or rather that *she* believed what she was saying. It couldn't hurt looking into it. But helping her would mean aiding and abetting a criminal, because that's what she was at the moment. If he agreed to her proposal, he'd be putting himself and his career in jeopardy, not to mention compromising his beliefs. He did things by the book, and what she proposed went against everything he believed in.

Only then, he looked at her and saw the vulnerability she hid deep down. He remembered the way she felt, snug against his body, and for once in his life, he didn't make a decision with his head but his heart. Muttering under his breath, he cranked the engine and put the car in drive.

"Where are we going?" she asked, the distrust evident in her voice.

He shot her a glare as he pulled out of the parking spot.

"If I find out you're lying to me again, I'll lock you up and throw away the key."

She nodded slowly. "You didn't say where we're going."

"Home." May all Lita's spirits help him.

Chapter Seventeen

Willow leaned sideways in the passenger seat, facing Ramirez. The car didn't allow for handcuffs, and her hands tingled with pins and needles from the circulation being restricted.

Ramirez didn't look happy. In fact, he looked like he was chewing glass, and that made her grin for a second.

He said he was taking her home, but what did that mean? Was he going to help her? Hope lifted in her chest. What other reason would he have for taking her to his house?

Her cell vibrated. It'd been going crazy for the past hour. It had to be Morgan, but it wasn't like she could answer it with her hands bound. She shifted her legs, conscious of how close it was to her already thrumming crotch.

Damn the cop. His slow frisk-tease had turned her on more than she wanted to admit.

"You're staring," he said, never taking his eyes from the road.

"Just wondering."

"About?"

"If you do everything so precisely."

He glanced at her. "Like?"

She nodded at the steering wheel. "Driving. Dressing. Working. Makes me wonder what else is included in the list."

He raised his eyebrow. "What do you think?"

Willow thought wondering about *that* would get her in trouble. Instead, she laid her head against the back of the seat and said, "I think you're perfect at everything. You follow the rules, cross your *t*'s and dot your *i*'s."

"You make it sound unappealing."

"Sometimes rules need to be broken. Sometimes being wild is so much more fun than being safe."

He pulled into a parking spot, killed the ignition, and faced her. "Being wild has landed you in a lot of trouble."

Didn't she know it. But she shrugged and smiled, like she didn't have a care in the world. "It always works out."

He scowled at her, muttered something under his breath, and then came around to her side. Opening the door, he helped her out, rewrapped her in his coat, and turned her to face the car. "Why didn't you tell me to uncuff you?"

"I was indulging you in your kink." She felt him fiddling with the handcuffs. Suddenly her hands were free. Sighing in relief, she rotated her wrists and rolled her shoulders. When she faced him, he looked pissed, only this time at himself.

She reached out and played with his tie. "Don't worry. Next time I'll truss you up and then we'll be even. I bet you'd like it." As she went to move past him, he caught her elbow and held her still. He searched her face, his expression stony. She wanted to ask him what he was looking for—she wanted to tell him whatever it was, he wouldn't find it. But before she could do anything, he ran a finger down her cheek and across her lips.

The trail he mapped on her skin tingled. The sensation confused her, forcing her to rely on the only defense she had: being aloof. "Want to try it now? We can use this instead of the cold handcuffs. I'll be gentle with you."

His face flushed—with anger but also with desire. He grabbed her arms and shook her. "Look. If you want me to trust you, you've got to stop pretending to be someone you aren't."

Even though his grip was firm, she noted he took care not to hurt her. No one had cared about her in a long, long time. Feeling her lips tremble, she dropped her arms. "What makes you think I was pretending?"

"That was fake. This isn't." He gripped the back of her neck and brought her mouth to his.

His caring had weakened her, but his kiss was what made her crumble. It was achingly sweet, hitting an Achilles' heel she didn't know she had.

The softening began in her chest and spread through her body, until she was relaxed against the length of him. She didn't know she had it in her to soften, much less to that extent.

It scared her.

Just as she was about to pull away to shore up her defenses again, his hand tightened in her hair. His lips and tongue became insistent. Impassioned.

Scorching.

She felt the roughness of his beard growth, reminding her of bark's pleasant scratching. She tasted how much he wanted her, in the flick of his tongue against hers. She smelled the scent of their lust, verdant and earthy, and felt herself melt into him some more.

Ramirez broke away first. Breathing heavily, he gazed into her eyes. "Come inside."

It was a request and command all at once. She thought about what he might do to her in the privacy of his home. He wouldn't play dirty, but he'd be thorough. Just the thought made her already damp panties wetter.

Fear shot through her. She didn't need this kind of complication. Not now. Not ever.

"Come inside, Willow," he said again. His thumb caressed a spot just under her ear, next to her jaw.

Shocks of electricity shot through her body, and she knew she wouldn't be able to resist. Barely nodding, she let him lead her to his home. They walked up the set of steps at the side of the house, to the second story. He unlocked the door and guided her into the kitchen. Flipping on an overhead light, he loosened his tie.

She watched him unbutton the top of his shirt, mesmerized by the patch of dark skin revealed. Low on the right side of his neck there was a tattoo of what appeared to be a series of concentric circles fanning out in waves.

She nodded at it. "Is that regulation, Starsky?"

"It's youthful folly, before I went into the force." Tugging his collar aside, he bared his neck for her.

At the edge of the circles was a stylized spider, simply done in crisp, solid black, stark even against his dark skin. She wanted to reach out and run her fingers along the smooth lines. "An unusual choice. Do you have a thing for arachnids?"

"I got it to remind me of my grandmother's wisdom. She used to tell me that we live in a web of our own weaving. It's a hard lesson to learn."

Was he talking about himself? She wanted to ask, but she had the impression he wouldn't appreciate how much she knew of his past.

Ramirez tapped his neck. "This is a visual reminder, that we control what we get caught up in through our own decisions and actions."

She studied the tattoo, conscious of the soft inhale-exhale of his breath close to her ear. "What about outside forces?"

"Like fate?"

Like the Bad Man, but Willow just shrugged. "Sure. Your grandmother believes in it."

"She has many beliefs I can't share."

By his tone and the way he was watching her, it seemed like there was hidden meaning to his words. She had no idea what he could mean, though. "So are you caught up in your own web, Inspector?"

He smiled faintly and righted his collar. "My grandmother thinks so."

Realizing she was still staring at his neck, she looked away, blushing, and pretended to check out the kitchen. What an idiot, getting excited over a little glimpse of neck. It wasn't like she was a virginal Victorian chick.

Ramirez, thankfully, had no clue about her thoughts. He gestured to a short hallway beyond an archway. "This way."

Good, a distraction. Following him, she noted the pristine kitchen. There was no sign of what one expected of a bachelor residence—no food-crusted dishes piled around the sink, no discarded take-out boxes cluttering the counters. It was simple and fastidiously clean, but still warm and inviting. Was this his grandmother's doing or his own?

She took notice of the potted plant in the hallway. To the right, there was a spacious living room. It was too dark to check out, but she bet it was every bit as perfect as the kitchen. Beyond it, she saw a set of stairs, which was where Ramirez was headed.

"This isn't like any bachelor pad I've ever seen," she commented casually as she trailed after him. The only time regular guys were this clean was if they had a woman in their life. Who that woman was burned a hole in her chest.

He glanced at her over his shoulder. "Been in many bachelor pads?"

"A few." Although they'd all been assignments. She'd never gone to a guy's place for anything intimate. That got too personal. But she'd let Ramirez think whatever he wanted, especially because she knew he'd never accept the truth. "Do you have maid service, or is this your grandmother's doing?"

He turned around on the top step and stared at her knowingly. Finally he said, "There's no woman, Willow. There hasn't been in a long time."

She scowled, entirely uncomfortable. "I wasn't…"

He turned around and continued without waiting for her to finish. Eyes narrowed, she glared at him for a moment before following. He opened the door to a room and stepped inside. She waited in the doorway until he turned on the light.

The room was perfect. Masculine but relaxing and warm, just like the rest of the house. She looked at him and tried to compare the man she was coming to know with the no-nonsense cop she knew.

He opened a drawer and extracted a couple items, holding them out to her. "You can use these."

She sauntered over to see what he offered. She took the bundle and held it up. "A sweatshirt and boxers." She arched her brow at him. "Are you a leg man, Inspector?"

"I don't have any pajama bottoms."

"Really?" She tipped her head. "Are you blushing?"

A look of suspicion crossed his gorgeous face, but he didn't say anything. Instead, he grabbed a couple things and left the room, shutting the door behind him.

Willow walked around his bedroom slowly, noticing the absence of dust. There were several pictures of his grandmother over the years, but no pictures of other women or even parents and other siblings. She wondered what his story was. She should have asked his grandmother when she had the chance.

The bathroom was attached. It wasn't lavish, but neither was it bare-bones like the one in the motel. The bath was a modern ceramic rendition of an old-fashioned claw-foot tub, and the shower was separate.

Impulse spurred Willow to plug the tub and run the water. She hadn't indulged in a bath in longer than she remembered, and it seemed the perfect place to think. She found some bath salts under the sink and dumped a generous handful in. Sighing in relief as she slipped off her shoes, she stripped out of her clothes and eased into the tub.

A refreshing lemon scent teased her nostrils. His scent. She pictured him lying there, stretched out, naked, head resting on the rim, right where hers was. Gloriously naked.

Her cell phone buzzed, skittering on the floor next to her meager pile of clothes. Dripping water, she leaned out of the tub and picked it up. Morgan, of course. She flipped it open.

Morgan was already talking before she had the chance to say hello. "—ere the hell are you? I lost connection to your system and haven't been able to reach you. Did you think to call me to let me know what's going on? *Noooo.* I'm just the grunt in the background. Who cares about me? I—"

Knowing Morgan could go on forever, Willow interrupted. "I was going to call you in the morning."

"It *is* morning."

"There have been developments."

Pause. "Uh-oh. Whenever you say that, it always costs thousands of dollars to fix."

Willow thought about all the equipment and clothing in her motel room. "That's a fair assessment to make."

"Jesus Christ. What happened?"

"I went to speak with the club owner, but he was dead—killed by a silver star."

"Aw, crap."

"I took the opportunity to go through his things, which is where Inspector Ramirez found me."

"*Crap.* You aren't in jail, are you? Wait, you answered your phone. Do they allow cell phones in jail?"

"I'm not in jail. I'm at Ramirez's house."

Silence stretched over the line. And then Morgan said, "Because hiding out in a cop's house is smart, since that's the last place he'd look for you?"

"No, since I asked the cop to help me find the Bad Man."

"*What?* Are you smoking crack?"

"He has resources I no longer have. It's to my benefit to have him help me."

"You never work with anyone," her partner pointed out. "*Ever.* It took me months to convince you to go into business with me."

"Then this will be the first and last time."

Morgan didn't say anything for a long time, but Willow could feel her thinking. The manic tapping on the keyboard across the line was a dead giveaway. Morgan typed like crazy, but when she needed to think, she typed even faster.

Finally she said, "I'm arriving in San Francisco at two in the afternoon. I'll find you." She hung up.

Great. Willow closed the phone and tossed it onto the pile of clothes. She didn't doubt that Morgan would find her, since the woman had mysterious ways Willow had never understood. Which made the Bad Man that much more clever for evading all the cybertraps her partner had set for him.

She wondered what Ramirez would make of Morgan. Men normally preferred her—Morgan was petite, bubbly, and smart. Not intimidating or cold, as some had called Willow. The only person who seemed not to notice Willow's cold nature was Ramirez.

She frowned, brushing the surface of the water. Then again, he wasn't beating down the door to the bathroom, trying to get with her, either. Why was that? A misplaced sense of chivalry? She remembered the way he'd tucked his coat around her and felt a queer flopping in her belly.

Disgusted with herself, she put her head on her drawn-up knees. She needed to pull herself together and make a plan. The Bad Man had left her a message, and she wasn't going to let it go unanswered. She *couldn't* let it go unanswered, not even for a righteous man who kissed divinely. She owed it to her mother. She needed it for herself.

Chapter Eighteen

Ramirez set the kettle on the stove top a little too hard, based on the sharp clang. He took down the tin of herbs his grandmother kept stocked in his kitchen. Lita said there was nothing tea didn't cure. She said this particular blend encouraged relaxation, and that he needed to drink it morning, noon, and night.

If he ever needed help calming down, it was now.

He looked up at the ceiling. Overhead, Willow was taking a bath. He could hear the water running, and that was all he needed to get his imagination going. He could picture her slowly shimmying out of her clothes, letting them fall at her feet. Her bending over to unstrap the phone from her thigh. Her long legs folding into his tub, the water lapping her hardened nipples.

Shaking his head, he set a couple mugs on the counter. He needed to get his head back where it belonged, on his neck and not in his pants. He was sitting at the table, with a mug in his hands, wishing it was a tumbler of tequila instead, when she walked into the kitchen. She had on the sweatshirt he'd given her, the boxer shorts missing.

She shrugged. "They kept sliding down."

The sweatshirt covered just as much as her leather skirt had, but for some reason, it looked more enticing, almost illicit.

Any bit of calming effect the tea had on him faded in the presence of her bare tanned legs. Swallowing thickly, he gripped the mug so he wouldn't be tempted to run his hands along them. It didn't help knowing how soft her skin was.

She shifted her weight to one leg, cocking her hip. "I wouldn't have figured you as the silk-boxer type."

"I hate elastic." Plus, silk was roomier, except for now. He felt like he was going to combust. He waved to the mug he'd set opposite him. "I made tea."

"Hmm." She strutted toward the table in that sensual way that muddled his thinking, picked up the mug, and breathed it in. "Your grandmother's blend."

He nodded, wondering what had gone on between the two women that day. Lita didn't give her special tea to just anyone.

Willow took another deep inhale and then sank onto the chair that was next to him. "Your home is lovely."

"Thank you."

"It suits you." She cradled the tea in her hands as she looked around the kitchen. "It must be nice having some-place this peaceful to come back to every night."

If he didn't know better, he would have thought that sounded wistful. "A condemned building isn't peaceful?"

"Actually, it's great. My neighbors are never home." Her lips quirked as she raised the mug.

"You must have a place to go to at the end of the day."

Humming noncommittally, she took another sip. When she set the cup down, she said, "Your grandmother thinks you need calming, too, huh?"

"Among other things. I'm surprised she didn't give you the rundown."

"Oh, she did. I kept expecting her to show me your resumé." She chuckled, lifting her feet to prop them on one of the other chairs.

Was she trying to drive him insane? He tried not to stare at the long length of skin, but it was impossible. He was having a hard time not placing them in his lap and massaging them.

He wanted to hear her purr.

Yet, he still couldn't understand, why her? Why *this* woman?

He stared at her, trying to figure it out. Of course he was a guy, and a stunning woman would attract his attention, but he'd known stunning women before, ones who weren't implicated in several murders. Why was it he wanted to kiss the insolent smile off her face and strip her bare, body and soul, for his eyes only?

So much for staying professional. He watched her lick a stray drop from the lip of her cup, and he knew it was a lost cause. He'd been moving to this point from the moment he saw her walking away from his crime scene, her hair gleaming in the moonlight. Lita would reiterate that Willow was his fate; it was futile to struggle against it. In other words, he was doomed.

If he was going to do this, it'd be on his terms. He'd make sure to mitigate any potential damage up front. "We need to establish the ground rules."

Her eyes went flat, all the ease dissipating in a blink. "The only ground rule that needs to be established is that I'm going to hunt down the Bad Man and deliver him to you."

"No."

She put her mug down so hard it made a sharp *clack*. "That's the deal."

His temper rose in his throat, and he had to suppress it. He hadn't had so much trouble controlling it since he was a teenager. "As I see it, you don't have any bargaining power here. You're only here by my good graces."

"I'm here because you need me to catch the bastard who's killing people on your turf." She stood up, hands on her hips. "You'll only get in the way, with all your rules and laws."

He stood and faced her. "Rules and laws are what keep people in order."

"Yeah, rules have worked *really* well with the Bad Man thus far." Her voice dripped with sarcasm.

He ignored it, focusing on the issue. "Why do you call him *the Bad Man*?"

She blinked. "That's what he is, isn't he?"

He sensed her discomfort. "That's all you've called him. Doesn't he have a name?"

Glaring at him, she picked up her mug and dumped it in the sink.

"You don't know his name," he said with sudden clarity. He walked to her and turned her around. "You don't know who he is."

"I know who he is." Her eyes shot daggers at him. "Not knowing his name is a mere formality."

"A mere formality?" He barked a disbelieving laugh. "I'd like to see what you call a complete unknown."

Willow poked him in the chest. "I told you I'd deliver him. That's all you need to know."

"I need to know a whole lot more than that." He crowded her until her back pressed against the edge of the sink and his body was crushed against hers. He gripped the counter around her and leaned in. "I don't think you understand the situation here. I've put my career on the line for you."

"You've put your career on the line to bring your perp to justice." She lifted her chin, avoiding his eyes. "I'm only the means, so don't go romanticizing what's going on here."

"What is going on here?" he asked through gritted teeth, because he sure as hell didn't know. One minute she flirted with him, like she wanted to eat him whole, and the next she was all business.

"We're using each other to catch the man we both want."

She said it so matter-of-factly that he saw red. He wasn't an idiot. He'd known all along she was using him. He just wanted it to be for more than catching her mother's killer. "So that's it? That's all you want from me?"

"That's all either of us could want," she said coolly.

He almost believed she meant it. She delivered it so convincingly, without the tiniest bit of feeling.

But he didn't believe. Or he didn't want to believe. Whatever the case, he wasn't going to let her lie to him again. Running his fingers through her soft tresses, he felt her body relax against his touch. Easing her head back, he saw something flare in her piercing gray eyes.

Desire.

He placed his free hand around her neck, so his thumb feathered over her pulse. It beat fast, and he realized it was in response to his touch. Then, as if to verify it, her breath hitched and she shivered. She was so tall, he didn't have far to lower his head, stopping right above her mouth. Her lips parted, and he felt a surge of satisfaction. "Both of us want more, and you know it."

She put her hands on his waist. "The only thing I want—"

"You want me as badly as I want you. Admit it." His hand in her hair kept her from shaking her head. He pressed his body to hers. "Admit it, Willow. You're shaking for me."

"I don't need anyone." She whispered it unconvincingly.

"You need me." He lowered his lips to brush the side of her neck. "Your mind may disagree, but your body tells a different story."

"I—"

Before she could say another word, he kissed her. No pretense of softness, no illusion of gentleness, just passion and desire mixed with frustration from the past few days.

Her grip tightened on his hips, and for a second, he thought she was going to push him away. But then her hands snaked around him, and she gave in. There was nothing submissive about her surrender. She yanked his shirt out of his pants and slipped her hands under, kneading his back with surprisingly strong fingers. Those fingers dipped into the waistband of his pants from behind, teasing. Then she skimmed around the front.

Lifting her, he kissed his way down her neck as he set her on the counter. "Not yet."

"I thought this was what you wanted," she said, reaching for his fly again.

He shook his head, loving it when she shivered from

the scratch of his five-o'clock shadow. Setting his teeth to the sensitive spot at the base of her neck, he trailed his hands up her bare thighs and under the sweatshirt. "This is what I want."

She wrapped her legs around his waist and dragged him closer. "I can't believe I'm going to be the voice of reason here, but I feel like I need to reiterate that this isn't a good idea."

"I can't believe I'm going to say to hell with reason." He pushed her sweatshirt up and then froze, staring into her eyes. "I don't feel any underwear."

The corner of her lips quirked. "That's probably good, considering I'm not wearing any."

He leaned back. The sweatshirt bunched around her waist. Below it was skin toasted by the sun, no tan lines. A tiny patch of hair pointed the way down to full, glistening lips. As if his dick weren't hard enough, it surged painfully in his pants. He wanted to pull it out and sink into her. Badly. But he couldn't—not yet. He feathered his thumb over the crease of her sex, rubbing the moisture across her skin. She gasped and widened her legs.

He didn't need any more invitation than that, but he wasn't ready to take it further. He watched her face as he ran his thumb over her. He loved the feel of her, plump and soft, belying her angularity and toughness.

She leaned back on her hands, her eyes half-lidded as she watched him. "For someone who wanted this so badly, you're certainly taking your time."

"This deserves to be savored." He parted her just a little, opening her to his view.

Her eyes glazed over with passion. Her back arched, her chest heaving with her heavy breathing.

As he slipped a finger into her folds, his other hand traveled the length of his sweatshirt.

She tugged at her sleeve. "Take it off."

"No. The window's open." His palm grazed over a hard nipple.

Crying out, Willow's head dropped back and she thrust her hips forward. "Kinky, Starsky. I think you just like it this way."

"What is it *you* like? This?" He drew his finger through her wetness, careful not to touch her clit.

Moaning, she squirmed, trying to direct his touch where she wanted it. And he knew where that was. He glanced down. Her clit rose swollen at the top of her sex, begging for attention, and so tempting. He knew it would swell under his tongue. He wanted to lick it, to suck on it until she screamed for him, until her strong, tanned legs gripped him like she never wanted him to stop.

Not yet, he commanded himself, breathing heavily. He abraded the tip of her breast again. "Or do you like this?"

She moaned and opened her eyes to glare at him. "Get on with it already."

He shook his head. Her nipples stabbed through the thick fabric. He rubbed one tip between his fingers and leaned down to bite the other one through the sweatshirt. Her exclamation was sweet and sharp. Needing to hear it again, he relented and let his thumb brush over her clit.

Her legs fell open wide and she arched up. She cried out, over and over, her head thrown back and her body trembling in her release.

He watched her face, admiring her beauty. He kept stroking softly over her until her hips stopped undulating and she wilted on the countertop, her back resting against the window behind her. She half opened her eyes as she tried to catch her breath.

Not enough. He bent his head between her legs and kissed her. Because he wanted to know her taste, he ran his tongue through her folds and up to the hardened little spot.

"In case you missed it, I finished already," she said, moaning again.

But the way she propped her feet on the counter told him she wanted more, so he lapped at her. Soft and slow at first, he let her build again. It wasn't long before she was writhing on the counter, panting.

"Yes." Her fingers speared through his hair, holding him close. "Again."

He licked her softly, pinching her nipple. "I'm in charge here."

"Do I need to point out that you're the one kneeling in front of me?"

"But you're the one who's going to beg." He dragged his teeth over her.

Her hips jerked and she gripped his head tighter. "In your dreams, Starsky."

Ignoring her false bravado, he took her in his mouth and sucked. The little noises she made told him she was close. He sucked harder, using his tongue to flick at her.

"Oh, Rick." She pulled his hair to the point of pain as her hips lifted off the counter, trying to get closer to him.

Abandoning her nipples, he took hold of her ass, pulling her closer to him. She must have liked the angle, because she skyrocketed again, harder than the first time. Something jolted him, like the ricochet of a branch snapping back. Startled, he lifted his head. Before he could question it, she brought his mouth to hers, kissing him deeply. She mewled in pleasure, wrapping her legs around his waist. Hell, he probably imagined it.

He hissed into her mouth when his dick pressed against her, then almost came when she reached down between them and rubbed him through his pants. Pulling away, he put his hand over hers to stop her.

She licked her lips, moist and red and swollen from his kisses. "What? Don't you like?"

"I like it too much," he said in a gravelly tone, barely recognizing his own voice.

She smiled with wicked sweetness as she unzipped his fly with her other hand. "That can't be so bad, then."

It was, when he was seconds from coming in his pants. He stepped back and tried to pry her hands off his crotch.

Willow reached inside his waistband.

They both froze as soon as their skin touched. They looked up at the same time and stared at each other.

Willow moved her hand up and down his length. "Rather impressive, Inspector."

He swallowed, closing his eyes. Her slow strokes became sure and fast as she rubbed over him. He couldn't help surging into her hand with a helpless growl.

She used his cock to draw him close, closing him in her fist. "Who's going to beg now?"

He wrapped his hand around hers to stop her arousing movement. "This isn't how it's going to play out."

"It seems like I hold the power at the moment." She smiled knowingly. "But I'm willing to let you help."

She began to work him again. Despite his efforts, he found himself helping, their hands moving in unison. She felt so good, the pleasure running through his body. His toes even tingled with each pull of her capable hand.

"Wet," she said as she circled around the crown. She squeezed again, as if milking him, before spreading the wetness all the way down to his balls. "And here I was thinking of licking it."

He knew what she was doing—he knew she said it on purpose. But he couldn't stop from picturing her tongue lapping at him, her mouth taking him as deeply as she could. He groaned, his weight pressing against the countertop, trying to hold it together. It was useless, especially when her other hand cupped his balls and began to massage them.

He thrust forward, his hand tightening around hers. She tugged him toward her, and he could feel her breath on his neck a moment before he felt her teeth scrape his skin, right over his tattoo. He roared as an intense orgasm overtook him.

He missed her lips nibbling at him the moment she drew away. She let go of his still-firm cock and slid off the counter. "Between that and the tea, I should sleep well tonight. And thanks for giving me your room."

Wrung dry, Ramirez slumped against the counter and watched her saunter out of the kitchen, her perfect ass peeking at him from under the band of the sweatshirt.

Willow had to use the wall to help herself up the stairs to Ramirez's bedroom, her legs were so noodly. How she made it out of the kitchen, she had no idea. All from unspent lust. Yes, he'd got her off—twice—but somehow it wasn't enough.

Letting herself into his bedroom, she stumbled to the bed and dropped on the covers. She didn't have words for what had happened, so she borrowed some from Morgan. *Jesus Christ.*

It wasn't like she was a virgin, but she'd never experienced *that* before—helpless pleasure, where she had no control over anything. She'd even come close to letting *mù ch'i* slip, which she'd *never* done before.

She wished she would have gotten to taste him, like he'd tasted her. She remembered the way he'd licked her, like she was a dessert to be savored; she felt herself get turned on again.

Drawing her sweatshirt over her head, she tossed it aside. She was about to pull the covers down, when the door opened. She whirled around to see a rumpled Ramirez standing in the doorway.

She didn't know what she expected from him, but it wasn't the clear, calm light in his eyes. For some reason, that freaked her out more than anything.

She took an involuntary step back. "It's late. I'm going to bed."

"Good idea," he said, still staring at her. He unbuttoned his dress shirt and dropped it on the floor.

She felt her eyes widen at the sight of his beautiful chest. Sprinkled with enough hair to be manly, it was broad and muscled, and she wanted nothing more than to run her tongue along every ridge and ripple.

She cleared her throat. "I'm sleeping in here."

"Good," he said, undoing his pants and stepping out of them. "Because I am, too."

Jesus. Christ. She ogled the black silk boxers he wore, the same as what he'd offered her earlier.

"Except we're not going to sleep right away." He tugged the shorts down.

She watched his erection pop free from the waistband, and a need so strong, so potent, overcame her. She wanted him, too, badly. The intensity of that want terrified her.

"Do you want to know what we're going to do?" He stalked toward her, slowly, as if he thought she'd bolt, which was a distinct possibility.

She locked her knees to stand still, cursing that her nipples got harder with each step he took. "Are you offering to draw me a diagram?"

"Why would I draw a picture, when I could just show you?" He stopped in front of her. "Get in bed."

Her eyes narrowed in defiance, but before she could tell him what he could do with his bed, he pushed her back. She lay stunned for a second before she glared at him. "If you think I enjoy being manhandled, you've got a rude awakening coming."

"That wasn't manhandling, but I'm happy to show you the difference."

"Not in this lifetime." She rolled and scrambled across the mattress, looking over her shoulder in time to see him lunge for her. He landed to the right of her and quickly shifted Willow onto her back, pinning her in place.

Willow froze, unable to breathe. Not from his weight—he kept that off her. It was the feel of him covering her. His arms holding hers down. His chest, broad and strong across her back. His erection nestled at the crux of her legs.

Closing her eyes, she imagined his hands reaching under her belly to touch as he inched his way into her. She wanted that so badly. Before she could help herself, she nudged him with her butt.

"Willow," he whispered, brushing her hair aside. His teeth scraped the tendon where her neck and shoulder met. Like he'd read her mind, he slipped a hand under her and cupped between her legs. He held her there for a long, breathtaking moment before he eased a finger into her folds.

She buried her head into the comforter to muffle her groan.

His tongue traced a line up the nape of her neck. "Tell me you want my hand there."

"It figured you'd be this autocratic during sex, too," she said, wishing she sounded more unaffected. But the base of his finger pressed her right there, and it was all she could do to breathe, much less pretend like she didn't want to beg for him to stroke her to orgasm again.

He pressed harder, but his finger remained still. "I'm waiting."

"Impatiently." She rolled her hips back and opened her legs enough so he slipped between them.

Nipping the side of her neck, he felt his way to her opening and pushed in. The shock of him there made her gasp. He stretched her wide. Full. His slow, deep thrusts caused goose bumps to rise up and down her body. His teeth scraped her skin before a soft murmur caressed her ear. "I just want to know that you like it, too."

She fisted the covers, trying to ground herself. "It's all right," she teased.

She felt his smile against her skin a moment before he levered her hips up, found the right angle, and drove all the way into her. As if that weren't enough, his finger got busy, gliding through her wetness until the tip focused on her clit. Her cry was high and keening. She panted, trying not to come. Not yet—not until she got to savor it for just a little longer.

"Come for me," he commanded, softly, but it was a command nonetheless. His weight rested on her, heavy, but she didn't care, not after his right hand snaked under to join the left. His fingers strummed her in tandem, insistent, as he slid in and out. The focused touch short-circuited her brain. She rocked back against him, over and over, and screamed as she came.

He gripped her, controlling her frantic motions so she didn't dislodge him, driving into her with increased fervor until his triumphant cry echoed in her ears. He stiffened behind her, rigid both inside and out, and then collapsed slightly to her side.

She tried not to think of his consideration. Of course he wouldn't want to continue to rest his full weight on her. For a man like Ramirez, that'd be a given. She stifled the part of her that wanted that caring to be special, specific to only her.

She squeezed her eyes shut, trying to move away from him. She needed a little space to regroup. Somehow she felt flayed open, and Ramirez was the kind of man who'd not only sense that, but would use it to his advantage. Surprisingly, he only allowed her enough space to move his weight off her. His strong hands held her between her legs as he scooted her back, and he spooned her again. "Just relax. Be still."

That was easy for him to say. He didn't have long, skilled fingers nestled intimately into him, waiting to drive him crazy.

He kissed her neck. "Sleep, Willow."

Right—like that was possible.

Only, with him wrapped around her, warm and solid, she found herself relaxing. She felt his heart at her back, the rhythm strangely comforting. She could feel herself settling into it, meeting it, and something odd struck her chest.

What was that?

Something she hadn't felt in twenty years. *Safety,* she realized right before drifting off to sleep.

Chapter Nineteen

The pier was deserted, which was exactly how Edward wanted it. Some business needed to be conducted in the dark of night, and the piers along the Embarcadero were excellent for that. During the day, they teemed with people, but at night even the seagulls disappeared.

Edward scanned the bay, the surface reflecting light from the bridge and surrounding cities. The arms shipment slated for the Russians had been delayed, and he goddamn hated waiting.

Slipping his hand in his pocket, he ran a finger along one of the sharp edges of the silver throwing star. He had been so awkward and unskilled with them when he'd first picked one up. Even with the five edges, he hadn't been able to sink it into his practice target. But once he discovered Lani's weakness with metal, he'd been determined. He'd practiced for hours on end, until he could nail his target to the millimeter. Now he always carried one. It was his signature weapon. He loved the choked gasp a person made when it sank into his victim's flesh.

"Edward."

He turned to watch Deidre totter up the walkway in her high heels. As usual, she was dressed to perfection. If it weren't for her uncharacteristically pinched face, he wouldn't have suspected anything was wrong. But that expression spoke volumes.

"I have unfortunate news." She strode up to him, stopping three feet away. "She got away."

Of course she did. He felt that usual mixture of pride and fury whenever Willow evaded him. "Tell me what happened."

"My men surrounded her, but somehow she managed to escape." Deidre shifted her weight, but she never dropped her direct gaze. "I don't know precisely what happened. The tales my men recounted were fantastical."

He nodded. Willow used her powers. He wondered just how strong she was.

"And then there was the man."

"Man?" Edward stilled. "What man?"

"The one who helped her. I have no idea who he was." Deidre's lips formed a peeved moue. "You never told me she had an accomplice."

Because he hadn't known, and that infuriated him. Who the hell was it?

Deidre continued, oblivious to his anger in her own agitation. "She shouldn't have been able to escape. I sent my best men. They've never failed me. Who is she, Edward?"

"It doesn't matter who she is."

"The hell it doesn't." Her voice rose, shrill and grating. "I feel like I was set up to fail. You led me to believe she was a simple woman with some survival skills, but I've come to find out she's Wonder Woman. And now she's gone—"

"Gone." The word fell off his tongue flatly. "What do you mean *gone*?"

"I mean she disappeared with that man who helped her." Deidre glared at him as though it was his fault. "My men couldn't trace her. Now she's going to be doubly hard to find, because not only will she be extra vigilant, but she apparently has someone watching her back. You might as well chalk her up to lost."

Edward gritted his teeth, fighting back a sudden surge of irritation. "She is not lost."

"She is," Deidre insisted. "Only an idiot wouldn't go into hiding after being attacked twice, and by so many people. And this woman is no idiot. She's gone, and not even you will be able to find her."

Rage filled his chest. He gripped the throwing star, feeling the blades pierce his palm.

Deidre pointed at him. "You better not blame me for this, Edward. You didn't disclose all of the information. If I knew what I was up against—"

"What? You would have sent more men?" he asked derisively.

"No, I would have used a different tactic."

"And you would have still failed." He withdrew the star and held it up to the streetlamp light.

Eyes widening, Deidre stepped back. "Come on, Edward. You can't blame me for this."

"Of course I can." He followed her, step for step. "You yourself said Willow was going to be harder to track now. Whose fault is that?"

"*Yours. You* didn't give me the full picture of what I was up against."

Her desperation rolled off her in waves. He wanted to gag, it reeked so badly. Lani had been many things, but she'd never been desperate, not even at the end.

Deidre tripped on an uneven slat of wood, grabbing the railing for balance. "It's not hopeless. There's still a chance we can get her."

He smirked at the *we*. "A moment ago, you said just the opposite."

"I said this before, if we just offer her something she wants, we can lure her to the surface." Deidre stumbled again as she hit the corner of the pier. The expression on her face was priceless as she realized he'd backed her into a corner. When she spoke, her voice held a thread of hysteria. "What does she want, Edward?"

"Me." He tucked the star back into his pocket.

Deidre wilted in relief. "For heaven's sake, you had me scared there. I thought—"

"What did you think, Deidre?" he asked softly, walking up to her and taking her in his arms.

She laughed shakily. "I thought you were going to treat me like one of your employees."

"You aren't an employee." He lifted his hands to hold her face up to his. "I trusted you more."

Confusion lined her brow, but he caressed it away. He let his fingertips linger across her cheeks, soft and plump—so unlike Lani's sharp angles. Then he lowered his hands to her neck.

Closing her eyes, she hummed and dropped her head back. It was feigned for his benefit—he could tell from the start. Deidre recognized how much he enjoyed lavishing attention on her neck and tolerated it.

Lani used to love having her neck touched and kissed. It was one of the few times he felt like he had her under his control.

His thumbs caressed the pulse points under Deidre's jaw. He felt the delicate fluttering of her heart beneath her skin.

And he squeezed.

Her eyes flew open. The alarm in them was almost as satisfying as her strangled gasp.

He leaned in and whispered. "I might be able to tolerate failure in some instances, but not where my daughter is concerned."

Her mouth opened, but no sound came out. Her hands came up to grasp his wrists. He'd always been mesmerized by the agile elegance of his wife's fingers, especially as she played her flute. This slut's pale, delicate fingers repulsed him.

He'd choked Lani, too. He'd squeezed until he'd felt her weaken in his hands, saw the fear in her eyes, just like what he saw in Deidre's. But it wasn't until he saw her body go limp in submission that he knew he'd won.

When Deidre's eyes glazed with defeated resignation, he let go. She slumped backward, swaying and coughing weakly, hands holding her neck.

Edward stepped back and took the throwing star out of his pocket.

Her expression didn't change. *Pity.* Lani's had sparked with hate, a last surge of life. It had excited him. He should have known Deidre would ultimately disappoint him in this way, too.

He lifted his hand and flicked his wrist, releasing the star in one fluid motion. It sank deep into her heart. The irony of it made him smile.

Deidre fell to the ground, her eyes startled.

Edward bent down in front of her. He stared into her face, watching the life drain from her, metaphorically drinking it in. He waited until her gaze was flat and empty in death; then he picked her up. He carelessly tossed her over the railing into the bay, wiped his hands with a handkerchief, and walked away.

Her staff clacks against her mother's as she blocks.

Mama nods. "Good. Try again," she says, and then launches into a series of moves so fast that each movement blurs into the next.

Willow struggles to keep up, but her mother comes at her with fury. She stumbles backward and trips, tumbling to the ground.

Her mother swings her staff at Willow's head, stopping an inch from her temple. "You dropped your guard, Willow. Never drop your guard, not even with me. It could prove to be fatal."

Willow laughs at the silly idea. "You won't hurt me, Mama."

Her mother pauses, her face serious. "Never trust anyone, Willow. At best, they'll leave you. More likely, they'll betray you first. The only person you can rely on is yourself."

"What about you, Mama? You won't leave me."

Mama smiles at her sadly. She bows, her weapon at her side, and then turns to run.

"Mama." *Willow runs after her, through the* tarata. *Only the branches begin to grow, obscuring the path, tangling in her hair and grabbing her clothes. She looks forward, but she can't see her mother any longer.*

Her mother's voice, ghost-thin and tinny, drifts through the foliage. "Remember, Willow, trust no one…"

She tries to push her way through the thick bushes. "Come back!"

A branch wraps itself around her wrist, holding her there. The bush closes around her, the lemony scent strong in her nostrils.

"No. No." *She struggles against its hold, but she can't break free.* "Let go."

"Willow," *the* tarata *whispers softly.*

"Let go," *she yells. She has to find her mama.*

"Willow, wake up…"

She looks ahead, but the bush has closed her in. There's nothing but darkness. Her mother is gone.

Sobbing, she cries out. "Mama!"

"Willow."

She woke with a start. She would have bolted upright, but she was caught up in the *tarata*.

No—not the *tarata*. It was a warm body that held her pinned down. *Ramirez.*

Still breathing heavily, she looked up at him. The whites of his eyes were stark in the darkness. He watched her, observant without betraying any thoughts. A cop's gaze.

She swallowed and wiggled. He was not only on

top of her, his weight holding her down, but he had her by the wrists so she couldn't move her arms. "Off," she said.

"Promise not to try to hit me again."

She stopped moving. "I tried to hit you?"

"You only got one punch in, though." He slid off her slowly, resting on his side. "I'd like to believe it's because I was asleep when you attacked."

She winced and started to get up. "I can sleep some-place else—"

"I didn't ask you to leave." His arm snaked around her and pulled her close, until she was tucked into him, his body spooning hers. "I asked you not to maim me."

"I think I can manage that." She relaxed against him, which wasn't difficult with the way he ran his hand soothingly through her hair.

"Where did you learn to fight?" he asked.

"Mostly, my mother. At least in the beginning. After…" A lump formed in her throat, just like it always did when she thought about that day. "I studied with other random people when I was older, but my mother gave me the foundation for everything I know."

"Your mother seems unusual."

She smiled wryly. "That's one way of looking at her. She didn't live like most people. She was strong and brave. She did what she had to do."

"You take after her."

Did she? It wouldn't have taken her mother twenty years to find the Bad Man. "I'm not as good as she was," Willow said finally.

She waited for him to comment on that, but he said nothing. She wasn't sure if she was relieved he didn't offer her false platitudes, or disappointed that he didn't reassure her.

But then he brushed her hair aside and kissed the back of her neck, and that was better than anything he could have said. "Tell me about your dream."

She tensed. "It was just a dream."

"I'm not sure I believe that." He wrapped his arm around her middle, holding her firmly. "You called out for your mother."

Great. She tried to move away from him, but his arm tightened around her. He shifted, resting his weight on her just enough to make her feel secured in place without feeling smothered.

But she did feel trapped by the strange intimacy he was weaving around them. Normally, she would have run—fast and far.

Only, she couldn't run this time. Even if she had somewhere to go, she didn't want to leave this spot. She didn't want to leave him.

That was the scariest thing that had happened to her in forever.

Not wanting to think about that, she focused on the moment, instead—specifically how she felt in his arms. He was hard, nestled behind her. Despite their nearness, she wanted to get closer. Needed to feel his body against hers. She snaked her hand between their bodies to take hold of him.

"Later." He drew her hand away and held it in his, cradling it against her chest. "I want to hear about your dream."

"There's not much to tell," she said evasively.

"Willow, tell me."

She closed her eyes, fighting the need to do just that. "Withholding sex for information, Starsky?" she tried to joke, but it fell flat even to her own ears.

He just dropped another barely-there kiss on the nape of her neck.

She sighed, defeated. "Fine. I was dreaming that my mother and I were sparring, and then she ran away and disappeared, and no matter how hard I tried to find her, I couldn't. Happy?"

He kissed her again, his thumb massaging circles in her palm. She could practically hear him processing. She wondered what he'd make of it.

"How old were you when she died?" he finally asked.

"She was murdered," Willow corrected, "and I was ten."

"She didn't want to leave you."

"What do you mean?"

"She was taken from you. She wouldn't have left you if she had a choice."

Frowning, she wiggled until she had enough room to turn around and face him. His eyes were hooded, and she couldn't read his thoughts.

He cupped her face. "That's something to take comfort in, that she loved you and would have stayed with you."

"I'm not sure we're just talking about my mother."

His smile was rueful. "No."

She ducked her head, not sure how to deal with this. Multiple attackers? Piece of cake. Offering emotional comfort? Unfamiliar, frightening territory.

"I'm not sure which is better. Knowing your mother, but then losing her, or not knowing her at all. Maybe it's merciful not knowing what you're missing." He tucked her head against his chest. "I don't even remember what my mother looked like," he added, almost as though he was talking to himself.

"What happened to her?"

"She left. She was young when she had me, not much more than a child herself." He caressed the base of her skull with his fingers. "It was the best decision for everyone, but as a kid, you can't see that."

"She left you with your grandmother?"

"Yes."

"At least you had your grandmother." She hadn't had anyone. Yes, her mom had arranged a caretaker for her in the event of an emergency, however Willow might as well have been on her own. The woman who'd taken her in was hardly maternal—or caring, for that matter.

"A blessing and a curse," he said, his voice lightening into teasing amusement. "That woman scared the shit out of me when I was a child."

Willow smiled. "I can imagine."

"My friends wouldn't come over because they were afraid she'd curse them. Looking back, I realize what a good thing that was. I'd fallen in with the wrong crowd, and it prevented me from getting in too deep over my head." He rested his chin on her head. "Lita saved me."

Tipping her head back, she looked at his tattoo. "And you spun a new web for yourself."

He nodded. "Before the one I was weaving trapped me in its grip."

"You're lucky you had her."

"I am."

She traced the styled circles with the tip of her finger. He was falling into the wrong crowd again, this time with her. "What if your new web trips you up?"

"It won't." He speared his fingers in her hair and tipped her head back. "I'd rather wonder if my new web will help me catch what I want."

He lowered his mouth to hers and kissed her, and she knew he meant he wanted to catch *her*. She just wasn't clear on why: for a murder suspect, or for himself?

Chapter Twenty

Ramirez awoke pressed up against a taut backside, a mound of whitish-blond hair tickling his face, and a Texas-sized hard-on. He moved the hair and considered the backside, running a hand down the curve of Willow's hip. In the end, he decided his hard-on could wait until she woke up. She needed more sleep, and he needed to check in with work.

Untangling himself from her, he eased off the bed, stopping to soothe her when she stirred. Satisfied that she'd drifted back to sleep, he retrieved his boxers, grabbed a T-shirt, and used the bathroom down the hall. After washing up, he went downstairs into his office, closed the door, and called his partner.

Taylor answered with his usual good-natured enthusiasm. "Ricky, you'll never guess what the team found in that woman's room last night."

Ramirez scrubbed a hand over his face and sat in the window overlooking his grandmother's garden. "Tell me."

"We found a cache of driver's licenses, passports, and credit cards in what looked like a getaway file. She likes files, because she had others, including one for each of our victims. Pretty incriminating."

Damn it, Willow. "What else?"

"Her laptop's state-of-the-art. Weinberg's in geek heaven over it. He's locked himself with it in his office. I don't want to think about what he's doing in there." Taylor shuddered audibly.

"Has he found anything on the computer yet?"

"No. The thing locked down like a virgin the second the kid tried to get in."

Good. He'd have to ask Willow about that.

"Hey, Ricky, you know what else?"

He wasn't sure he wanted to know. "What?"

"You sitting down?"

"Just tell me," he growled.

"She had a dossier on you." His partner hesitated. "It looks like you were her next victim."

No, he wasn't. She didn't have any intention of killing him, or if she once did, she didn't anymore. She wouldn't have been able to give herself to him the way she had last night. She wouldn't have been able to sleep cocooned in his arms.

Would she?

He gritted his teeth and stared out the window. Was he being a fool, letting his dick lead him around? He'd seen it happen before, with guys on the force. He'd thought those men idiots for risking their solid careers for a woman. He never figured he'd join their ranks.

"Ricky?"

Ramirez frowned, looking down at the garden. Lita was down there, weeding and talking. He looked left to see who she was talking to. Willow, of course. She sat on a stone bench, legs crossed and sipping from one of Lita's mugs. She wore his sweatshirt and a pair of bottoms she must have found in his drawers. Her hair shined in the sun, glints of gold warming its cool pale. She looked at ease, but on closer inspection, he saw the little bit of stiffness around her shoulders. It couldn't have been easy chatting with your lover's grandmother the morning after.

Lover. He stared at her, wondering what she was to him. She felt like more than a lover. He shook his head. He couldn't think about that right now. First order of business was to find this Bad Man she kept talking about. Until she was cleared of any potential charges, they didn't have a future.

"Ricky? You okay, man? You seem distracted. This isn't like you. What's going on?"

"Just tired." He stood. "I have some things to take care of today. You good on your own?"

"Sure," Taylor said, not sounding too certain.

"Call me if anything comes up."

"Of course." He paused. "You'll tell me if you need help, right? You know I'm here for you."

"I know. Thank you." Except he couldn't drag his partner down with him, if anything went wrong. "Tell May I expect to be invited to dinner soon. It's been too long."

"Anytime, Ricky. You know that." His partner hung up.

Ramirez didn't miss the double meaning behind Taylor's parting words, which was why he was going to do everything he could to keep him out of this. Setting the phone down, he walked through the kitchen and out the back door to the garden.

Both women looked up when they heard him coming down the stairs, Lita with her usual love and genuine pleasure in seeing him, and Willow with cautious desire. He wondered if she even realized it.

Eyes on Willow, he went to his grandmother and kissed her upraised cheek. "Good morning."

"Is it still morning?" Lita teased.

He arched his brow.

She returned the look, a knowing half smile curling her lips before she returned her attention to the plants. "Your young lady and I were just getting to know each other. She knows a fair amount about shrubbery and trees, but her knowledge of herbs is lacking. No doubt because her mother didn't have time to complete her education."

He noticed the way Willow's face went blank at the mention of her mother. She'd said her mother had been killed, but not how or why. He couldn't help the twinge of sadness that plowed through him at the idea that Willow had spoken to his *abuelita* about her mother. He wondered if she'd tell him. He realized it was important to him for her to want to tell him, and he sighed.

When Willow spoke, her tone was light. "Despite what it looks like, I'm not certain the inspector would call me his lady, young or otherwise."

Lita smiled indulgently as she plucked a few stray growths from the dirt in the herb bed. "Ricardo is stubborn, but he's not stupid."

Both women looked at him.

He shook his head. "I know better than to enter this conversation."

"See?" his grandmother said.

"You've trained him well." Willow shot him an undecipherable look.

He felt a sense of satisfaction when she shuddered as his bare leg brushed hers. He wondered how she'd react if he leaned in and kissed her right here in front of Lita.

He was such a fool. He stuck his hands in his pockets, instead. It was better he didn't touch her, even if it made him a coward. "Can I talk to you a moment?"

Willow glanced at his grandmother. "Of course," she said, standing up.

Knowing Lita's sharp ears would be tuned to their conversation, he led Willow to the other side of the yard and faced her. He searched her features as though he'd find answers there.

She regarded him curiously. "What is it?"

"I need to ask you some questions."

"What else is new?" she asked with a wry smile.

Despite her casual reply, he felt her body tense in preparation. He frowned, trying not to imagine all the things she could be hiding. "They found information on the victims in your room."

"Of course they did." The exasperation in her voice was real. "I do a detailed background check on everyone I do business with. So, of course, I had a file on the PI."

"And Joel Rocco?"

"I ran a check on him after he died." She crossed her arms. "If you'd been set up to take the fall for someone's murder, you'd want to know who he was, as well."

He didn't point out that he wouldn't have been set up in the first place. "Did you compile the file on Quentin before or after he died?"

"Before. I needed to talk to him, and I wanted to know about him first." Her steady gaze told him she was telling the truth.

"And why did you have a file on me?"

She dropped her arms and looked away. "Know your enemy."

He lifted her gaze to meet his and saw defiance—like she dared him to call her a liar—and something else. Subterfuge? "You're not telling the whole truth."

"So you at least believe part of it." Her lips pursed and she nodded her head. "I guess that's something."

Those lips were pure temptation. "It's the other part that I'm concerned about."

She pulled free and shrugged.

He told himself that he stepped closer to force her attention on him, not because he wanted to inhale the fresh scent of her. "Tell me why you checked up on me."

"There's nothing to tell." She frowned at him. "So is that it? Are you done with me now?"

He had the feeling he'd never be done with her, and he wasn't sure if that was a great or terrible thing. "I'm done. For now."

Without a word, she turned and walked back toward the house. He stayed close behind, and based on the stiff set of her back, she was very aware of it.

Willow stopped next to his grandmother. "Thank you for the talk. I'm going to take a shower now, if you don't mind."

"Of course not, *mijita*." Lita sat back on her heels. "Take your time."

The corner of Willow's mouth quirked. "So you have enough time to discuss me?"

God, he wanted to kiss those lips. He vaguely registered that his grandmother said something in reply, but he didn't miss a moment of Willow sauntering up the stairs. He wanted to follow her. He wanted to turn her around and take her in his arms, to slowly strip his clothes off her, tuck her in bed, and make love to her. He could so clearly picture her tanned skin against his white bedding, and just the thought of the erotic contrast was driving him to distraction.

"You're drooling, *hijo*."

He waited to face his grandmother until Willow had walked inside and closed the door. "You're taking this well. It wasn't long ago that you would have lectured me for bringing home a woman I didn't know."

"You know Willow," she said without hesitation. "And she isn't just any woman. You and the white witch are fated for each other."

He knew better than to say anything.

Lita shook a trowel at him. "I can feel your skepticism. Silence doesn't mask it."

"I respect your beliefs, Lita, but you can't ask me to subscribe to something that I don't feel."

"You feel it. Otherwise, you would never have offered her sanctuary." His grandmother's eyes reflected ages of wisdom. "You would never risk your career for her, otherwise."

He looked up at his bedroom window.

"She's been trusted to you, *hijo*," his grandmother said softly. "It's a great gift. One you're worthy of."

"It's not a question of being worthy," he said, standing up.

His grandmother's only reply was to look at him suspiciously.

She had no idea what he was up against. It wasn't as if he could tell her he was harboring a wanted murderer. He dropped a kiss on her forehead and walked up to his home.

Ramirez could hear the shower running. Not allowing himself to stop to think, he quickly went upstairs to his room, stripping out of his shirt and boxers before entering the bathroom.

It was cloudy with steam. Through the glass shower door, he could see her form. A side view of her curves and her head bent back, arms raised to rinse soap from her hair.

He opened the door and stepped in.

Her eyes snapped open. Her gaze went up and down his body, stopping to watch his dick reawaken, which only turned him on more.

"Lean your head back again," he said.

He thought she'd argue, but she didn't put up a fight, because she wanted him as much as he wanted her, he hoped. Stepping forward until he was as close to her as he could be, he reached up and began to work the fresh water through her long hair. She melted against him with a sigh, letting her head fall back even more.

He tried not to think about how perfect she was for him—how his dick was aligned to enter her with minimal effort. How her nipples stabbed his chest. The feel of her fingers biting into his biceps. He concentrated on rinsing the rest of the shampoo from her hair, massaging her scalp and neck in the process.

She hummed. "You're good at this. Ever thought of becoming a hairdresser?"

"Stylist," he corrected.

She opened one eye and looked at him with amusement.

He took the bottle of soap off the shelf. "That's what my barber tells me these days, so he can charge me more money, I think."

She watched him squeeze some soap onto his palm, her lips tipped with a smile. "He sounds like a marketing genius."

Ramirez grunted. Lathering the soap between his hands, he shifted them so she was away from the spray of the showerhead. He put his hands on either side of her neck and rubbed circles into her muscles.

"What did I do to rate the deluxe service?" She sighed as her body went limp, but she watched for his answer. "Assuming you don't treat everyone under the suspicion of murder this way."

"Not hardly." He massaged her shoulders, working his way down each arm. "You know we're going to have to discuss that."

She studied him. She must have seen what she was looking for, because she finally nodded. "Yes, I know."

Something inside him relaxed. He nodded. "But not right now. Right now, I'm busy."

A smile touched the corner of her mouth. "Too busy for me?"

He loved that small show of amusement. It felt real, like her true self was breaking through the thick facade she'd built around herself. He kissed her mouth, flicking her lips with his tongue to taste how it felt. "Too busy *with* you," he corrected.

"In that case." She leaned back against the shower stall, offering herself to him with open arms. "You better get on with it."

No arguments from him. He lifted her arms and held them high over her head. "Don't move."

She rolled her eyes but didn't fight him. *Good,* he thought as he ran his hands down the insides of her arms, stopping to press inside her underarms with his thumbs. She squirmed for a moment before holding herself still.

"Ticklish?"

"Of course not."

He stopped. "You're lying."

"Why do you say that?"

"Your eyes tell me. They go flat when you lie," he pointed out.

Rolling those beautiful eyes, she said, "Sure they do. Next you'll tell me they darken, too."

"Only when you're coming." He slid his hands down her chest, pausing once to knead her breasts before wrapping his arms around her and washing her back. He could feel her heartbeat against his chest, a short staccato rhythm that showed him just how excited she was. "Want to test my theory?"

She rubbed her pelvis against his erection, which didn't mind the attention. "I think you're the one who wants to test things out."

Reaching for more soap, he continued lathering her back, all the way down to her ass. He slipped his fingers in its crease, liking the gasp he got in response. He let his fingers caress down into her folds, and her mouth parted, along with her legs—an invitation he wasn't ready to take. He withdrew his fingers from her sex and massaged the firm globes of her rear. Then he got to his knees and started working his way up from her feet.

After a moment, she said, "I like you kneeling before me."

He glanced up at her. "Makes you feel in charge, huh?"

"Aren't I?"

She was, because right now he would do anything for her—the scariest thought he'd had in his life. Scarier than facing a strung-out perp with a gun.

He bit her above her ankle; then he rotated her foot. Right above her anklebone was the small image of a sword, one of those curved Chinese swords he'd seen in magazines. "What's this? A tattoo?"

She shook her head. "A birthmark."

"A birthmark." He looked at it closer, rubbing his thumb over it. He felt a shock, which he would have dismissed if he hadn't heard Willow's gasp. He looked to find her eyes wide with fear. He surprised himself by asking, "It's not just a birthmark, is it?"

She hesitated, but then said, "It is, but it represents more."

He touched it again, feeling another shock of electricity. "You'll tell me about it later."

She frowned.

Satisfied that she didn't argue, he kissed over the spot and continued up her legs. When he reached her thighs, he got to his knees, positioning himself so his mouth was level with her sex. His fingers worked the inside of her legs until he couldn't wait any longer. He moved his hand up so his thumbs ran over the bare skin there. "I like this."

Her chest heaved with each short breath she took. When she spoke, her voice was huskier than usual. "Glad to know it meets your approval."

"More than approval." He worked the soap across the surface, rinsed her, and then dipped his fingers in.

She moaned, her head falling back to rest on the tile behind her.

He lifted her leg to his shoulder for better access. He'd intended to take his time, but the sight, along with her moans, was too much to handle. He set her foot down and stood. He soaped his own body in record time, rinsed himself, and then turned the spray onto her.

She shrieked when the water hit her. "It's cold!"

"It has been for a while."

"I'm freezing." She glared at him.

"I'll warm you up." He turned off the water. She opened her mouth, and he kissed her to stop any arguments. He picked her up so her legs straddled his hips and carried her to his bed, easing inside her as he laid her against the plump pillows. They lay there, motionless, both of them panting. Then she said, "My hair is soaking the sheets."

He kissed her lovely neck. "I'm not sure that's a punishable offense."

"Damn," she said in her facetious tone.

Biting her softly at the top rise of her breasts, he arched into her. "Careful, or I'll get the cuffs out."

"Promises, promises."

Her arms were wrapped around him, actively holding him, and he liked that. A lot.

In fact, he liked it a little too much.

Chapter Twenty-one

A doorbell woke Ramirez a short while later.

No one ever came to his door, and Lita had a key. Figuring it was someone's TV, he checked the time and mentally groaned. It was after noon. He couldn't remember the last time he'd slept so late. He couldn't remember the last time he'd had such fantastic sex, either.

He spooned Willow closer, knowing he should get up, but he was unwilling to disrupt the peace. Or would-be peace, if the doorbell would just stop buzzing. That's when he realized it was his door. It had to be a Jehovah's Witness or salesman. He usually wasn't home during the day, so whoever it was would get the idea and move on.

Willow rolled toward him, her eyes wide open. "I think you have a visitor."

He grunted, gathering her onto his chest.

A slow smile curved her lips. "Again, Starsky? Aren't you afraid it might fall off from overuse?"

He started to answer, but the person laid on the buzzer, continuous and annoying, until Ramirez was forced to push the covers back. "Who the hell is it? Not even Taylor drops by without calling first."

"Uh-oh." Willow's eyes grew distant for a moment before she snapped back to herself. "I think I know who it is."

Grabbing his boxers, he gave her a dark look. "It's not a disgruntled husband, is it?"

"Of course not." She glared back at him as she swung her legs out of bed and reached for his shirt. "You can't seriously think I'd be married."

"I know nothing about you," he said as he walked out of the room.

"You know enough." She buttoned his shirt that she wore as she followed him downstairs. "You wouldn't have let me in your house if you didn't trust me a little."

He rounded on her, causing her to walk into him. He held her hips to steady her. Hell, he held her hips because he wanted to keep her close. He glanced at her eyes, her lips, swollen from their lovemaking, and was overcome by some piercing emotion he had no time for. "Maybe I was thinking with my dick. Any guy would, around you."

She studied him unwaveringly. Then she shook her head. "No, your grandmother is right. You're not just *any guy.*"

He wanted to rail at her for thinking that but still not trusting him enough to be completely honest. He could tell there were things she was still hiding from him, but the buzzer began an obnoxious staccato. He growled and strode down the hall to answer it.

As he swung the door open, the person standing on his stoop looked up with big Betty Boop eyes. She had a mop of springy curls tied back in a ponytail. She wore jeans, an asymmetrical jacket that hit her midthigh, and army green tennis shoes. Around her shoulder hung a laptop bag, and she held in her hand a small overnight bag.

She blinked her thick-lashed cartoon eyes as she looked him up and down. Her gaze darted beyond him to Willow, her eyes widening impossibly. "Um. Okay. Of all the scenarios I imagined, this wasn't one of them."

Ramirez glanced back at Willow. "You know this person?" he asked.

"Unfortunately. Although I'm not entirely certain how she found me."

"The GPS transponder in your phone." The woman shook her head. "Duh."

Willow rolled her eyes. "Let her in, Starsky. We can discuss everything over breakfast." She turned and headed into the kitchen.

Ramirez and the woman on his doorstep watched her walk away. Then the woman said, "You must rate."

He glanced at her. "What?"

"Willow hardly ever cooks. She must like you if she's willing to cook for you." She smiled like a demented pixie. "But then based on your attire, I'd say you two like each other a lot."

Not willing to comment on that, he took her overnight bag and stepped aside to let her in.

"Thank you, Inspector Ramirez."

"Have we met?" he asked as he closed the door, knowing that they hadn't.

"Nope, but I've done some research on you." She held out her hand. "Morgan, Willow's office manager."

"Willow has an office?"

She shrugged. "Metaphorically speaking."

He set the bag by the stairs and ushered Morgan into the kitchen, where Willow stood at the refrigerator. In a flurry of motion, she extracted an armful of ingredients and set them on the counter.

"Oh, boy." Morgan rubbed her hands together. Setting her laptop bag on the floor, she pulled out a chair from the table and sat, eagerly waiting. "She hasn't cooked for me in ages. You're in for a treat."

Willow's movements were confident and quick. It shouldn't have surprised him that she'd be as expert in the kitchen as she was fighting on the street, but it did. She looked at home, dicing vegetables while wearing his shirt. It rode up her thighs whenever she reached for something, and that turned him on. He should have nibbled her there, too.

Feeling as though he were being watched, he found Morgan's eyes on him with narrow suspicion. Acutely aware he wore only boxers, he excused himself to get dressed. He quickly pulled on a pair of jeans and a T-shirt, returning to overhear Willow and Morgan talking. He stopped in the hallway, out of sight, to listen.

"—can't believe you're getting it on with a Homicide detective." Morgan placed extra emphasis on *homicide*.

"They're inspectors in San Francisco. And you yourself said he was hot."

"Well, duh. He's totally hot, but that doesn't mean I'd do him. Does he know who you are?"

A pause. "Not yet."

Ramirez felt his gut churning with unease. Who was she?

"*Not yet?*" The leg of a chair scraped on the hardwood floor. "You're actually considering telling him?"

"I need him in order to get to the Bad Man. I'm out of choices, Morgan. The police confiscated everything, and I'm wanted for questioning in three murders."

"Yeah, but that would never have made you tell someone who you are."

In the long pause, he heard something sizzling on the stove.

Then Morgan spoke again. "Are you in love with him?"

"That would be stupid, wouldn't it?" was Willow's calm answer.

He released a breath he hadn't realized he was holding. She hadn't denied it, and he found that surprisingly important.

"Because I shouldn't have to tell you, this is an impossible situation." Morgan's voice sobered, the sadness in it loud and clear. "Someone like you would never be able to hook up with a cop. It just wouldn't work."

The thud of the oven door banging shut was followed by Willow's angry voice. "You think I don't understand that?"

"I'm just checking."

Having heard enough, Ramirez strolled into the kitchen.

Both women looked up, Morgan blinking guiltily and Willow watching him with her steady gaze. "It smells good," he said mildly, getting water glasses out of the cabinet.

Neither woman said anything, and he felt a surge of satisfaction that he had them guessing. The kitchen door opened and his grandmother walked in. She gave Willow a handful of fresh herbs before turning to inspect Morgan.

"Morgan, my grandmother Elena. Lita, this is Morgan, Willow's *office manager.*" Somehow he managed to say it with a minimum of irony.

His grandmother eyed the young woman and then said, "Your rival is also your greatest ally. Don't let your pride keep you from realizing true happiness with the one person who would appreciate your worth."

"Um." Morgan blinked. "Okay. Thanks. I think."

Lita went to inspect the skillet that Willow had pulled out of the oven. She nodded in approval and pulled four plates out from the cabinet. Without looking at him, she said, "Business after sustenance, Ricardo. Your woman hasn't eaten. I know I taught you better than that."

Ramirez exchanged a look with Willow, who smirked a little.

Morgan had the good sense not to comment. She rubbed her hands together. "I'm so starving. Airplane food sucks."

"Where did you fly from?" he asked, getting out the silverware.

That instantly sobered her. "Paris," she answered cautiously.

"Careful, Morgan," Willow said, setting the pan on a trivet on the table. "The inspector won't hesitate in resorting to subtle torture to get answers out of you."

He cocked his brow, taking a seat. "Is that all it'll take? Subtle torture?"

"I'm not sure subtlety is your forte." She sat next to him, angling the serving utensil to his grandmother, who served a portion to Morgan.

"You didn't complain last night," he said softly.

"Jesus Christ." Morgan let her fork clatter onto the

plate. "The table is *not* the place for foreplay. And there's a grandmother here, for Christ's sake."

"That's all right, *linda,*" she said, taking a portion for herself and passing the spatula to Willow. "They need to work it out of their systems."

"They keep this up and they'll be working it out on the tabletop," she muttered.

Not the table, the counter, he thought. Glancing at Willow, he was surprised to find her cheeks turning pink. *Good.* He'd hate to think he was the only one affected here, because every time he washed dishes, he was going to remember her offering herself, her beautiful legs splayed open for him.

Morgan waved her fork. "Will, this is awesome. You make the best omelets."

"Frittata," Willow corrected halfheartedly.

"Whatever. The point is, I've missed the rare occasions you cook for me. Since you've been trying to track down—" Morgan blinked and then quickly shoved a large forkful of food into her mouth.

Willow shook her head. "He knows. Not all of it, but that much."

Morgan choked. She slapped the table, trying to control her coughing.

Ramirez kept an eye on her—as long as she was coughing, she was okay, but he didn't want her to asphyxiate on his watch. "Why don't you finish eating, and then we can hash everything out?"

"Good idea," she said hoarsely, clearing her throat.

Morgan was right—the frittata was excellent. He ate another piece, despite his impatience to discuss the situation. By the way her foot tapped on the floor, he knew

Willow wanted to get it over with just as badly—also in the way she jumped up to clear the table when his grandmother finished eating.

"*Mijita,* I'll clean," Lita said, waving her away from the sink. "You have important matters to discuss."

Willow frowned at the plates. "If you're sure."

"Your fate lies in the balance." She smiled gently. "A few dishes are a small price to pay to make sure your path is secured."

Willow didn't look pleased by Lita's statement. He prepared himself to defend his grandmother, the way he always had from people who disrespected her talents. But Willow quietly thanked her and led the way out of the kitchen.

"*Hijo,*" Lita called as he went to follow.

He turned. "Yes?"

She hesitated, something so rare for her that he frowned. Finally she said, "Sometimes gray can be washed away to reveal pure white."

He mentally sighed, not needing a PhD to figure out what his grandmother meant. So he just nodded and went to find Willow.

Willow sat cross-legged in the window seat of Ramirez's office, waiting for him to follow. Her stomach fluttered. Nerves, she realized, tucking his shirttail demurely under her. Ramirez strode into the room and came to an abrupt stop when he noticed Morgan on all fours under his desk.

Willow couldn't help but be amused. "She's checking out your computer."

"I see," he said, even though he sounded like he didn't.

Morgan turned and scowled at him. "I can't believe the city's finest has such a poor excuse for a desktop. Jesus. No wonder crime's on the rise. How can anyone be expected to fight villains with machinery built in the Stone Age?"

"The machinery doesn't actually do much," he pointed out.

"No kidding. It's like a square wheel. Totally useless." She got up, dusting her hands on her jeans. "Okay, what's going on here? I thought Will was on the run from the fuzz, but I come here and find her shacked up with one, instead."

"The police want me for questioning in the murder of three men." She paused, glancing at him to see if he would offer anything. He remained impassive, so she continued. "They've confiscated everything in my motel room."

Morgan's face fell in dismay. "Including the lappie I gave you?"

She nodded. "Including the laptop."

"Aw, man." Morgan dropped heavily onto his office chair. "I knew I shouldn't have trusted you with it."

"We need to start at the beginning. I need to know everything." Ramirez crossed his arms and stared at her with his cop's steady gaze.

She pushed aside the fleeting thought that it was a shame he'd put clothes on and got to the crux of the matter instead. "I told you I believe the man who killed my mother is the same one who killed the three you think I offed." She frowned. "At least I'm positive he killed Quentin. I only strongly suspect he killed the other two."

"Why are you positive about Quentin?"

"The method. He used a ninja star." She swallowed back the image of her mother lying on the floor, the gleaming silver protruding out of her chest. "The same way my mother was killed."

"Ninja stars aren't exactly a common method for killing," Morgan chimed in.

Willow frowned at her before facing Ramirez again. "He left it as a calling card for me. We've been circling around each other for over twenty years."

"Why?" Ramirez asked.

"Frankly? I don't know. He wants me. I assume to kill me, too, although I have no idea why, or who he is beyond a photo I have of him." She pursed her lips. "*Had.* Your team would have that, too."

"Hey, if you're so interested in helping Will, why'd you sic your team on her? Seems like she'd bend over for you." Morgan smirked. "I only meant that figuratively, of course."

"I didn't *sic* my team on her." He looked at her. "My partner said there was an anonymous call."

Willow nodded. "The Bad Man. We need to figure out who he is."

Morgan threw her hands in the air. "Like we haven't been trying for the past ten years. That man is a master of deception. The moment we get close, he slithers away again. As solid as my defenses against being hacked are"—she scowled—"*were,* he's got an entire different scope at his disposal. If we had backing like that, I could work miracles, too. Money talks."

Ramirez rubbed his cheek as he stared thoughtfully at Morgan. "You're very knowledgeable about computers for an office manager."

Morgan clamped her mouth shut, blinking owlishly. After a moment, she said, "I took an online course."

Willow shook her head at Morgan and faced Ramirez. "You have an idea."

He nodded. "I know someone who might be able to help."

"Not a systems expert, right?" Morgan sniffed disdainfully. "If I couldn't get past his firewalls, I can't see anyone else being able to do it."

"Not even the person who broke through yours?" Willow asked skeptically.

"The bastard." She banged her fist on the desk and then shook a finger at Ramirez. "Is that who you're talking about? Because that sucker better be careful when he walks down the street at night."

A trace of humor lightened his expression. "No, Weinberg works for the force. I'd ask him for help if I could, but that would compromise him too much."

"The force," Morgan spat. "What a waste. What's his first name? And you wouldn't happen to know his Social, would you?"

"Morgan." Willow shook her head, facing Ramirez. "What do you have in mind, Inspector?"

"I know someone who has backing, as Morgan says. And connections. I'll call him and we'll go from there."

Morgan wrinkled her nose. "You make it sound so easy, but this dude isn't going to just let us find him."

"She's right," Willow said. "He's been playing cat and mouse with me for over twenty years. He's not going to let anything slip, unless he wants it to slip."

"But you're here, chasing him." Ramirez paused, his

expression darkening. "Are you saying you knew he was luring you, and you still came?"

She shrugged. "As long as I know he's trying to pull me, I can take precautions."

"That's ridiculous." Ramirez faced off in front of her, legs braced, his jaw twitching with tension. "If everything you've told me is true, we're dealing with a psychopath. What precautions can you take against a psychopath?"

"I've been careful."

"So careful you've lost all your belongings and are one step away from serving a lifetime sentence for murder?"

So she hadn't exactly handled everything perfectly. *He* was the one messing with her plans. "Tell me how you really feel."

"Okay, I will." He stepped in front of her and pulled her to standing so his angry face filled her vision. "This senselessly putting yourself in danger is stopping right now. From now on, you don't do anything that stupidly jeopardizes your safety."

"Uh-oh," she heard Morgan mutter.

Ramirez, however, was oblivious to the peanut gallery. "I don't think you realize the stakes here. I'm risking *everything* on a gut feeling that you're telling the truth. So if there's anything else you need to tell me, you better lay it on the table now."

She pointed a finger in his face and raised her voice. "You're risking everything because you wanted to get laid."

"I'm risking everything because I'm falling in love with you."

The shock of hearing him say he might love her paralyzed her. No one had said that to her since her mom. The temptation of giving in to it was overwhelming.

Somewhere in the back of her mind echoed the thought that this was it—this was as close as she'd ever get to true happiness. Because once he found out the things she'd done, he'd never want her.

As if sensing her withdrawal, he sighed and let her go. "I'll call my contact."

"Okay." For some reason, she couldn't look at him. She toed the wood floor, looking for something to say. "If only we still had the Bad Man's photo."

"I'll check it out of property."

"Don't jeopardize yourself any further." At one time, she wouldn't have cared, but now the thought of him in trouble was oddly disturbing.

"Is there anything else you need to tell me? Anything that could help?"

She laughed mirthlessly. *How about that I'm an assassin and Guardian of ancient Chinese powers?* She looked at him, and her laughter was replaced by bone-deep sadness. "What else could there be?"

Chapter Twenty-two

He'd told her he was falling in love with her.

Ramirez snorted as he strapped himself in the car. *Falling in love.* He wasn't sure he had much further to fall.

He turned the key in the ignition and pulled away from the curb. He didn't know how it happened. He'd gone from levelheaded to completely illogical, because there was no logic in aiding and abetting a suspect. He knew there was only one way this could end for him: badly. Yes, he trusted her, but he knew she was still hiding things from him. He'd learned early in his career that you couldn't hide anything from your partner and expect to win the day.

Shaking his head, he went on autopilot to the station, slipped his headset onto his ear, and called someone who had more connections than God.

The man answered right away. "Prescott speaking."

"Max, it's Ramirez."

"Ramirez." Pause. "By the tone of your voice, this isn't a social call for my wife."

he reached the bottom. He pulled out a Baggie that contained a thin, six-inch stick. A flute. If it was handmade, it'd been done by an expert. It was beautifully carved, yet simple.

That night in Buena Vista, he'd thought he'd heard a flute playing. Was it possible that it was this flute? If so, there was no doubt that he could place Willow at another crime scene. She'd admitted she was supposed to meet with those two men, but he wanted to believe she had nothing to do with their murders. After a quick glance at Jenkins, to make sure he was still diverted, Ramirez pocketed the flute. He had a feeling Willow would want this, plus he knew giving it to her would warrant him some answers. He couldn't check it out legitimately because it'd raise eyebrows, not to mention that he'd have to get supervisor approval to keep anything longer than twenty-four hours. Feeling sure in his decision to keep the flute, he repacked everything else into the box.

Jenkins was eating a candy bar while reading *People* magazine when Ramirez approached with Willow's belongings. Jenkins set the candy down and reached to take the box out of Ramirez's hand. He chewed madly and then asked, "Got what you needed?"

"Yes." Ramirez held up the photo.

"Let's just get that checked out to you." Jenkins handed over another slip and a pen. "Just fill this out, Inspector."

Ramirez wrote in the case number, the evidence number, and his name. Hoping he wasn't signing his pink slip, he handed it back to the officer. "Thank you for your help."

"Sure thing. Good luck nabbing this broad."

Ramirez nodded, thinking about how he'd already nabbed her, and how much he was dying to do it all over again.

"I can't believe you made me do your shopping. You know I hate to shop," Morgan grumbled, handing over a bag.

Willow wheeled Ramirez's office chair around and took the bag. She was going to be so glad to be covered in something other than his shirt. Being mostly naked around him wreaked havoc on her concentration. "You don't mind whenever I send you out to buy me a laptop."

"That's not shopping. That's pure joy."

Shaking her head, Willow opened the bag and looked inside, blinked, and then raised her eyebrows at Morgan, who flashed an unrepentant grin.

"Like them? I picked them out specially."

Everything in the bag was black, which was actually perfect. People who dressed in black faded into the background. And if there was ever a time to be anonymous, it was now, with every cop in the city on the lookout for her.

She pulled out the thin and luxurious cashmere top. A surprising choice, given Morgan's style or lack thereof. But then she set that aside and extracted the rest from the bag. "Leather pants?"

"They're so you. You can't deny you like leather."

"I do, but these are hardly inconspicuous."

"They're black," her partner stated logically.

Willow nodded. At least they had that going for them. But the underwear... She held up the two scraps of red lace that served as a bra and panties. "And these?"

Morgan smiled wickedly. "I got those for the cop."

Willow narrowed her eyes. "I'm not sure you got the right size."

"He won't want them on long, anyway." Snickering, she handed over another bag. "Your shoes."

Good. She only had the heels she'd been wearing—not the most practical thing for running someone down. She pulled out the box, relieved to find a pair of fancy but functional boots. "I'm surprised they aren't thigh high."

"I thought the double layer of leather coating your legs would be overkill." Morgan batted her eyes innocently. "But I'm happy to go back and exchange them."

Shooting her partner a peeved look, she took her new things and went up to Ramirez's room to change. Unfortunately, Morgan followed her, all the way into the room to flop on the bed. Setting the clothes on the dresser, Willow ignored her and went into the bathroom. When she emerged, Morgan was still there, sprawled on her stomach, reading a computer magazine she brought with her. Willow shook her head and reached for the underwear, if it could be called that.

Behind her, there was the rustle of a page turning. "Your cop is quite a guy."

Willow glanced over her shoulder at her partner calmly perusing an ad for some sort of alien-looking machine. "He's not mine."

"Isn't he?" Another page turning.

He couldn't be, except he'd said he was falling in love with her. Willow hooked the bra behind her back and pulled on the straps. She stared at herself in the half mirror hanging above the dresser. How could he possibly be falling for her? He hadn't known her but for a few days.

It had to be because of the sex. Men got crazy over good sex, right? And it'd been more than good, so it would make sense that he'd be overtaken by the feelings evoked. But Ramirez wasn't the type of man to make idle comments. From the moment she'd first seen him, she could tell he was no-nonsense—grounded and very clear in his purpose. She turned and faced Morgan. Morgan had more experience with men though she was a couple years younger. She'd know if Ramirez really meant it, or if it was the sex talking.

Her partner must have felt the scrutiny, because she lifted her head and whistled. "Damn, I know my lingerie. You're rocking that red, babe. Your cop is going to drop to his knees when he sees that."

"I told you, he's not mine."

"He could be if you wanted." Morgan tipped her head. "Do you?"

Yes. No. Willow scowled. "I've been after the Bad Man for over twenty years. Do you think I'm going to screw everything up by taking up with a cop?"

Morgan looked around the room. "Funny. From my perspective, that looks exactly like what you've done."

No, it wasn't. Willow grabbed the leather pants and shimmied into them.

"I take it you haven't told him about your occupation," Morgan said, idly flipping another page.

Willow pulled the sweater over her head and glared. "Of course I haven't told him. That'd be a one-way ticket to maximum security for life."

Morgan set the magazine aside and rolled onto her back. "I think he likes you."

"What is this, high school?"

"Which is why I think you need to break it off with him." Morgan pursed her lips. "Soon. He's the type of guy who won't like being deceived. The longer you go without telling him, the more he'll hold it against you. It's trouble waiting to happen."

Willow yanked the sleeves on and gathered her hair into a high ponytail. That was the problem—the thought of leaving tore at her gut.

"Leave it to you, Will, to pick the most upstanding guy on earth to hook up with."

"I didn't pick him."

"It just happened, huh?" Morgan rolled her eyes. "Yeah, I can see that, because you're so given to peer pressure. And you're always whoring around. I can't count all the guys you've been out with. I'm not sure a number that high exists. In fact—"

"*Shut up.*" The second the words came out of her mouth, she regretted them. Shame flushed her cheeks.

Morgan sat up and pointed a finger at her. "I won't shut up. How long have we known each other? Ten years?"

"Almost eleven."

"Eleven fucking years, Willow," she yelled, her face flushed. "I know you better than anyone else in this world, and I *care.*"

All Willow could do was stare blankly, taken aback by her friend's vehemence.

"Yeah, I care. How could I not? After everything we've been through? You're the closest thing I have to family, and I like to delude myself that you feel the same way. But that's what I'm doing, isn't it? Deluding myself?"

"I—" She tried to think of what to say, but she was so stunned by the outbreak, her mind was blank.

"Tell me I'm not deluding myself," Morgan yelled. "We're friends. No, we're *family*, damn it."

"Mor—"

"Get that through your thick skull." Hopping off the bed, Morgan stalked toward her. "We're family, and family cares about each other, which is why I'm telling you that cop can't be your future. You're just setting yourself up to be hurt. What are you going to do after you take your mother's killer down? Sneak away to go on jobs? Retire? To do what?"

Honestly, she hadn't thought that far. She'd only had one goal: the Bad Man. "That day hasn't come yet."

"But it will, and then you'll be shackled to someone who can't possibly approve of who you are." Morgan crossed her arms, looking more pissed than even the time Willow had knocked over a cup of tea onto her hard drive. "I think the cop is more important to you than the Bad Man."

"Of course not," Willow said automatically.

"Uh-huh." Morgan shook her head, disbelief radiating from her. "Whatever. But don't tell me I didn't warn you, because when he finds out who you are, your little paradise is going to be over."

"Who are you?" asked a cool masculine voice from behind them.

Both women whirled around. Even Morgan was struck silent by Ramirez's sudden appearance. His gaze met Willow's before it roved down her body, and back.

"I'm outta here." Morgan poked Willow in the side and said, "Don't fuck this up," then she walked out the door.

Willow watched her partner—friend—until she'd disappeared from view, only because she had no idea what to say to Ramirez. She faced him and opened her mouth, but nothing came out.

"Who are you?" he asked again.

She swallowed. "You know who I am."

"Obviously, I don't." The muscle in his jaw twitched. "Are you going to tell me?"

If it were up to her, she'd never say a word. For the first time in her life, she wished she'd taken a different path, but there was nothing to be done about that now. She was who she was, and she only had one goal: to bring the Bad Man to justice. Morgan's words echoed in her head. *"What are you going to do after you take your mother's killer down?"* She could tell Ramirez something to pacify him, but he'd know.

She looked him in the eye and realized that she didn't want to lie to him anymore. "Can you trust me? Just until after I take the Bad Man down? I'll tell you everything *after* it's over. If you still want."

"We," he said after a moment.

She frowned. "What?"

"We're bringing your Bad Man in. *We,*" he said as emphasis.

"Right." She nodded.

"Why do I feel like you're placating me?" He stepped forward and took her arms. "I told you, I'm not going to let you do this alone. I have as much vested in this as you do."

She searched his face. "I don't see how you could."

"Don't you?" He lifted her chin and lowered his mouth to hers.

The kiss was soft. She tried to keep her distance—she tried not to notice how well he *fit*—but he engulfed her and she melted against him. With one last caressing brush of his lips, he let her go and studied her. His stare was so shuttered, she couldn't tell what he was thinking, and that bothered her. She resisted the urge to shift from leg to leg, instead waiting for the verdict.

Finally he said, "Is what you're keeping from me in regard to this case?"

She shook her head. "No."

He paused, obviously weighing her answer. "You'll tell me after we clear you from any potential charges?"

"Yes." Her answer sounded less sure, even to herself. But he didn't comment. He stepped back and pulled a plastic Baggie from his inside jacket pocket. "Is this him?"

She took the bag from him. Inside was the worn photograph she knew so well. Those familiar cold eyes stared back at her, and she shivered. "That's him."

"I'm going to take this to a friend of mine."

"To try to ID him? Morgan and I have done an exhaustive search. I don't know what else your friend can do."

"My friend has connections and resources that you and Morgan don't have. He may know someone who knows this man."

"Then I'm going with you," she stated quickly.

He nodded like he hadn't expected anything less. "We'll leave in an hour." He reached into his coat again. "Even once you're cleared, it'll take a while before the evidence collected will be released to you. I'm sure you'll want to replace some of it before then."

She shrugged. Material things didn't matter in the whole scheme of things. Her scroll was safe, and the only thing she really wanted back was the flute. Her heart squeezed with the possibility that the flute was lost to her forever.

"I thought you might want this." He pulled out another bag.

The flute. She took it, almost afraid she was imagining it. She looked up at him, brows furrowed in confusion.

"That night at Buena Vista Park, I thought I heard someone playing the flute." He stuck his hands in his pockets. "You?"

She nodded, too dumbstruck to say anything.

"It sounded"—he glanced up at the ceiling in thought—"heartfelt. Like it was coming from someplace deep inside you. It was beautiful. When I saw the flute, it seemed like you'd want it back. It looks well loved."

Hands shaking, she took the flute out of the bag and let the plastic fall to the floor. She rolled the flute in her hands, the pulse of the wood under her fingertips. She closed her eyes and reached out to the energy, feeling the echoes of her mother's and her own *mù ch'i* deep in the grain.

Tears prickled her eyes, falling down to her nose, but she pushed them back and lifted her chin. "My mother made this flute."

He nodded solemnly. He understood. She could see it in his eyes; yet she couldn't wrap her mind around it.

"You stole this for me?" she asked.

"I requisitioned it out of the property room," he corrected, his expression neutral.

"But isn't that against the rules?"

"The flute has no bearing in this case."

She shook her head. "That doesn't matter. They collected it as evidence, which means it stays listed as evidence until otherwise released."

Ramirez still didn't say anything.

Frustration ate at her. "You broke the rules, which

is noteworthy considering you're a by-the-book kind of guy. You risked your job to bring this to me?"

He stared at her, his gaze dark and intense, waiting for her to get it.

It didn't compute.

Yes, it was just a flute, and he probably wouldn't suffer any consequences for bringing it to her. But his job defined him. If she'd learned anything about him, it was that he took his work very seriously. It was something she related to. But what did it mean?

"I'm falling in love with you."

She looked back up at him, but all she saw was his back as he walked away.

Chapter Twenty-three

There was an old apple tree in Ramirez's backyard. Its limbs were barren of fruit, but they stretched out like welcoming arms, full of sheltering leaves. Willow went to it and sat at its foot. She put her hand on the dirt and let her energy flow into the earth, feeling how grounded and sure the tree felt. It knew its place and thrived in that security.

Willow immediately recognized Elena's hand in that. Anyone would have—evidence of her love and caring was all around the abundant garden. Mama would have been like that. Willow pulled out the flute and rolled it under her fingertips. If they'd been able to stay in one place for any length of time, her mom would have had a garden sanctuary much like this one.

Swallowing the bitterness, she took a deep breath and raised the flute to her lips. On her exhale, a note floated into the air. She closed her eyes and let the note extend into a pure melody. It began soft and tentative, but with each breath, her chest loosened more. Soon everything inside her poured out through the pipe. One moment the tune lulled in sadness, the next it rose in anger.

She felt the tree sway overhead, dancing to her emotions. She felt the brush of a leaf against her face and she shivered, remembering the touch of Ramirez's lips there. Just like that, the music changed, becoming complicated with longing, dark with need. Finally it trilled in careful hope. The last note expired in a slow, long breath, and Willow opened her eyes to find Ramirez's grandmother sitting on a bench, eyes closed, face uplifted to the sun. Inhaling deeply, Elena opened her eyes and smiled sadly at Willow.

"If you were truly as dark as you believe you are, you would never be able to make music so pure."

Willow cradled the flute in her hands. "If you knew how I made my living, you'd change your assessment."

"Would I?" The older woman cocked her head and studied Willow; then she patted the bench next to her. "Come, *mijita.*"

Without a thought of resisting, Willow got up and sat next to her. She waited, her body tense. What was his grandmother going to say? Much to Willow's surprise, Elena said nothing. She looked over her domain, her pride evident. Consciously or not, her breathing matched the garden's ebb and flow.

Sitting next to her, Willow found herself settling into the same peaceful rhythm. She became aware of the insects buzzing and the occasional squawk of tiny birds dive-bombing each other. The tension in her shoulders melted, and *mù ch'i* hummed contentedly through her body.

"This is a special place," Willow murmured. The only thing it needed was a *tarata* and it would be perfect.

Elena nodded. "It is. Not many people see that. Instead, they see a tangle of weeds and herbs that need to be cut back. Even Ricardo doesn't fully understand, though he respects my talents." Elena faced her. "He doubts what he can't see and touch, but he accepts both in those he loves. Do you understand?"

Willow swallowed thickly, not sure what they were talking about: her past or her Guardianship. She had no idea how Elena would know about either one. "Why don't you explain it to me?"

The woman sighed. "Ricardo's mother was my daughter. She didn't understand my vocation, and I couldn't understand her needs. She was such a volatile girl, one moment ecstatic, the next wallowing in misery. I made mistake after mistake with her, trying to push her to accept a destiny that wasn't hers.

"She finally ran off." Elena's body seemed to droop, and for the first time since Willow had met her, she looked her age. "For a long time, I didn't know where she'd gone, but she came back with a baby boy."

Ramirez. "And his father?"

"I don't think she knew who his father was. If she did, she never told me." The woman's smile was bitter. "Not that I deserved her trust."

Not knowing what to do, but needing to do something, Willow enveloped Elena in a warm blanket of *mù ch'i*. Elena lifted her head, turning to Willow with a sharp gaze. Then she reached over and squeezed her hand. "I knew I wasn't wrong. If only I'd known then, what I know now. Perhaps I could have helped my daughter."

"What happened?" Willow asked, very aware that Elena's hand still covered hers.

"She withered and died, like a plant that didn't receive the care she needed. It's the age-old story of a young woman spiraling out of control, taking a path that led to her eventual destruction. They found her dead of a drug overdose. Ricardo was only two at the time." Her eyes went distant, as if she were watching a scene replaying in her mind. She shuddered as she came back to herself. "My fault, because I couldn't accept her as she was."

"I don't think—"

"*My fault.*" She pounded her chest with her fist. "I carry that with me every day."

Willow nodded. That she could understand.

"I could have altered my daughter's fate. If only I'd been less stubborn." She turned to Willow, the grip on her hand firm. "But you couldn't do anything to change your mother's fate."

Willow stiffened. She tried to extract her hand, but the woman wouldn't let her retreat. Finally she cleared the guilt from her throat. "You said yourself you didn't know my mother. You can't know anything about it."

"Can't I? There's much in this world that defies explanation. You of all people should recognize this."

She fell into the woman's eyes, their depths fathomless. They extended into the past and future, and in them she could see everything. Dizzy, she gripped the bench with her free hand, trying to ground herself.

Elena smiled humorlessly. Then she sighed, and her

gaze returned to normal. Her behavior was odd—even to Willow, who was no stranger to odd things.

"I tried to do better with Ricardo. I think I did a good job," she said with a faint proud smile. "But he inherited my stubbornness."

"Did he ever," Willow muttered.

Elena grinned at her. "He's a good man. Despite the stubbornness, he sees reason. Which is why you need to tell him about yourself."

Herself, as in her career? Or her Guardianship? "I can't tell him who I am, but I can tell him what I've done."

"They're one and the same, *mijita*." She must have looked doubtful, because Elena smiled and patted her hand. "Do it sooner rather than later."

"Have you been talking to Morgan?" Willow asked suspiciously.

"No, but she's next." The woman smiled.

Willow tried to think of something to say. What came out was "I don't deserve him."

"You'll find no argument with me there." The older woman grinned mischievously. "I raised him, so I'm inclined to believe he's too good for any woman. However, if I were to give him to someone, it would be you, *mijita*."

Tears flooded Willow's eyes. "How can you say that?"

"Because I see what's in your heart." She cradled Willow's face. "The future is more important than the past. He'll see that. But his honor is strong, and if his trust is lost, it will never be regained. You need to tell him, or you'll risk losing him."

She shook her head. Telling him would get the same result.

"You don't know that," his grandmother said.

Willow held Elena's stare, realizing she hadn't spoken the words out loud. "That was freaky, and coming from me, that's saying something."

Chuckling, Elena pulled Willow into her arms. Elena smelled warm and earthy and comforting, and Willow had a pang of longing to stay there forever. She felt a tear sneak down her cheek and drip onto Elena's shoulder.

"Is everything okay here?"

Ramirez. Willow started to disengage herself, but his grandmother held on to her for a beat longer, squeezing her. She had the impression the woman was trying to infuse her with courage, and that made her squeeze back in gratitude.

Elena let her go and smiled at her grandson. "Everything is perfect, *hijo.*"

Ramirez didn't look like he believed it, but he didn't argue. "We need to go, Willow."

She nodded and started to stand, when his grandmother grabbed her arm. "Willow has something to tell you. Sit under the apple tree and listen to her, *hijo.*"

Willow's heart pounded. She wanted to say, it could wait—she'd promised him she'd tell him after everything was settled with the Bad Man, anyway. But his grandmother was looking at her like she was going to be supremely disappointed in her if she didn't come clean. Fighting to gain strength, Willow nodded in his direction. "You heard your grandma, Starsky. It'll just take a minute, anyway."

Elena pushed her toward the tree. "It'll bring you comfort." She stood and pointed a finger at Ramirez. "Listen with your heart, not with your head."

His jaw tightened as if expecting a blow, but he nodded.

Willow exhaled a shaky breath. If he knew what she was about to tell him, he'd ask for the blow, instead.

The biggest obstacle seemed her career, so she figured she'd start there. She just hoped he wouldn't drag her to prison the moment she finished telling him.

Striding to the tree, Willow sat in the same spot as before. Hands on the ground, she felt the roots and let their stability bolster her. Mama had told her one day she'd meet someone she'd want to share her Guardianship with, but that she had to be careful of her choice.

Was that person Ramirez? Could she tell him? Would he believe her?

One thing at a time, she told herself. *Better to get this over with first.*

Ramirez approached and stood over her.

She frowned. "I can't talk with you towering over me."

"Is that really necessary?" he asked, gesturing to the ground.

"It is if you want me to say what I need to tell you." When he just stared at her, she blew out an exasperated breath. "Sit your ass down."

He looked like he was going to argue, but he sat cross-legged, facing her.

Great. Now what? She ran her hands over the tree's roots.

Exhaling, he took her hand in his. "Just tell me, Willow."

"Okay." She took a breath and let it go. "After my mother died, I was afraid the Bad Man would find me, even hidden away with the caretaker Mama had arranged in case something like this happened. When I turned eighteen, I ran away and hid, traveling from place to place."

He nodded, his attention completely focused on her.

"I was scared he'd find me." Such an understatement, she realized and swallowed thickly. "I used to have nightmares. Like the one I had the other night, only worse. Every night I'd see my mom's body lying there, just like the Bad Man had left it. But then the face would change into mine and I'd hear him laughing."

Squeezing her hand, Ramirez brought it to his lips and pressed a kiss to her knuckles. She looked at their entwined fingers, puzzled by how such an innocent gesture could feel so comforting. Safe.

"I knew the Bad Man was trying to track me. I narrowly escaped him a couple times, but I kept running. Eventually I ended up in Paris. It's easier to stay lost in a big city. I spent a lot of time in the Metro, riding the trains aimlessly, because I felt safest in the crush of random strangers. But I wasn't hanging out in the most reputable places, and I attracted the attention of a man who was exploiting young girls. Selling their bodies.

"I got ambushed and taken. They put me in chains." Willow shuddered, remembering how the metal hurt. How helpless she felt, with the metal inhibiting her use of *mù ch'i.*

Fury sharpened Ramirez's features. He tried to pull her into his arms.

"Don't, or I won't be able to do this." She stared at him steadily. "I'm not saying this to gain your sympathy. It's just the way it was. Do you understand?"

"I understand." His voice was hoarse with rage.

She swallowed. Here went everything. "That's where I

met Morgan. She'd been captured a few days before me. We devised a plan, not just to escape but to stop the man from doing this to other girls."

She could see Ramirez working out the different scenarios in his mind. She smiled bitterly. "Imagine the worst, Inspector."

He froze, his face a stony mask.

Sigh. She drew some energy from the tree to finish her story. "I stopped him the only way I knew how. We escaped, free and clear."

Not really clear. Morgan had been a mess, both of them plagued by the memories for a long time.

She looked up at the tree, trying to draw comfort from the branches curving overhead. "I'd hit my threshold. I was sick of running, sick of powerful people—men— terrorizing the weak. So when Morgan suggested we do something about it, I jumped at the chance."

She knew Ramirez got what she was saying by the way his hand slipped free of hers. She tried to steel herself against the cutting pain. *Try* being the operative word.

"Morgan said we'd clean up the streets. It appealed to me." She gave Ramirez a look. "A lot. But I couldn't risk the Bad Man tracking me. So Morgan said she'd act as my partner, fielding the assignments, and I could remain incognito. She had the skills to do it, too. She's amazing with anything electronic, but especially with computers. She was some sort of cyber child prodigy. Anyway, we were selective about the assignments we took."

"*Assignments?*" He stood up, raking his hair back. "They were people, Willow."

She stood up, too. "People who preyed on the weak. Of all the contracts offered to us, Morgan and I only accepted the ones where the target needed to be stopped. Society is better off without them."

"That's not for you to decide. That's up to the justice system."

"The justice system doesn't apply to the rich. Do you really think the police would have done anything to stop those people? That guy in Paris was kidnapping girls and selling them to the highest bidders. Several of those bidders were officials from foreign governments."

"That doesn't make being a vigilante right." His voice sounded tight.

She glanced down and saw that his knuckles were white from being clenched so tightly. She surprised herself by wanting to take his hands in hers and soothe him. Not that he'd be open to any kind of comfort from her right now. "I'm not saying I was right or wrong. I'm telling you about my past."

"You're telling me you killed people."

She met his accusing glare. "Yeah, I am."

"Shit." He began to pace. "Did you conveniently forget what I do for a living?"

"No."

"Willow..." He rubbed a hand over his tattoo and stopped directly in front of her. "I could haul you in. There's no statute of limitations on murder."

"I know." She gazed at him unwaveringly. She heard her mother whisper, "*Trust no one*," but she ignored it for the first time in her life.

"That seems like a big leap of faith, especially for you."

"I know," she repeated. Hopefully, she wasn't making a mistake.

He just stood there, staring for longer than she could stand. When he finally spoke, she wasn't expecting the question he asked. "Were you approached with those assignments, or did you methodically target these people?"

"Does it matter? The end result is the same."

"You accepted money for this?"

She shrugged, pretending to be unaffected. She was really good at pretending. "Even Robin Hood needed funds to do his good deeds."

"This isn't a joking matter," he said, his voice low. "What you did was dangerous. You could have been locked away forever. You can *still* be locked away, and for what? For revenge?"

She preferred to think of it as justice, but she knew better than to tell him that. "To get those men off the streets, it'd be worth it."

"Damn it, Willow." Ramirez reached out like he wanted to shake her, but, instead, he began to pace again. "Those people had children and people who cared about them. Regardless of what they'd done, it wasn't your job to judge them."

Was he angry or repulsed? She couldn't tell. Her heart cracked at the thought that he could hate her.

But she was used to the pain, and she pushed it aside for later, where she could let it all out in private. "Six months ago, I stopped."

"Why? What happened six months ago?" he asked in his cool detective's voice.

"I read in a paper about the death of a professor at the university in Berkeley."

He stilled, his face suddenly alert.

Strange. She frowned at him but continued on. "The

professor specialized in these specific Chinese artifacts, artifacts the Bad Man seems obsessed with. I thought he was probably responsible for her death. Even if he wasn't, he'd be drawn by it. So I waited and watched, until I got word that he was here."

"And you followed him."

She nodded. "He won't relent, and I won't give in to him. He's destroyed a lot of lives, and I need to stop him."

Ramirez shocked her by grabbing her shirt and pulling her close. "You will not kill again, Willow. Not on my turf. I won't hesitate to arrest you."

"I know," she said softly, bracing herself on his arms.

"But you're still going to do it, aren't you?" His grip tightened on her. "You can't let go of this vendetta? Not even for me?"

She heard the desperation and hopelessness and love in his tone. Her heart cracked a little more.

Standing back, he looked at her, waiting for her to make a move. What could she do? She couldn't let the Bad Man get away. Not again. Not when he was so close.

Ramirez raked his hair back. "I don't know how to feel about all this."

Swallowing her emotions, she nodded and tried to strike a logical note. "I'm sure you've had to kill in the line of duty."

"That's different, Willow."

"How is it different?" She grabbed his shirt and made him face her, logic slipping into passionate defense. "Because you have a tin badge, that makes it okay? It's the same thing. You take down bad guys in your way, I take them down in mine."

"It's not that cut-and-dried."

"You're the one who believes everything is black and white."

He scowled at her. "I need to separate you and my *abuelita*. She's a bad influence."

"You know I'm right," she said, shaking him once.

He covered her fists with his hands, stilling her against him. "Do you want to know what I know? I know that I swore an oath to uphold the law, and you've moved outside the law."

"I—"

"Stop," he ordered. "It's my turn to talk."

She clamped her mouth shut, but she put all her anger and frustration into the death glare she aimed at him.

"You are the most aggravating woman I've ever met." He kissed her so suddenly, it took her by surprise. Just as quickly, he stopped. She noted with satisfaction that he was as breathless as she.

His voice was gravelly when he spoke. "The other thing I know is that the thought of anyone hurting you drives me *insane*. I would do *anything* to take down anyone who harmed you. I'd make sure they suffered for the rest of their lives. But I would abide by the law. I wouldn't hunt them like they were animals and kill them."

A weird jumble of feelings caught in her chest: hope and dread circled each other, dread the most prominent of all. She cleared her throat. "What are you saying?"

"I'm not sure. Excusing your actions is the same as condoning them. How can I do that and continue to be a cop? Being a cop is what I am."

"I know," she said, losing hope.

He stared at her, his gaze blazing with turmoil. Then he said, "Damn it to hell, Willow." He turned and stormed off.

She watched him leave, grateful his back was turned so he couldn't see the single tear rolling down her cheek. Watching him walk away was one of the hardest things she'd ever done. She knew she was losing the one person she truly loved.

Chapter Twenty-four

The thick silence in the car was cut only by Morgan's occasional impatient rustling in the backseat. Willow was thankful Morgan had insisted on coming along. Her presence eased some of the tension. Ramirez hadn't said more than five words to her since her confession. Like she could blame him.

She glanced at him from under her lashes. She couldn't tell what was going on in his head. He'd closed himself off from her, and it hurt. So much it eclipsed the discomfort of being in the metal box—and that surprised her. But it pissed her off, too, because he had no right to judge her. Not without walking a mile in her shoes.

"So," Morgan said brightly from the back.

Neither she nor Ramirez said a word. Her friend allowed a few moments of silence before speaking. "I've never been to San Francisco before. What do you guys say, after we drop off the picture, we go somewhere, like the Ferry Building, for lunch? We've got to eat, and I can get some sightseeing in at the same time."

Willow turned in the seat. "You aren't serious."

"Of course I'm serious." Morgan frowned. "Not as serious as you two, but I doubt morticians are as serious as you two."

Apt analogy. After the talk with Ramirez, Willow felt like part of her had died. She faced the front again, crossing her arms to contain the hurt.

"I don't think it's unreasonable to want to see the Golden Gate Bridge," Morgan continued blithely. "Coming to the city and not seeing the Golden Gate is like going to Paris and not seeing the Eiffel Tower. Like going to Florence and not seeing Michelangelo's *David.* Like going to Athens and—"

"We get the picture," Willow cut in.

"If you got the picture, you'd take me to see the bridge," her friend mumbled from the back.

Ramirez kept his clear gaze on the road, weaving carefully through city traffic. Willow stretched her legs, trying to act like she was unaffected, trying to act like she didn't want to take his hand and put it on hers, just to be connected.

Fortunately, she didn't have to pretend for long. As Ramirez parallel parked, she looked around the neighborhood. Calling it industrial would be generous. There wasn't anything resembling a house around them. "Your friend lives here?"

"Converted loft." He unbuckled his seat belt and got out of the car without waiting for the two of them.

Morgan popped her head between the seats. "What'd you do to him? You've got his panties in a twist."

"I told him."

"Told him what?" Her eyes widened and she gasped. "Wait. You didn't tell him about..."

"I did."

"How much did you tell him?"

"Everything."

"Are you smoking crack or something?" Morgan yelled, her eyes bulging. "He's a *cop*. A *Homicide* cop. He could toss you in jail and throw away the key. Holy shit—he could toss *me* in jail. I'm just as complicit in all this as you are. Damn it to hell, Willow, didn't you think about that?"

"He won't throw you in jail." She hoped she sounded more certain of that than she felt. She didn't know what to expect from Ramirez at this point. "I won't let him. You know I'll always protect you."

"Even if it meant hurting *him*?"

The thought of hurting Ramirez was like a stake through her heart. It wouldn't come to that.

"I knew this was going to happen." Morgan slammed her palm into the driver's-side headrest. "You haven't been acting like yourself since you met him."

Scowling at her supposed friend, Willow unbuckled her seat belt and opened the door. "Thanks for your show of support."

What a fool. Morgan was right—she was falling off the deep end. Shaking her head in disgust, she surveyed the block and caught up to Ramirez. "Where are we going?"

"This way." Ramirez led the way to what looked like a warehouse. Gritting her teeth, she breathed past the stabbing sensation caused by the metal around her. They took an elevator up to the top floor and rang the doorbell on an unmarked door. The door opened to reveal the blonde she'd seen Ramirez so chummy with the other night.

Great.

Like before, the strawberry blonde smiled up at him like he was a sun god. "Twice in a matter of days, Rick. My husband is going to get suspicious."

He tugged on one of her curls. "Your husband is the one who invited me."

Willow kept her face carefully blank. Hopefully, no one would hear her teeth grinding.

The blonde took him by the arm before she noticed Willow and Morgan behind him. Her smile was no less friendly, if a little cautious. She stuck out her hand. "Hi, I'm Carrie Prescott."

Willow smelled the salty tang of marine air as she took the woman's hand. Feeling something amiss, she probed the woman with *mù ch'i*. She didn't get anything except the fact that the woman was pregnant.

Morgan nudged her. "Usually, when someone introduces herself, it's polite to introduce yourself back."

The blonde—Carrie Prescott—laughed as she withdrew her hand. "No worries. I'm used to it. My husband isn't the most socially ept guy, either."

"Well, I'm Morgan, and my mute friend here is Willow."

"Come in. Max is in the living room." She ushered them in and closed the door. "Can I get you anything? Tea? Coffee? Water?"

"I love tea," Morgan said with her usual pep. "Ramirez's grandma makes the best blend. I swear it boosted my mental alertness."

"You've met his grandmother?" the blonde asked with interest.

"Yeah, since we're kind of staying with him." Morgan

cast a sly glance at Willow as she answered. Willow glared back at her partner. If only she had one of her dirks with her.

Carrie looked at her with increased interest, but she just said, "What can I get you, Willow?"

"Nothing. Thank you."

Carrie slipped an arm through Morgan's. "You can help me while they talk. It's not like we won't hear, anyway. The kitchen is right next to the living room."

They walked into the main space of the loft. To one side, there was the kitchen and, just like Carrie had said, the living area took up the rest of the space. Furnished in clean, modern lines, it looked homey with splashes of color. A spiral staircase led to the second floor.

A man, presumably this Max they were there to see, stood in front of one of the couches. The shift in the air warned her a second before his energy hit her. Like that time at the bar, a shock wave reverberated through her. Unlike that time at the bar, this was a lot stronger. And more painful, like a thousand razor blades slicing her skin.

Guardian of the Book of Metal. She recognized him without introduction.

Gasping, she wanted to drop to her knees. She forced herself to endure, drawing *mù ch'i* up like a shield. She narrowed her eyes with satisfaction as he himself paled. Something in his cold gray eyes shifted. She saw his intent to withdraw his power and an offer of truce—plus, the threat she was sure he'd carry through on if she didn't cooperate. She focused her will and drew energy inward despite the way it wanted to rise and match his. The effort left her panting for breath, sweat lining her brow.

"Willow."

She turned her head, suddenly aware Ramirez had her in his arms.

His grip was gentle, and his concerned face frowned at her. "Are you okay?"

She managed a shaky laugh, glancing at the other Guardian. She noticed his wife had returned, resting her head on his chest as if nuzzling him into calmness. At least he didn't look any better than she did.

Ramirez's frown deepened, and he moved her to sit her on the couch. "Do you need water?"

She shook her head. Her stomach still roiled with the extra energy. If she had anything to drink now, she'd vomit.

"Can you tell me what happened?"

She glanced at the other Guardian. He settled onto the couch, his arms around his wife as if to protect her. His eyes gave away nothing, and he didn't seem inclined to explain.

"Willow?"

She looked at Ramirez. "I forgot to eat. I got dizzy."

Morgan snorted. Willow could see the disappointment written on every line of Ramirez's face, but he didn't push it.

"I'm going to make that tea," the blonde said, not making a move to go anywhere. Her curious eyes were glued on Willow and Ramirez, like she was unraveling all their secrets. A blush heated Willow's face, and she conspicuously stepped away from Ramirez.

Morgan snorted again.

"Well. Here I go." The blonde patted her muscle-bound Guardian on the chest. "You reel it in, big boy."

His eyes narrowed, but he didn't say anything. At least not until his wife walked away. Then he turned a scowl onto Ramirez and growled. "You better have a good reason for bringing her here."

Ramirez looked back and forth between the two of them. "I didn't realize you knew each other."

"We don't," Willow and Max replied in unison.

"Do you want to explain what that was about, then?"

"No," they both said together, again.

Ramirez searched between the two of them, clearly not buying it. One thing was certain to Willow: he didn't know about their Guardianship. She would have suspected this little field trip was a setup—especially given the other Guardian at the bar—but Ramirez seemed genuinely clueless as to what had just transpired.

That didn't explain why there were two Guardians other than herself in San Francisco. Mind-boggling, to say the least. She glared at Metal, wondering what his deal was. And wondering why Ramirez believed he could help them identify the Bad Man.

Morgan elbowed her in the ribs. "Let's try to keep the objective clear, shall we?"

Right. Willow tried to rein herself back. The sooner they asked about the Bad Man, the sooner they could leave. It couldn't be fast enough—her skin still crawled with the taint of his power. "Show him the picture."

Ramirez pulled out the photograph from his pocket. If Willow had been Catholic, she would have crossed herself, the picture creeped her out so badly. His eyes seemed to follow her everywhere she went.

Ramirez handed it over to Max, who held it in his hands and studied it for a long time. Then he lowered it and peered at her. Before Willow could ask him what he was thinking, his wife returned with cups of tea. She set a tray on the table. "I brought sugar and cream. Can I serve—"

Max pulled her down and cuddled her into his side. "They can serve themselves."

"But, Max—"

He just squeezed her closer until she squeaked.

"*Max.*" Carrie elbowed some breathing space for herself. She gave Ramirez an apologetic look, which he shrugged off.

Willow stared daggers at him. What was up with the silent communication between Ramirez and the blonde? They may be just friends now—the Neanderthal Guardian across the room would demolish anyone who even thought about touching his wife—but that didn't mean they hadn't been lovers before. *Mù ch'i* stirred inside her, echoing her growing anger.

Max lifted his head as if he could scent her unease.

"Behave." The blonde pulled her hound back.

He ignored her, instead glaring at Willow. "So let's get this straight. I help you find out who this man is, and then you leave town?"

"Max!" His wife gasped.

Ramirez nodded calmly, seemingly undisturbed by his friend's belligerence. "We believe he's involved in a series of recent murders."

"It's got to be more than that if you've gone in on this with a civilian." Max's eyes didn't waver from hers. "She's not in law enforcement."

Willow smirked. "Don't be deceived by the leather pants. I've got handcuffs, and I know how to use them."

Max leaned in, his entire demeanor as steely as his element would imply. "Let me rephrase that. You *will* leave town once this business is concluded."

Morgan groaned. "Oh, Jesus. Ordering her is *not* a good idea."

"Once this business is concluded." As hard as Willow had worked to track down the Bad Man, it was difficult for her to imagine it being over. Morgan had asked her what she was going to do when this was all done. She'd said she didn't know, but she found herself studying Ramirez. Not that he'd want her to stay. And actually, there was a good chance he'd try to put her away for life if everything went down the way she intended. Still, there was a part of her that wanted him to want her to stay.

Ridiculous. She smirked at herself. "I'll leave town when I'm ready. But I'm not looking for a turf war, so don't work yourself into a lather."

Max didn't look like he believed her.

Which pissed her off. "You have no reason to distrust me. And, frankly, how do I know *you're* not the one setting me up?"

Ramirez didn't move, but she felt him snap to attention nonetheless. "What are you talking about?"

She didn't look away from the other Guardian. "The inspector doesn't have any idea, but you can hardly claim innocence. Two of you, tied so closely together? Cause for suspicion if I ever saw one."

"What are you talking about?" Ramirez repeated.

Ramirez may not have understood the subtext, but she knew she didn't have to spell it out for Max. He knew she was talking about him and the other Guardian from the bar, and she silently dared him to contradict her.

He didn't.

His wife attempted to intervene. "Listen, Willow, there isn't any—"

"Carrie," Max said in warning.

"Don't *Carrie* me. This is what we were talking about the other night. There's something—"

"Not now, Carrie."

The petite woman huffed in exasperation but didn't say another word. Willow studied them, wondering what they'd been talking about the other night that was so sensitive she couldn't be told.

Max waved the picture. "Is it okay if I bring Rhys in on this?"

"If that's what it takes." Ramirez sounded amiable, but his face was all stone.

Who was Rhys? She glanced at Morgan, who gave her a small nod. *Good.* She could always count on Morgan for information.

"I'll get on it right away." Max stood, obviously ending the meeting.

Willow smiled sardonically, also standing. "The sooner you're rid of me, the better?"

"How could you tell?" he asked coolly.

"Well," the blonde said perkily, hopping to her feet. "Hasn't this been fun? We should do it again soon."

Morgan grinned. "I want a ringside seat. And I'm putting ten bucks on the chick in the leather."

If anyone had told him he'd be going to his onetime best friend, onetime enemy, for help—again—Max would have directed the person to the nearest psych ward.

"I'm so curious about Willow." Carrie shifted in the

passenger seat, adjusting her seat belt over her barely rounded belly. "There's something going on between her and Rick. Did you see the sparks between them? Hot."

He'd been more distracted by the friction the other Guardian caused when she had entered the room. He'd felt it with Gabrielle, Rhys's partner, but not this strongly. Of course, Gabrielle hadn't grasped the full extent of her powers yet. The Wood Guardian was much stronger.

"I've been worried about Rick, but I have a feeling Willow is just what he needs," Carrie continued. "She's strong enough to stand up to him, and deviant enough to keep his life from being boring. Did you see her pants?"

Max glanced at his wife. "Do you really want me to notice another woman's leather pants?"

She laughed, lifting his hand to her face. "You can't keep your hands off me, and I'm getting fatter every day. I'm pretty secure in how you feel."

"Your curves are delicious."

"My curves are your fault." Carrie shifted again.

"How are you feeling?" he asked, running his hand along her leg. She'd been having backaches lately. Not that she'd admit as much to him, but he could tell from the way she moved. She claimed he was being overprotective. She hadn't even seen protective yet. If it were up to him, he'd keep her cocooned in bed 24/7.

"I'm great. Really." She squeezed his hand. "Do you think Rhys will be able to track down this mystery guy?"

"If anyone could, it'd be Rhys." Rhys had connections that stretched even into the underworld.

"I wonder what Willow's story is, and how she's mixed up with this guy."

Max had a suspicion, but he wasn't ready to voice it—only because he didn't want his wife getting involved doing any of her research.

"Maybe we should have called before barging in on them," Carrie said as they pulled into Rhys's long driveway.

"Because they always call before they barge in on us?" Max asked with a lift of his brow.

She laughed as she started to scoot out of the car. "You know you love them coming over all the time."

Not like he'd ever admit that, even if it were true. He went around the car to help his wife to standing and led her to the front door.

Brian, Rhys's majordomo, answered the door. He nodded at Max but greeted Carrie with a huge grin and a careful hug. "Hey, kid. You eating croissants every morning? You're a little padded around the middle."

She punched him playfully on his massive arm. "Not hardly. But if you've got any, I wouldn't turn one down."

"You got it." He faced Max. "Assuming you're here to see the boss? They're in the workout room. You know the way."

"As if we could miss it," Max mumbled as he escorted Carrie down the hall. "His workout room is twice the size of mine. He's compensating."

"Play nice."

"Compensating for his youth and growing up an orphan." Max smiled slyly. "What did you think I meant?"

She shook her head. "You know what you meant."

As they arrived in the doorway of the workout studio, they heard a grunt and a thud. Max paused in the entrance, holding Carrie behind him to check the scene before letting her in. Rhys was probably just working out, but it was better to play it safe.

Sure enough, on the blue matted area in the middle of the room, there were two people. Rhys lay flat on his back, arms splayed like he was recently thrown. Above him stood Gabrielle, looking pleased with herself. Rhys's arms swung in, grabbing her ankle and sweeping her onto the floor with an *oof*. Before she recovered, he rolled on top of her and pinned her down, wrists by her ears.

"Give up, love?" he asked, his British accent less crisp and more heated than usual.

"Never."

"You sure?" He lowered his head and nuzzled her neck.

Arching her back, Gabrielle made a happy noise. Then she raised her arms, crossed her wrists, and broke his grip. Straightening his leg, she flipped them over so she was dominant.

She smiled down at him. "How do you feel, now that the tables are turned?"

"Actually, I feel good." He tangled his hand in her hair and brought her mouth down to his.

Max felt a finger poke in his side, and he looked at his wife.

Her eyes lit bright as she nodded at the spectacle in the workout room. "If you taught me kung fu, we could have foreplay like that, too."

"Our foreplay is fine the way it is."

"Yeah." She watched the other couple with avid interest. "But that looks fun, too."

"Don't make me blindfold you."

"Promises, promises." Carrie gave Max a sultry look that shot directly to his cock. Then she walked straight into the room. "Break it up, guys. We need your help."

"Go away," Gabrielle said, lifting her head for just a second before launching into another lip-lock.

"This is serious. It's about the other Guardian."

That got their attention. Still, they broke off their kiss reluctantly.

Gabrielle hopped to her feet with an unconcealed scowl at him. "This better be good."

"Rick Ramirez brought the Guardian of the Book of Wood to our loft this afternoon." He arched an eyebrow. "Is that good enough?"

Pursing her lips, Gabrielle nodded slowly. "I'd say that has some merit."

Rhys stroked the scar bisecting the corner of his mouth. "Ramirez, of course, didn't know who she was, correct?"

Carrie nodded her head. "He didn't, but he knows something strange is going on. He said as much, the last time he and I got together."

Gabrielle wrinkled her nose. "Why would the other Guardian want to hang with Ramirez?"

"Maybe because he's hot," Carrie replied with more emphasis than Max liked. She must have realized it, though, because she patted his chest reassuringly.

Max pressed her hand to his heart. "Ramirez and this Willow—"

Gabrielle chuckled.

They all looked at her.

"*Willow?* Guardian of the Book of Wood?" She chuckled some more. "I'm so happy my mom named me something decent, even if it's girly. Can you see me as a *Terra?*"

Max frowned. "Do you want to hear what they wanted or not?"

"Go ahead," she said graciously.

"They're looking for a man wanted for questioning in several murders."

"This sounds familiar," Gabrielle muttered.

He held out the picture to Rhys. "I went through my network, but I came up empty-handed. I thought you might check some of the other avenues you have open to you."

Rhys's brow furrowed as he stared at the photo.

"What?" Gabrielle asked. "Do you know this guy?"

He didn't answer, but Max knew him well enough to know his former best friend knew exactly who this guy was—and it wasn't good. "Can you pull some information together for Ramirez?"

Rhys nodded and headed for the door. "And perhaps we can arrange a little chat with his Guardian. Excuse me. I'll be right back."

"She's staying with him," Carrie said to fill Rhys's absence.

Gabrielle gasped. "No way."

"Seriously." Carrie grinned like an imp. "I think he likes her quite a lot. He was almost drooling over her. Of course she *did* have leather pants on. Any guy would drool over a woman in leather pants. But I think he *likes* her."

"Yeah, but you're also knocked up, and you know how they say pregnant women are totally insane because of their hormones."

Carrie looked at Max. "Am I insane?"

"Less so than some people," he assured her.

Gabrielle laughed. "That's not saying much."

As Gabrielle and Carrie chatted, he wandered over to the weapons mounted on the wall. He ignored the variety of knives and sticks, focusing on one sword in particular. The sword he'd forged for Rhys back at the monastery, where they learned how to be Guardians, when they were brothers in every way but blood. He ran a finger along the well-cared-for blade. The metal whispered in pleasure, and he heard the echo deep inside him.

"I have the information."

Max turned around to find Rhys studying him, only several inches behind. It bothered the hell out of him that he hadn't heard his approach. Max glanced at the women, still engrossed in whatever conversation they were having. Just as well. He had a bad feeling.

Rhys held out a portfolio. "I thought I recognized him. It's been a long time, and I'd only met him briefly, but he's who I thought. I opted out of dealing with him once, years ago."

"That bad?" Max whispered so the women couldn't hear as he took the folder.

"Worse," Rhys replied, equally hushed. "Tell Ramirez to watch his back, because based on the information in that dossier, if the man wants Willow, she's as good as his."

Max opened the file and skimmed it, his bad feeling increasing with each word. For once, he couldn't argue with Rhys.

Chapter Twenty-five

Edward cut into his rack of lamb, aware of the large presence standing over his shoulder. Anger inflated his chest, and his knife screeched on the plate.

He stopped, exhaled, and calmly took a bite of the meat. Perfection. Boulevard's chef obviously took the same kind of thorough pride in his work as Edward did in his.

Too bad his employees didn't understand the importance of quality work. All he asked was for them to bring him one lone woman. How was that difficult? He'd delivered her to them practically on a plate.

He savored another bite and took a sip of the Château Margaux. He set the glass down and cut another piece. "You had better have tracked her down."

"I did."

Ah, it was Frank behind him. Frank was marginally less lacking than the rest of his bodyguards. "Where is she?"

"She's staying here."

A piece of paper appeared in front of him. Edward took his time with another mouthful before he plucked the paper from Frank's fingers. An address. He refolded it and slipped it inside his shirt's pocket before taking up his fork and knife. "I take it that's a residence."

"Yes."

"And who lives there?"

"Ricardo Ramirez." Frank paused. "He's a cop. In Homicide."

The fork slipped out of his hand with a clatter. A Homicide policeman. A slow smile crossed his face as he waved his employee into the empty seat across from him. "Isn't that interesting?"

Frank unbuttoned his suit coat as he sat down and took out an envelope from his inside pocket. "Not as interesting as what they're doing together."

Pictures. Excitement shivered through him as he held his hand out. That night at the club he'd caught a glimpse of her distinctive hair—the same as Lani's—but he hadn't seen her face. He hadn't looked upon her in years. The last time one of his employees had managed to photograph her, she'd barely been a teenager.

He touched the cheap white paper of the standard envelope. Her pictures deserved something finer. Vellum. Handmade and fine. Should he open it now or wait? He ran a finger along the open flap. He couldn't wait—he needed to see her face. Opening the envelope, he pulled out the first photo, a telephoto close-up. She took his breath away. High, royal cheekbones and almond-shaped eyes. Full lips. The perfect melding of Lani and himself, made into something unique and exquisite. The only thing on her that belonged completely to Lani was her hair.

Her pale gray eyes, however, were all his. He stared into those eyes. Even flat on a piece of paper, they sparked with intelligence and cunning. He felt a thrill of pride and anticipation. He was going to enjoy making her bend to his will.

Edward flipped to the next picture. She sat on the kitchen counter, a dark-haired man in front of her. Not only a bitch like her mother, but a whore, too. He clenched his fist, wrinkling the picture. Edward knew without a doubt that this was the man coming between him and his daughter.

He scanned through the rest of the batch. The policeman was featured in most of them, in various states of undress. He studied one particularly provocative one of them staring at each other. Edward slipped the photos back into the envelope and set them next to his plate.

Clever of her to take up with a cop. But if she thought she was going to circumvent his plan, she didn't give him enough credit. Nothing was going to keep him from claiming her powers.

Picking up his wineglass, he held it up to the light to inspect the deep ruby color. "Continue to watch her."

"Yes, sir." Frank pushed back from the table.

"And, Frank?"

"Sir?"

"I want the police officer out of the picture. Understand?"

His employee nodded. "Yes, sir."

Chapter Twenty-six

Ramirez woke early and quietly slipped out from the house. Scowling, he put the car in drive and pulled out of the parking spot. He had an assassin in his bed, and he didn't know what to do about it.

Well, he knew what he *wanted* to do about it. He wanted to crawl in next to her. Only he couldn't. He growled as he stepped on the accelerator. Cops didn't sleep with criminals, and Homicide cops certainly didn't get together with hit men. He wanted to, though. Badly.

The hard-on he'd had all night was testament to that. But he also plain missed her. He'd hovered at the foot of the stairs for longer than he cared to admit, trying to decide whether he should just go up to her. He couldn't. In the end, he'd huddled on the couch, staring at the wooden stilettos he'd confiscated from her garter. She had turned his world upside down. He'd lost his bedroom, and his guest room to Morgan. He'd even lost the support of his grandmother, who seemed to be on Willow's side. Losing his mind was just a short step away. He was pathetic.

Ramirez gripped the steering wheel. He needed to concentrate on the task at hand: bringing in her Bad Man. If he could do that, then Willow wouldn't have to kill anymore. Hopefully, by that time, he'd have a better handle on what he was going to do about everything else.

He parked his car and strode into the Hall of Justice. Barely acknowledging the guard, he took the elevator up to his office. Even though it was early, there was already an assortment of people working, either from the night before or this morning. He nodded at a couple guys who called out to him, but he headed straight to his desk. His goal was to catch up and get out quickly.

His plan was shot when his partner walked in a short while later. Instead of going to his desk, Taylor snagged a chair and set it next to him. Taylor unbuttoned his suit jacket, which already had some sort of stain on the lapel, leaned on the desk, and rested his chin in his hand.

When there was nothing forthcoming, Ramirez cocked his brow. "Well?"

"I'm waiting," Taylor said.

"For?"

"For you to tell me where the hell you've been."

"I told you I had some personal matters to take care of."

His partner shook his head. "I'm not buying it. In the years we've worked together, you've never let personal matters come before the job. Suddenly that's changed. Are you going to tell me what's going on, or do I have to guess?"

Ramirez stilled. There was no way Taylor could know about him and Willow. "I don't know what you mean."

"Don't you?" Taylor stared at him in a solemn way that wasn't natural to his character. "Officer Jenkins called up."

Ramirez cursed mentally, but he tried to maintain his stoic demeanor.

Taylor watched him like a hawk. "He said you checked out some evidence from the property room."

"I did."

"And what about the evidence you didn't check out?"

Shit. "I don't—"

"Don't bullshit me, Ricardo. Jenkins went through the evidence box and found an item missing. A wooden flute. You aren't being busted, because I covered for you. I managed to convince him you were distracted."

It wouldn't do any good to deny it, so he just nodded. "Thanks."

"I want to know why," his partner demanded. "You owe me that much."

"I'm doing my job."

"A big part of your job is to communicate with me. You're the one who's always telling me that. Now you're going off half-cocked and I have to wonder what's going on." Taylor leaned in. "So what is it?"

Ramirez stared impassively at his partner. "I'm working to solve this case."

Taylor's gaze narrowed. "Yeah, I believe that, but something's still hinky. You're acting strangely. You're not focused. It can't be just the pressure to solve this. We're always under pressure."

Yes, but this time there was much more at stake. "I'm working an angle. You need to trust me."

"Goddamn it, Ricky." His partner ran a hand over his head. "Just tell me what's going on."

He wished he could.

The phone ringing saved him. He held up a finger and

grabbed the receiver. Ignoring Taylor's imaginative cursing in the background, he answered the call. "Inspector Ramirez."

"It's Max."

Turning his back, he spoke softly. "What do you have?"

"We need to meet. What time is good for you?"

"Give me an hour." Hopefully, he could find something to occupy Taylor by then so he could slip out undetected.

"See you at the loft," Max said, hanging up.

Taylor pounced even before he'd put the receiver back down. "Who was that?"

"A friend," he said, happy not to lie. Taylor, for all his bumbling charm, had a keen sixth sense.

His partner snorted. "Please. Try to come up with something a little more believable."

He frowned. "Why isn't that believable?"

"You don't have a social life, which indicates an absence of friends."

"Maybe I've finally listened to your lectures on life being more than work."

"See? Another indication that something is very wrong." Taylor hefted his weight up, pointing a finger at him. "I've got your back, even if it means I have to protect you from yourself."

Ramirez watched him amble out of the pen. He just had to keep his partner occupied long enough to set everything right.

Max was leaning in the open door, waiting for Ramirez, when he arrived. "How well do you know Willow?"

"Well enough." Scowling, Ramirez walked in. "Why do you ask?"

Max walked past him into the kitchen and picked up a folder placed on the table. "Are you sure?" he asked, handing it over.

Ramirez stared at the file, wondering what it could contain that had Max so leery. "This is about the man we needed to ID, isn't it?"

Max nodded, sticking his hands in his pockets. "And then some."

"About Willow?"

"Yeah."

Ramirez studied the other man's face, but his metallic countenance gave away nothing. How bad could it be? She'd already told him she was an assassin—what could be worse than that?

He reassessed that statement when he opened the file. The picture he'd checked out from the property room was clipped to the front. Shaking his head, he backed up and started reading the profile from the beginning. Slowly.

Edward Rodgers-Dynes, age sixty-two, born in Johannesburg, South Africa. Dark hair, gray eyes. List of crimes attributed to him: piracy, theft, prostitution, murder. Never been convicted.

"You ready to reconsider your answer?"

He looked up at Max. "This information is accurate? No chance of discrepancies?"

"None." Max's response was absolute. "Rhys is many things, but his information is never suspect. In fact, he'd considered a partnership with the man at some time in the past but decided against it. That's a testament to the guy's character, or lack thereof. Rhys operates in a pretty big gray area. Rhys deciding someone was unscrupulous is saying something."

"Understood." He re-read the one line that caused his teeth to clench:

Widowed. Only surviving relative: one daughter. Willow Rodgers-Dynes.

He looked at the picture of Rodgers-Dynes. Ramirez had thought there was something familiar about him. Now he saw it was the subtle resemblance to Willow. You had to stretch your imagination to see it—except for the eyes.

Did she know? He had to force his hands to relax before he crumpled the pages. All he could think about was whether or not she'd played him for some personal vendetta.

But she'd told him her Bad Man had killed her mother and that she was out for justice. The only piece of information she'd omitted was that he was her father. Ramirez grimaced as reason penetrated the wild flare of emotions. Why would she not tell him? She'd even confessed to being an assassin. This was hardly on the same scale. It had to be because she didn't know.

Shit. He slapped the file closed. "Thank you. I owe you for this."

Max shrugged. "We'll call it even. In appreciation of you looking out for my wife."

The not-so-subtle inflection on *my wife* wasn't lost on him. He flashed a sardonic grin. He was beginning to understand that sense of possession, because he was beginning to feel that way about Willow. Beginning to? Hell, he was halfway to chaining her to his side.

"You have a lot to process," Max said as they walked out.

"That's stating the obvious."

"You'll let us know if you need anything else?" Max opened the door.

"Are you offering because Carrie would want you to?"

"Of course. I'm not stupid," the other man said with a smile. Then he sobered. "But we have a vested interest in Willow, as well. I may not trust her, but seeing her hurt wouldn't benefit anyone, either."

Ramirez paused in the doorway, frowning. "What sort of vested interest?"

"The sort that is Willow's to tell, if she feels so inclined." Max tipped his head. "Happy hunting."

Ramirez hesitated, wanting to ask more questions, but he knew Max wouldn't answer. So he nodded and headed to the elevator. When he walked outside, Taylor was leaning against his car, waiting for him.

What the hell? His eyes narrowed as he strode to his partner, who obviously had no compulsion against following him and invading his privacy. "What are you doing here?"

Taylor squared off for the confrontation, arms folded across his barrel chest. "Saving your ass, you ungrateful cur."

"*Cur?*" That was over-the-top, even for his dramatic partner.

"Beats *asshole*. If I'm going to risk my hide for you, I want to know what's going on."

Heaving a sigh, Ramirez ran a hand over his head. "Listen—"

"No, *you* listen." Taylor pointed a finger at him. "I'm done with this. You're going to tell me what the hell you're up to, even if I have to sit on you until you relent.

And I ate almost all of May's meat loaf for dinner last night, so I've got a couple extra pounds to back me up."

Ramirez started to tell his partner what he could do with his extra pounds, when a shot rang out. They both turned their heads as a volley of bullets rained down on them.

Chapter Twenty-seven

Where the hell was he?

Willow looked out the office window for the millionth time. No sign of his car. No sign of Ramirez. He left without saying good morning or good-bye. Hell, he left without saying anything. He hadn't even joined her in his room last night. What did that mean? She'd stayed up half the night, listening to him puttering around downstairs. She thought he'd come up eventually, even if it was after she'd fallen asleep.

Hadn't happened.

Now here she was, freaking out from this growing sense of impending doom. Something bad was brewing—something involving Ramirez—and she didn't know where he was and couldn't stop it. She kept imagining the worst, and the thought that she might never see him again was unbearable.

The bastard. He should have told her where he was going. A phone call, was that too much to ask for?

She knew why he'd withdrawn from her, too. Because

she'd told him that she'd killed people. She rubbed her forehead, a headache throbbing dully at her temples. That had to be why he'd left.

"It's unrealistic to think a Homicide detective would want a relationship with someone who killed people."

"It is, if the Homicide detective in question is Ramirez," Morgan answered absently, engrossed with her computer. "That man's shorts are bound so tight, I'm impressed you were able to shimmy them off him."

"That's the thing. He's not really wound as tight as I thought." Because if he had been, he would have taken her straight to jail when she'd told him. Instead, he'd given her a chance to prove that she was innocent. "He's helping me track down the Bad Man. That's got to mean something."

"It means that the Bad Man is a worse criminal than you are."

She glanced at her so-called friend. "Thanks."

"Just keeping it real."

If only Morgan would keep it real elsewhere. "What are you doing?"

"I'm on Twitter."

"Now?"

Morgan glanced up, her nose wrinkled with disdain. "Don't mock it. I've found some guy who tweets on local police activity. I'm checking up on your policeman, since you're obviously so concerned about him."

"I'm not concerned."

"Which is why you're wearing a groove in the carpet?"

Willow stopped abruptly, but she couldn't stay still and started pacing again. Damn it, where were her whittling tools when she needed them? Oh, right, being held in the police station.

Damn it.

"Listen." Morgan swiveled her chair around and leaned forward. "He's fine. I've found no evidence that anything's happened to him."

"This isn't about his safety."

"So you haven't been doing laps in this room all day because you're worried about him?"

"Of course not."

Morgan rolled her eyes. "You're such a liar."

"You wouldn't say that if I had any weapons in my hands."

"You're not only a liar, you're delusional. Especially if you believe that."

Hands on hips, she faced her friend. "You're pushing it."

But Morgan wouldn't back down. "Just admit that you're scared. You don't have control, and that's driving you crazy."

"This isn't about control," Willow said, hands clenched tight. "But I don't know why he would think I could sit at home while he runs off doing God knows what without telling me what's going on."

Morgan blinked. "You've fallen for him."

"Please."

"Jesus Christ. I thought it was a possibility, but I didn't really believe you would." She fell back against the chair. "Only you have."

"Right."

"The hard-assed warrior all aflutter because she's in love for the first time." Morgan shook her head. "It'd be cute if you'd picked someone other than a cop."

Elena walked in, carrying a tray. "It makes me happy to hear light voices and feel life in this house."

"Good thing someone's happy here, because Willow sure isn't." Morgan moved her laptop so Elena could set the tray on the desk. "She was about to rip me a new one."

"Which is why I brought tea for you two," the older woman said, pouring two cups.

Willow stepped forward. "Did you have a premonition? Is there something I should know?"

"The only thing I know is that you're tromping back and forth over my head." Ramirez's grandmother smiled warmly as she handed Willow a mug. "I thought you could use the soothing."

"Have you talked to him today?"

"He often keeps his own counsel," Elena said, pouring Morgan a cup and then wiping some stray drops from the desk. "There's no cause to worry."

"I just have this feeling." Willow cradled the hot beverage, wishing the warmth would seep in and ease the nervousness in her belly.

"Everything works out the way it's supposed to in the end, *mijita.*" Elena brushed a hair from Willow's face. "You have to have faith. In him, but also in yourself. You have everything you need inside you."

"Yeah, grasshopper," Morgan chimed in.

"Taunting a tiger is a sure way to get your hand bitten." A smile flirting with her lips, Elena picked up the tray. "If you need to resist the temptation, come down and help me in the garden. You need some sunlight."

"I didn't know there was such a thing as sunlight in San Francisco," Morgan said as she got up.

Willow listened to their chatter as they walked out. Then she pulled out her cell phone and called Ramirez again. His phone rang four times before it transferred to voice mail. Ending the call, she tapped the cell phone against her chin. She couldn't just sit there and not do anything. She pulled up a chair and dragged over the laptop.

"Morgan will have a fit if she knows I'm using her computer," she said aloud. Not that it was going to stop her. She pressed a key and a log-in box popped up.

Expected. Morgan was a freak about security and privacy.

"Good thing I know her password," she observed out loud. Willow flexed her fingers and began typing, feeling a twinge of guilt. Morgan didn't drink, except for one day a year, and then she drank until she was incoherently pissed. Willow didn't know what significance that date had for her, she just made sure she was always around to make sure Morgan was okay. This past year during her binge, Morgan had blabbed her password. Hopefully, she hadn't changed it.

Willow hit enter. The password box closed to reveal the desktop and every open program and window Morgan had running. Including what looked like Ramirez's in-box.

"Morgan, you little devil." Willow clicked on that window. His in-box had a couple new e-mails in it. One was spam, the other was from Maximillian Prescott.

"Bingo." She clicked on it: *An e-version of the file, just in case.*

What file? She frowned and opened the attachment. The Bad Man stared at her from the first page of the PDF. Ramirez had gotten the dossier on the Bad Man, and he hadn't told her.

"What are you doing?"

Willow looked up to find an incredulous Morgan walking into the room.

Morgan pushed her aside, chair and all, and leaned over her laptop. "You cracked my password?"

"I listen sometimes when you talk about tech things," she said, not really lying.

"Dang. I should be angry, but I'm impressed." She pressed a few keys. Then she frowned, her expression suddenly intent. "Get off the chair."

Knowing better than to argue, Willow got up and passed it to Morgan, who promptly sat down and began to furiously type. "Oh, shit. Oh, hell."

Dread chilled her. "What is it?"

"There's an officer down."

Ramirez. Willow pulled out her cell phone. "I knew it. I knew something was wrong."

"What are you doing?"

"Calling the station." She walked back and forth, willing someone to pick up the line. Finally an operator answered, but she insisted she couldn't give out any information.

Willow hung up. "Damn it. She wouldn't crack."

"Of course they're not going to tell random people anything." Morgan's fingers flew over the keyboard. "But back up and let me work my magic. Here it is. *Oh, no.*"

"What?" Willow asked, already knowing.

"Two Homicide inspectors involved in a shoot-out."

Willow's heart stopped, and then beat so hard it echoed in her head. "Address."

Morgan scribbled it down on a sticky pad she found on the desktop. "Here. Be careful, okay?"

"I'm not the one to be concerned about right now." She frowned at the address. "Isn't this where Prescott lives?"

"Now that you mention it, yeah." Morgan bit her lip. "That doesn't bode well, does it?"

"No, it doesn't." Willow turned and hurried out of the house.

A cab was driving by as she walked down Ramirez's walkway. It stopped when she hailed it. Giving the driver the address, she sat back and tried not to go insane.

As they pulled up, Willow noticed the street was cordoned off, so she had the cabdriver pull up as close as possible. She paid him and walked the rest of the way. Drawing *mù ch'i* to cloak herself, she walked straight past the street cops, who were keeping the gawkers behind the police line, and to the building's entrance.

It was swarming with cops. She edged past a gaggle of them talking in somber tones. Ramirez's car was parked right in front. It was riddled with bullet holes. On the ground next to it, there was a large dark stain.

Blood.

Her vision wavered, and she swayed on her feet.

"Hey." Someone took her elbow. "You okay?"

She looked into a concerned policewoman's face. "Fine," she said weakly.

The officer looked at Willow quizzically. "You aren't supposed to be here. How did you get past the line?"

"I live inside," Willow lied.

"Let me walk you out." She kept a hand under Willow's elbow and guided her back toward the spectators.

This time Willow noticed the ambulance parked at the edge of the scene. She let her energy root through the ground to the truck. Ramirez was inside. He was alive—she could sense his energy—but she couldn't tell how hurt he'd been.

She stumbled.

"Careful there," the officer said. "Are you sure you're okay?" she asked with concern.

No, she wasn't. She stared at the ambulance, needing to go see for herself that he was okay. This had the Bad Man written all over it. She didn't need physical proof to be certain of that. And if he knew about Ramirez, he'd know about Elena and maybe even Morgan. She had to keep them safe. She had to pull it together and take care of this before anyone else got hurt.

With a last glance at the ambulance, she shook off the policewoman's hand and took out her phone as she headed away from the crime scene.

Morgan answered before the first ring ended. "What's going on? Is Ramirez—"

"On your computer, there's a PDF with the Bad Man's information. His name is Edward Rodgers-Dynes. I need a contact number for him."

"Um, Willow, did you read that file?"

"I didn't have time."

"Listen, there's something—"

"His contact number, Morgan," she said, unable to care that her tone was harsh.

"I'm texting it to you. Will, you need to know—"

"Tell me later. And lock down the house and don't open the door for anyone. Keep Elena inside, too." She hung up and looked at the new text waiting for her. She punched in the number and waited.

On the third ring, a man answered. "Speak."

A command. The accent was South African, and she

recognized the low, cultured voice as the same one she'd heard as a child right before her mother had been killed. "Edward Rodgers-Dynes?"

There was a pause. She would have said it felt like anticipation. And then he said, "Yes."

"I believe you've been looking for me. I'd like to set up a meeting."

Chapter Twenty-eight

Flagging down another cab, Willow had it drop her off two blocks away from her meeting place. She strolled, fingers hooked in what passed for pockets on her pants, as she checked out the buildings lining the piers.

There wasn't anything unusual, if deserted warehouses were typical. But nothing about this felt typical.

She ambled to the end of Brannan, where it connected with the Embarcadero, and pretended to admire the Bay Bridge, while she surveyed the rendezvous point. It was an old abandoned warehouse with a chain-link fence with countless KEEP OUT signs around it. How original.

She let *mù ch'i* branch out to take stock of the rendezvous point. There were three people, one outside, two in.

"I bet one of them is Rodgers-Dynes," she muttered as she headed to the fence. She walked around back to be out of view of the cars driving by and quickly climbed over.

The person outside was around the other side of the

building, to the right. Normally, Willow would have used *mù ch'i* to slip past the first guard, but she wasn't feeling generous today. And she wanted to make a statement. She strode right up to him, her boots clacking on the wooden slats of the pier. He pushed his chest out as she approached.

She smiled, small and mean. "If you're trying to intimidate me, you'll have to try harder."

Before he could say anything, she punched him in the solar plexus to make him lose his breath so he couldn't cry out. She followed with a left hook to his temple, not hard enough for permanent damage, but just enough to shock him into unconsciousness. Eyes rolling back into his head, he dropped to his knees. Slowly he tilted to one side and slumped onto the ground. She kicked him, just to make sure he was really out and not playing her, and then she headed to the obvious entrance to the warehouse.

Being bold was one thing—being stupid was another. She wanted to barge in and make a statement, but she didn't want to chance letting him escape. So she sneaked in. She'd take out the other guard, and then deal with Rodgers-Dynes.

Sensing two people on the other side of the building, she tiptoed through towers of crates until she found the second bodyguard. He didn't see her, and she used his inattention to creep behind him.

She wanted to take him out physically, too. Her hands itched to beat him up, even if it was a short-lived fight, like the guard outside. Instead, in the interest of not alerting Rodgers-Dynes, she planted somnolence in his mind, encouraging it to grow into the urge to take a nap. He wavered back and forth on his feet, shaking his head. She pushed the thought harder, picturing it rooting firmly in his subconscious.

Staggering to the right, he caught himself on a crate, sliding slowly to a sleeping heap on the ground.

Clapping rang out. "Bravo, Willow. Well done."

Behind her. She spun around, poised to strike.

He stood twenty feet away, far enough that she couldn't attack by normal means, close enough that she could see him in full detail.

Prescott's dossier said he was in his early sixties. In the club, she hadn't been able to see him in detail. Standing this close, he appeared younger. Fit and tanned, the only things that belied his age were his pale gray eyes.

He looked pleased.

And why not? He'd gotten what he wanted: her.

The doors to the ambulance slammed shut. Ramirez said a prayer as he watched it tear off for San Francisco General. Taylor had to be okay.

"Inspector." One of the remaining medics took his elbow. "If you'll come this way, we'll take you downtown and have your arm looked at."

He glanced down at the quick bandage someone had wrapped around the wound to stanch the bleeding. "It's just a graze."

The medic pursed her lips. If she were fifty years older and Latina, she could have been Lita. "It's a bullet wound. You're lucky it passed through without much damage, but it doesn't mean you don't need it treated. You need stitches."

What he needed was a shot of tequila and a long vacation. But right now, he had to make sure Willow was okay. He couldn't shake the bad feeling that she was about to step into trouble. "I'll have someone look at this later. I need to ensure that whoever shot at us is caught."

"You cops are so impossible. You aren't invincible, you know." She threw her hands in the air. "Fine. Go be a hero. But if you pass out from loss of blood, it's on your head," she said as she stormed off.

As long as he passed out after he brought Rodgers-Dynes in, he'd be okay. He flipped out his phone and called Willow on her cell. No answer.

Cursing under his breath, he called his home. It rang several times before someone picked up.

"Ramirez headquarters," Morgan said in a grumpy tone. "Lackey speaking."

"Let me talk to Willow."

"Ramirez?" She heaved a sigh that he felt all the way across town. "Thank God you're okay. Wait, you *are* okay, aren't you? We heard there was an officer down—"

"I'm fine. I need to talk to Willow."

Her pause was heavy. "She went to meet Rodgers-Dynes."

He started to scrub his face, but his wound burned and he dropped his arm. *Damn it.* "And you didn't stop her?"

"Stop her?" Morgan asked, her voice rising. "Willow is a force of nature. You don't just *stop her.* It's like trying to stop a hurricane."

"Where is she?" He waved an officer over.

"I don't know, but I can find out. Hold on."

He listened to the furious tapping of a keyboard. Moving the phone to the side, he nodded at the approaching officer. "Are you free to give me a ride? My car is decommissioned."

The officer grimaced at the bullet-ridden sedan. "Of course, Inspector. Whenever you're ready."

"Got it, Ricardo," Morgan said.

He held up a finger to the young man and turned away to talk with her. "Where?"

"She's on Embarcadero. I'd place her in what looks like a warehouse, off Pier Fourteen."

"Got it." He snapped the phone shut and motioned to the officer. "Let's go."

They drove in silence. Perfect—it gave Ramirez the space to figure out what he was going to do, which was difficult considering he had no idea what to expect. The young officer was competent and fast, getting them to the pier quickly.

"Drop me off here." Ramirez pointed to the corner at Brannan.

"Of course." The officer pulled over. "Good luck, sir. I'll be praying for your partner's speedy recovery."

Choked up, Ramirez nodded and got out. He waited until the officer drove off and then scanned the area.

The warehouse.

He knew without a doubt that's where she'd be. He headed there, staying alert. He needed to get to her before it was too late.

Chapter Twenty-nine

Smiling, Rodgers-Dynes glanced at the passed-out heap of his bodyguard. "Is Frank still alive?"

Willow frowned at his amused tone. "Yes."

"Good. Thank you for not killing my best associate," he said politely. "Good help is hard to come by."

She shrugged, standing ready. "You won't have to worry about that much longer."

He arched an eyebrow, humor lighting his expression. "I admire that you think you're going to stop me. Perhaps we may talk before you unleash your supposed fury on me."

"There's nothing supposed about it."

"Ah, that's where you're incorrect." He leaned against the crate behind him, crossing his legs at the ankles, arms akimbo. "I suppose you think I hurt your mother."

"I don't think anything. I was there."

"Yes, you were, weren't you." He regarded her inquiringly. "How old were you then? Twelve? Thirteen?"

"Ten." She watched him suspiciously. He was toying with her. He knew exactly how old she'd been.

"Ten." He nodded. "So young. So malleable, believing whatever you were told. Don't you think you could have had the wrong impression of what was going on?"

Conscious that he watched her like a hawk, gauging her every emotion, she stifled her anger and feigned nonchalance. "Are you insinuating that my mother lied to me?"

"Your mother was a woman who ran from her husband and took their child."

She stilled. "You know who my father is?"

His smile grew slow and delighted. "I know your father very well."

Studying him, she tried to figure out if he was leading her on. He'd say anything to get what he wanted. She had no doubt of that. But he was being sincere, at least as sincere as he was capable of.

She swallowed, wanting to ask about her father, wondering if he was alive. She couldn't, however, because giving away how important that was to her would give him an advantage. She knew better than that.

"But you want to know, don't you, Willow?" He smiled gently at her. "You want to know whether he's looked for you and whether he wants to know you. You wonder if he loves you."

She did—badly—but she shrugged. "It's not exactly startling that I would wonder some of those things."

"I can tell you."

For some reason, she felt like she was being offered a deal with the devil. She crossed her arms and set her stance. Ready. Just in case. "And what would you want in return?"

His eyes lit, like she'd performed a particularly amusing trick. "You're quite delightful. I'm going to enjoy getting to know you."

The hell he was, but she didn't say anything.

"You have the look of your mother." He gestured toward her. "Your hair and build. But you get your dogged determination from your father. That, and your eyes."

Eyes.

Her gaze snapped to his. There was indulgence and patience in the gray of his eyes. The same gray as hers.

"Oh, my God..."

He smiled. "Yes, Willow."

She stayed on her feet, but on the inside, she was staggering. She didn't want to believe him. She wanted to call him a liar. Only he wasn't lying. Deep inside, she knew what he said was true.

He watched her steadily. "No arguing? No calling me names and questioning the truth?"

She pretended not to care. She had to be careful, at least until she processed all this. "Why bother? Besides, the truth can't be altered, no matter how much we'd like it to be."

"Perhaps if you got to know me, you wouldn't wish to change your paternity."

"Perhaps." She couldn't picture getting to know him. What did fathers do with their grown daughters? She had no frame of reference.

His expression was knowing and amused. "You don't sound convinced. I'm going to persuade you. Why do you think I've been searching for you all this time?"

"Searching?" She raised her brow. "Is that what you call it?"

"I admit, a few times my overzealous associates got carried away in carrying out my orders to bring you to me, but I had your best interests in mind. You're my only family. I'd do anything for you."

Her mother would have done—*had* done—anything for her, too. It filled her with a longing so sharp, she felt it in her bones.

"Your little business with law enforcement, for example."

Willow glared at him. "What do you know about that?"

"I have connections. I hear things." His sharp gray stare belied his casual stance. "I can get any police interest in you dropped."

Something didn't ring true. "Just because I'm your long-lost daughter?"

He nodded. "I've dreamed of having a family. I may be well-off, but you can't buy a family and have it be genuine. That's all I've ever wanted. All these years, I've kept this with me, hoping I'd finally get to know you." He reached into his coat pocket and pulled out a piece of paper. No, a photo. Willow made no move to take it. As curious as she was about it, she didn't trust him not to use it to spring a trap.

Squinting, she realized it was a picture of a laughing toddler with a shock of white hair sticking straight up.

It was a picture of *her.*

She blinked. She'd never seen a baby picture of herself. She wanted to reach for it, to hold it in her own hands—to reconnect to that part of herself that was lost.

"Take it." He stepped forward, arm extended. "I'd rather have the real thing. I was cheated out of my time with you, and I only want to reclaim some of that. That's all I'm asking for, Willow. My daughter back."

She wanted to call him a liar, but she could tell he wasn't lying. He wanted her, and she wanted to be wanted. She wanted roots.

He held out the picture. "Take it."

Except he was offering more than an old snapshot. He was offering everything she'd lost so long ago: acceptance, home, and family. Everything that was missing in her life. That is, until recently.

"Take it," he urged.

"Why did my mother run away from you?"

He blinked, and his smile dimmed. "What?"

"I want to know what happened with my mother."

"She took what was mine."

Her blood froze. "Are you saying you took out my mother because she wouldn't give *me* to you?"

"She wouldn't share anything with me, despite the vows she took." A scowl twisted his face. "Nothing happened to her that she didn't deserve."

The loving dad mask slipped, the seductive web he'd woven fading. She glanced at the photo, at the happy little girl, and realized that girl no longer existed. For better or worse, she'd become who she was now. Yet she still wanted that dream of a family. Those roots. But her roots were planted right there in that charming house in the Mission. Her family had become a brilliant hacker, a mystical Latina healer, and a straightlaced cop.

A cop who was gunned down this evening.

By *him*—Edward Rodgers-Dynes, her father.

Eyes narrowed, Willow grounded herself and faced him. "And did Inspector Ramirez deserve what he got, too?"

He shifted his weight forward. "He wasn't good for you. I did you a service."

Willow wanted to scream. She clenched her hands into fists feeling *mù ch'i* react to her desire to lash out. Not yet. "Excuse me if I don't thank you."

His expression went cold. Any semblance of affection evaporated, and she was left with the Bad Man she'd been chasing for so long. "You're ungrateful, just like your mother," he said, letting the photograph drop.

She nodded. "Better to be like my mother than like my father."

"Unwise to provoke me," he said, his voice a low growl. He moved toward her, stepping on the discarded snapshot. "You'll regret it."

"I doubt that." She drew on *mù ch'i* so she was armed and ready.

"Oh, you will." He pulled out a throwing star, holding it between his fingers in front of him. It glinted in the harsh lighting of the warehouse.

She had a sudden flash of her mother lying on the floor, the star embedded in her chest.

"You seem to emulate your mother." Rodgers-Dynes smiled coldly. "The question is, will you take your place at my side or follow in her very dead footsteps?"

Chapter Thirty

Ramirez knew he was on the right track when he found a man passed out and propped against the building. It had been Willow's handiwork, of course. Ramirez hesitated and then leaned down to feel for a pulse. Strong. Of course the man was only knocked out. What did he expect, for her to leave a trail of dead bodies?

Actually, yeah. He shook his head in disgust at himself. Except for the confession about her line of work, he had no evidence to think that she would. Even if he thought she'd been misguided in her vigilante past, she wasn't bloodthirsty. She was quite the contrary. He had evidence that she was respectful of life. When she'd been attacked before, she'd been protecting her life and was justified in the eyes of the law of—well, anywhere. But she'd just disabled them.

Think about her past later. Right now, he needed to ensure she didn't make a mistake that would ruin her forever.

He crept around the back of the warehouse and found another knocked-out bodyguard. Not bothering to check his pulse, Ramirez unholstered his gun and held it down on his unhurt side. He heard a masculine voice from the back. Edging along a long line of stacked crates, he made his way toward the voice.

He spotted Willow first. She stood facing Rodgers-Dynes. Her father.

Her Bad Man smiled with delicious malevolence as he thumbed one of the points of the throwing star in his hand. "It's really quite disappointing. I thought you were more like me than your mother. What a waste."

Ramirez glanced at Willow. Her face masked her feelings, but her body didn't. He had come to know it very well. He could tell by the tension in her shoulders and the stiffness of her back, she was forcibly holding it together. Rodgers-Dynes circled her, an obvious effort to cut off any possible escape route. "I suspected it, especially when you were so surprised to find out I was your father. You should have known. *I* knew. The moment I saw you, I *knew*. *You* should have felt it, too. But you weren't that observant, were you?"

Ramirez glanced at Willow, his heart breaking for her. She hadn't intentionally kept that from him. And, God, what was going through her head, finding out her father was, as they would say at the station, a sick fuck?

"You don't count as a father," she said, shifting to keep him in her line of sight. "There's more to it than donating sperm. Which is why I don't get it."

Good work, Willow. Ramirez nodded. *Keep him talking.* He retreated behind one of the crates and pulled out his cell phone to do his part. He quickly texted Weinberg: *Need a conversation recorded. Set up surveillance.*

Weinberg's reply was just as immediate: *Got it, dude. Call 415-555-7745 in twenty secs.*

Ramirez punched in the number and stayed poised.

Willow continued to engage her father. "You could have had another kid. Why spend all the energy coming after me?"

"Need you ask?" Rodgers-Dynes looked at her with contempt. "For your powers, of course."

Powers? Ramirez looked at her sharply.

Willow appeared stunned, as well. "What do you know about that?"

"I was married to your mother." His voice was filled with contempt. "I discovered she was a Guardian. Imagine how delighted I was to find out she had more to offer than I expected. Of course, that was before she refused to enter a true partnership." His countenance darkened, and he flicked the ninja throwing star between his fingers. "She didn't want to share her powers with me."

Willow stilled. "So it wasn't me that you wanted? It was my powers. For what? World domination?"

"Crudely put, and without imagination." Rodgers-Dynes's smile was cruel. "But not entirely untrue."

Not taking his eye off the scene, Ramirez pressed the call button. He listened as Weinberg gave him a verbal thumbs-up and then set his phone on top of the crate so the kid could tape the conversation.

"Your mother was useless, in all ways except one," Rodgers-Dynes continued. "She gave me you, the next in her line. I realized it didn't matter if she didn't cooperate. I had you. But then she took you away."

"And you hunted us."

The tremor in Willow's voice made his chest ache. Ramirez wanted to wrap her in his arms and block her pain. However, he knew she didn't need or want that.

He'd have to settle for just loving her. But that would come after. Right now, he had to focus on the task at hand. He needed a confession so he could lock away Rodgers-Dynes. *Then* he could concentrate on his woman. *Come on, Willow, keep him talking.*

Willow's brow furrowed, and her eyes darted in his direction. But just as quickly, she returned her attention to her father. "You not only hunted us, but you mowed down anyone else who stood in your way."

"Starting with your mother." His smile radiated pure evil. "So satisfying, killing her. I'll never forget the sound she made as the blade sank into her heart."

Willow took a step forward, almost involuntarily, before she caught herself.

"You, I won't kill. But metal weakens you, doesn't it? A few well-placed throwing stars and you won't be able to fight me. Drugs should be able to take care of your reticence after."

Her father held up the star in his hands to inspect it in the light. "My preferred weapon, as you know. I didn't want to be obvious, so I had my associates take care of your investigator and that traitor who worked for me, but Quentin was all me. I only wish I could have seen your face when you saw his method of death."

Willow glared at him. "You set me up."

"Of course I did. I lured you to San Francisco. I had you implicated in three murders. I cut you off from everything and made it so you had no options. Even your last bit of hope, that cop, is taken care of. You have no one. No one but me."

Ramirez's heart sank. Did she think he was hurt?

The air around her shimmered, and she seemed to

grow taller. "No, not just you. I still have one person I can count on."

Her father smirked. "Who is that?"

"Me."

"Your mother couldn't defeat me. What makes you think you can?"

Ramirez held his gun ready, watching Rodgers-Dynes. Edward wasn't done toying with his daughter, but Ramirez would strike quickly—and thoroughly—when he was. Ramirez didn't want to be taken off guard. Willow, of course, took his dare. She walked toward her father, hands out, completely focused on him.

"Do you think I don't know what you're doing?"

Rodgers-Dynes tipped his head back mockingly. "What am I doing, daughter?"

Anger radiated off her in waves Ramirez could feel. "*Never* call me that," she growled.

"No one will call you anything soon." He lunged forward, a glint of silver caught in a flash.

With a gasp, Willow recoiled. She retracted her hands and looked down at her palms. Blood seeped from the left one, a thick rivulet that dripped down her wrist onto the concrete floor. She stared at it, transfixed, rooted to the floor.

Ramirez stepped out from his hiding place, his pistol raised and pointed at Rodgers-Dynes. "*Stop.*"

The gloating expression on the man's face slipped into irritation. "You were supposed to be disposed of."

"It doesn't look like that happened, does it?" Ramirez said, keeping the gun aimed. "Stop moving and drop your weapon."

Rodgers-Dynes shook his head, his lips twisted in mocking disdain. "Are you going to make me, Officer?"

"Ramirez?" Willow asked.

He kept his focus on her father. He didn't trust the man. "I'm here."

"You certainly are, but you won't be for long," Rodgers-Dynes said, circling, flashing another star. "It *is* considerate of you to come here to distract Willow. Her mother was distracted that last time, too."

Ramirez felt Willow stiffen and resurge with anger. He willed her to stay calm. The guy wasn't armed with anything other than a throwing star. A star was no good compared to a gun.

"Protecting the one she loved," Rodgers-Dynes said mockingly. "Her downfall. And based on how Willow is reacting, I'd wager it'll be hers, as well." Striking with the speed of a snake, he threw the star.

It was so sudden, Ramirez almost didn't see it coming. He dove for the floor, getting off a shot but knowing it missed its mark. He rolled as another throwing star landed with a *ping* on the ground next to him, right where his neck had been. Ramirez looked up as he scuttled, seeing Rodgers-Dynes extracting another throwing star.

"No," Willow yelled. She held her uninjured hand out. The air around it thickened before branching out like a lightning strike toward Rodgers-Dynes.

What the hell? Ramirez froze, unable to believe it.

The deranged man staggered back, surprise widening his eyes. And then he smiled, sinister and cold. "Is that all you have?"

"No," she said again, calmly this time. "Are you asking for more?"

Without waiting for a response, she flicked her finger toward him and he fell back, clutching his chest.

Ramirez stood up, not sure what was going on but knowing it wasn't good. "Willow, stop. Leave this for the police."

She glanced at him, her eyes reflecting an age-old hurt and wisdom so similar to Lita's when she got in a state. Her voice was sad when she spoke. "He has to be stopped."

"Yes, he does, but not by you." He reached for his phone. If anything happened, he didn't want Weinberg recording it. Besides, they had enough to put Rodgers-Dynes away. "Kid, you got all that?"

"Sure thing." Excitement had his voice high-pitched and wobbly. "What the hell is going on there? What were those metallic clinks? Should I come help? Where are you?"

"The warehouse on Pier Fourteen. Send backup. Do *not* come by yourself," he ordered. Ramirez ended the call, hoping the kid would obey. Slipping the phone in his pocket, he focused on Willow. "Leave this for the justice system."

Rodgers-Dynes managed a weak smirk, still clutching his chest. "I'll be released in an hour. There's absolutely nothing money can't buy."

Ramirez watched Willow's fury rise again. He stepped forward, putting himself between the two. "I had the conversation recorded, and it's enough to put him away. By taking him out yourself, he's only going to get what he wants. Your destruction."

"That may be worth having him silenced forever." She lifted her right hand.

He could see her focusing her energy again. Damn it, he had to make her listen to him. "I'll see to justice for you, Willow. You have to trust me."

She shook her head. "This has nothing to do with you."

"The hell it doesn't. If you do this, I won't be able to help you. You'll be lost to me," he said intently.

She paused, and her energy retracted just a little. "Does that bother you?"

"Of course it bothers me. I love you." He peered at her steadily, willing her to see how much, how completely. "The past can't be changed. I can't condone it, but I can let it go. The future is more important than the past."

Willow looked at him, and then at her father.

Ramirez could feel her will weakening. "Willow. Trust me. Please."

Chapter Thirty-one

Revenge or Ramirez?

Willow studied her lover. She trusted him. Even with her heart, but this was different.

She looked down at Rodgers-Dynes. She owed this to her mother. She needed to do this for herself.

Her father grinned at her, a twisted victory in his eyes that made her want to smash in his face. "Because cops helped you after your mother died, didn't they?" he taunted.

They didn't, but she also didn't try going to them. She was so young, and her mother had told her not to trust anyone, and certainly not to go to the police. They worked for the Bad Man, she'd said. The plan was to escape and hide without notifying anyone. To run. Either way, she was done running.

She looked at Ramirez. Not all policemen could be bought. Had he been a cop back then, he would have helped her.

Revenge or Ramirez?

"Weak, just like your mother." Rodgers-Dynes twitched in his effort to move.

In the distance, sirens wailed just like at the park, when she first saw Ramirez. She'd been drawn to him then, and she didn't even know him. Now she knew him and she loved him. There was no question about that. Was that enough, though?

She studied his beautiful, rugged face. Under his collar lay a tattoo. She knew his shape, every contour of his body. There was promise in his eyes, and he'd never renege on a promise. There was also love there. The kind of love she'd never imagined she could have. Full and blooming and healthy, just like his grandmother had said. He may not like her past, but he wouldn't hold it against her, not if he said he wouldn't. It was the kind of love her mother would have wanted her to have.

Revenge or love?

Put that way, there was no choice. She released her hold on Rodgers-Dynes. Only she couldn't resist one last crescent kick. It caught him at the jaw, knocking him out into a heap on the floor. She brushed her hands and turned to Ramirez. "He's yours."

As she stepped away from her father—and the anger—the wall inside her trembled. She froze, turning inward. Distantly she heard Ramirez's concerned shout, but she held up her hand to ward him off. The wall cracked. *Mù ch'i* pushed at it, and it crumbled into dust, revealing that elusive part of her she could never access before. It grew through her, healthy and vibrant, making her feel strong. Whole.

She blinked again and came back to reality, finding herself across Ramirez's lap, in his arms. Worry lined his face, and she smoothed his brow with her fingers. "Don't look like that."

"Don't look like that?" he said gruffly. "Damn it, Willow, you scared ten years off my life."

Before she could offer any other reassurances, he kissed her. At first, it tasted of fear and relief and desperation. But it warmed into promise, and then heated into love. She tunneled her fingers into his hair, rising up to meet him.

His hand slid under her shirt, and up her back, finding warmth there. "As much as I want this, this isn't the time or place. But later…"

"Later?" she asked.

He brushed a kiss on her lips, under the line of her jaw, and in the soft hollow of her collarbone. "Later."

"Is that a threat?" She tilted her head to one side, being cooperative.

"It's a promise," he whispered against her neck. He nipped her there and then lifted her up with him.

Feeling oddly light, she teetered on her boots before finding her equilibrium. She looked at her father one last time. Obviously clearing the aftereffects of her kick, he shook his head, lucid again. Hate glared back at her so forceful, it almost distracted her from the slight movement of his hand. His coat shifted, and she caught the glint of silver under the lapel.

"No you don't." She walked toward him and kicked his arm out, stepping on his wrist to prevent him from throwing the star.

"Remind me never to disobey you," Ramirez said mildly as he picked up the blade.

She rolled her eyes. "Because you're so obedient."

His backup arrived at that moment. With a squeeze of her arm, he walked to his team and quietly began issuing orders.

A couple uniformed officers went to collect Rodgers-Dynes. Willow watched as they hauled him to his feet, holding him there because his legs were useless. She felt a tinge of satisfaction. The big bad man wasn't so bad anymore.

Edward's head lifted and his pale eyes focused on her. As the officers dragged him past her, he chuckled, a breathy exhale that she felt more than heard. "This isn't over," he whispered. "Not in the least."

She waited for a surge of hate—and fear—to fill her. The distaste was still there, and a pale shadow of the anger. But that was it. She smiled coolly at her father. "I wouldn't count on that."

"*Willow.*"

She turned around in time to catch Morgan as she collided into her.

"How did you get here?" Ramirez asked. "You shouldn't have been allowed on scene."

"I ducked under the tape. As if anything would stop me." Morgan squeezed Willow hard before letting her go abruptly. "Are you okay? I was so freaked out. I tried to tell you he's your—"

"My father."

Morgan studied her closely. "And how is that for you?"

Willow shrugged, not sure how she felt. "It's been a tumultuous day."

"Jesus Christ, you're the master of understatement." Morgan turned and smiled cautiously. "Inspector, I'm happy to see you survived this whole thing."

"You don't sound certain."

"I'm certain about that. I'm not certain what happens

next. Or if my next residence is going to be a small cell shared with a big woman named Bertha."

Willow grinned at Ramirez. "She's asking in her warped way whether you're going to cart us off to jail."

"The only place I'm taking you is home. My home." He glanced at Morgan. "You can stay downstairs with my grandmother."

Her friend smiled at him, full and bright. "If you insist, Inspector. Like I'm going to argue. Your grandmother is an awesome cook." Her attention suddenly flickered away, and she flushed pink. "Who is *that*?"

Willow turned to look over her shoulder. There was a thin, geeky young man headed straight for them. He was obviously one of Ramirez's team, but he only had eyes for Morgan.

"Weinberg." Ramirez shook the man's hand. "Good work earlier."

"Thanks, sir," the geek said, still watching Morgan.

"Morgan, this is Martin Weinberg," Ramirez said, glancing back and forth between the two. "He's the one who cracked your firewall."

"That was *you*?" Morgan and Weinberg said at the same time.

Willow couldn't keep the broad grin off her face. Ah, geek love.

Ramirez's hand touched her elbow, and she realized she'd recognize his touch anywhere. Her face warmed with pleasure and anticipation, and she slipped her hand in his. "Take me home."

Chapter Thirty-two

Ramirez woke up the next morning alone.

He sat up, instantly alert from years of being on call 24/7. The covers next to him were pushed back, and when he ran his hand along the sheets, they were cool to the touch. Willow had been gone for a while.

But where?

Willow had made her statement to the police after the arrest and they'd arrived home late. He'd expected her to be completely wiped out and had intended on letting her bathe and then tucking her into bed, holding her all night while she slept. He hadn't counted on her jumping him. Now, thinking on it, he wasn't sure why he didn't expect it.

His eyes shot to the spot where he'd thrown her clothing the night before. The relief he felt when he saw it still there was ridiculous.

Getting out of bed, he pulled on a pair of shorts and grabbed a sweatshirt. Instinct told him to look out the window; so as he slipped the shirt over his head, he opened the drapes.

Willow sat crossed-legged on the bench in Lita's garden. She wore one of his sweatshirts, her long tanned legs gloriously bare just beneath the hem. He wondered if a pair of his boxers or underwear was hidden underneath. She rolled her flute between her fingers as she stared into space.

Something was still wrong.

He snorted. No kidding. Just because they'd caught her Bad Man didn't mean that everything would suddenly be okay for her. She'd spent pretty much all of her life running from her nemesis—there were going to be repercussions. What that meant for them, he had no idea. She'd told Ramirez she loved him. She hadn't told him she intended to spend the rest of her life with him. Which, amazingly, was precisely what he wanted.

He padded downstairs and out to the garden.

A quick scan showed that his *abuelita* was conspicuously absent. Not surprising—that woman had an uncanny knack for knowing when to disappear.

Willow looked up, smiling when she saw him.

He sat down next to her and took her hand. "You aren't supposed to slip out of bed before I wake up."

Her smile tilted mischievously, and she climbed on his lap, straddling him. "Is that in one of your rule books, Starsky?"

"If it isn't, it should be." He slid his hands up her thighs and under the loose leg openings of a pair of his silk boxers, so he cradled her ass. He kissed her, lingering until he was sure he had her attention. "Good morning, Willow."

"Good morning, Rick." Her lips curved under his. "Although technically, I think it's afternoon."

"So it is."

She tipped her head and looked at him. "No rushing to get to the office? No fretting about all your cases going unsolved?"

He tightened his arms around her. "Some things are more important."

"Are they?" she asked, sobering abruptly. She began worrying the flute again, which she held cradled between the two of them.

He sighed. Best to figure this out sooner rather than later. "Willow—"

"We need to talk," she said, beating him to the punch. "There's something you need to know."

The last time there was something he needed to know, she'd told him she was an assassin. He pulled back a little, his hands loose on her hips. "I'm not going to like this, am I?"

She shrugged one shoulder, a slight movement that conveyed enough to make him nervous. "Probably not. But before you say what I think you're going to say, you need to know."

Since he held her, he could feel her practically vibrating with nerves. This didn't bode well. As concerned as he was, he wanted to reassure her, too. "Tell me."

"Not right now." She framed his face with her hands. "I have a meeting I need to get to, and this isn't something to rush."

"Meeting?" He frowned. "What type of meeting?"

"With Maximillian Prescott." She must have sensed him stiffening, because she quickly added, "Don't get bent out of shape. It's not a big thing. I just need to, uh, check in."

"Check in," he repeated suspiciously.

Sighing, she dropped her hands. "You're not going to make this easy, are you?"

"No."

A smile flirted with her lips. "Okay, come with me."

That surprised him more than her saying she was going to see Max.

"It's fitting, in a way, that I tell you there," she said, as if trying to convince herself that it was a good idea. "I'd prefer doing it without an audience, but this particular audience is good backup to have in this instance."

"You need backup?"

She shrugged. "There's always a first time. So are you coming?"

Forty minutes later, they pulled up to Max's loft, behind a black sports car that he recognized as Gabrielle Sansouci Chin's. "It seems we aren't the only ones visiting," Ramirez said when they were on the sidewalk.

"No. The gang's all here." She turned to him and squeezed his hand. "Promise me you'll keep an open mind. That you'll listen objectively like the detective that you are before you judge."

He cocked an eyebrow, honestly worried. "You're not making this sound good."

"I know."

Before he could say anything else, the door opened and Max frowned at him. "Ramirez. What are you doing here?"

Steel infused Willow's backbone and her tone. "I invited him," she said, not giving Prescott room to argue.

Max narrowed his eyes at her, obviously wanting to say something but trying to hold his tongue.

Willow rolled her eyes. "You had to know it was inevitable."

"But I was holding out hope I was wrong."

Ramirez looked back and forth between Willow and Max. "Anyone going to clue me in on what's going on here?"

Max snorted. "Are you sure you don't want to cut and run? Now's your last chance."

Willow glared at Max. "Thanks for the support. And, I hate to point out, you were the one who called to invite us over."

"I invited *you* over." He pointed at Ramirez. "*He* wasn't included in the deal."

"Your wife is included."

"Because she's *my wife.*"

Willow glanced at Ramirez quickly before facing down Max again. "My point exactly."

Max went completely impassive, studying the two of them. Ramirez couldn't resist the urge to slide his hand around her waist.

Willow rolled her eyes. "Can we take this inside, guys?"

Max grunted and waved them in. In the living room, Rhys sat on a couch, his girlfriend, Gabrielle, curled next to him, her shoes kicked off and her legs curled under her. Carrie sat apart from them, obviously next to Max, based on the large impression in the cushions next to her.

When Ramirez and Willow walked into the room, they all stared in an array of different emotions. Gabe gaped, Carrie gave him a wicked wink, and Rhys surveyed them as impassively as Max had.

Ramirez felt an undercurrent, volatile and potent, course

through the room. It was almost tangible—like an electric shock—making his skin tingle. Strange.

Carrie was the one who spoke first. "I knew it," she said smugly. She turned to Gabe. "You owe me a hundred bucks."

Gabe looked back and forth between him and Willow. "I think that's a reasonable price of admission for the show we're about to see."

Willow frowned at them. "You people aren't helping matters."

"No, we're not," Rhys said sympathetically. "It might have to do with the fact that we invited you to come over, not Inspector Ramirez."

"Nevertheless, he's here, and you're going to have to deal." Willow exhaled deeply. "I'm going to tell him."

Gabrielle muttered things under her breath; Rhys squeezed her leg. She glared at Ramirez then, but at least she did it in silence.

Carrie watched with concern, which did little to relieve Ramirez's growing anxiety. He needed everyone to just get to the point.

He frowned. "Can we stop tiptoeing around this and let me know what's going on?"

"Good luck with this one, girlfriend." Gabrielle smirked. "I can't say I envy you."

"Thanks." Willow shot the other woman a dark look before she turned to Ramirez. She hesitated, but then took his hand in hers in the end. "I have special powers. We all do."

He stared at her, not blinking. "Okay, now that you got that joke out of the way, tell me what this is about."

"That *is* what this is about," she said. "It's a complicated story, but, in a nutshell, we're all Guardians of ancient Chinese scrolls. Our scrolls empower us with individual powers to help us do our duties."

"In short, we're Jedis," Gabrielle said gleefully. "Welcome to the Force, Inspector."

Ramirez was the one who gave Gabe a dark look this time. He returned his attention to Willow. "The thing with the tree? How you seemed to disappear?"

She nodded. "Part of my powers."

Ramirez wanted to scoff and deny existence of any such thing, only he'd witnessed Willow's powers, as she called them, with his own eyes. He couldn't explain them, and that made him want to refute any possibility that they existed.

And yet...

His grandmother was proof that the unexplainable did exist. While he was growing up, she defied everything he believed in, on a daily basis. He remembered how Lita told him sometimes shades of gray replaced pure black and white. He shook his head. It seemed Willow's entire life was a constant state of gray.

"What?" she asked softly.

"Is this it? Anything else in your closet?"

"This is it." She squeezed his hand. "I swear."

He nodded, trying to process. As he looked around the room, his gaze rested on Carrie. "You're a Guardian, too?"

She shook her head. "I'm in your boat. Although I knew about the myth. I just didn't know that it was more than a cool fairy tale."

He looked at Gabrielle, Rhys, and Max.

Gabrielle shrugged. "You knew something was

different all along. You smelled it. It's got to be good, knowing you were right."

"That's one way of looking at it."

Willow tugged his hand, pulling his attention to her again. "Metal—I mean Max wanted to discuss some Guardian business today. Let's get that out of the way and then you can ask me anything you need to. Okay?"

As if he had any other choice. Gritting his teeth, pissed but not sure why, he nodded.

She didn't look any more relieved, but she seemed to compartmentalize that and turned to Max, who'd sat back down next to his wife. "You said this was important."

"Carrie found some information that's pertinent to us all."

All eyes turned to Carrie.

Carrie looked at him. "Rick, you're going to want to be sitting when you get this information."

"Jeez, that bad!" Gabrielle exclaimed.

"It's a doozy," Carrie replied in her usual cheery voice. "You guys know how Wei Lin separated all the scrolls because together they wielded way too much power for anyone to control? And by 'you guys,' I really mean you, Rick. Because I think we can safely assume everyone else here is up on the myth."

Ramirez gave a curt nod. "I'll read the Cliffs Notes later if I need to."

Gabrielle chortled. "I can't believe it. You joked. This chick must be good for you." She turned to Willow. "Stick around. You seem to be humanizing him."

Willow bristled but said nothing.

Rhys sighed. "Love, is it really wise to provoke her?"

"Maybe not wise, but it sure is fun."

Carrie cleared her throat. "If you guys are done, I'll get on with this. It's important for all of you."

The room fell silent. Ramirez studied each person as they turned their attention to Carrie. They paid attention to her, like her words had weight, even though she said she wasn't one of them.

"Okay, here's the gist," she began, her cheeks flushing in excitement. "Wei Lin always knew the scrolls were meant to be together. '*The five elements coexist in harmony, an endless circle of give and take,*' he wrote. Separating them was a temporary stopgap that wasn't supposed to last forever."

"It wasn't?" Gabrielle asked, sitting up alert. "I thought the families were forever cursed to carry their burdens."

Ramirez frowned. "*Cursed?*"

Rhys smiled mildly. "Gabrielle is less than pleased with her role as a Guardian."

"Because it *sucks*," she said emphatically. "If you ask me, phenomenal cosmic power is overrated."

"Especially if you don't have a handle on it," Max commented quietly, obviously meaning for her to hear it.

"Hey." Gabrielle started to leap off the couch, pointing a finger at him. "You—"

Rhys tugged her back. "You can tear him to pieces later, love, with my blessings. After Carrie finishes."

Carrie wagged a finger at her husband. "Behave."

Max scowled, but neither did he say anything further.

Willow watched the other players like a tennis match. Ramirez wondered what she made of this. Her life sounded solitary—working as a group had to be a foreign experience.

"What was I saying before the children got out of hand?" Carrie tapped her chin in thought. "Right—Wei Lin and his vision. He always meant for the scrolls to be reunited."

"That doesn't make sense."

All eyes turned to Gabrielle, and Carrie sighed.

Gabrielle threw her hands in the air. "What? Am I supposed to raise my hand to talk or something? I just wanted to express that the third rule is that the scrolls need to be kept apart."

Carrie nodded. "That was a rule Wei Lin put into place, but it was only temporary. Until the messiah came to reunite all the elements."

"*Messiah?*" everyone exclaimed at once.

"Messiah," Carrie repeated resolutely.

Willow stared incredulously. "You're saying some religious person—"

"Not a religious person," Carrie interrupted. "I didn't mean *messiah* in the literal Christian sense. I meant there's going to be a Chosen One who unites the scrolls once and for all. And it seems to be happening now."

"How do you know that?" Rhys asked, his skepticism thinly veiled.

Carrie shrugged. "By virtue of the events. Gabe said that all her life she'd been told that you guys were supposed to stay away from each other. I think you're being staged."

Rhys nodded. "It'd explain why we all ended up in San Francisco."

"That we're all being lured into a holding pattern, waiting for this Chosen One to arrive and unite the scrolls." Max turned his wife's face toward his, his expression stonier than usual. "Does this mean we have to give up our scrolls?"

"I don't know." She held her hands out to forestall any other questions. "I only know that you guys have all gathered in San Francisco after centuries of being in separate corners of the world. I also know that, after all these centuries, I conveniently found a document that told me what was happening." She raised her eyebrows. "I'm a good researcher, but that's not just skill, it's luck. And I kind of think it was time for answers to surface, at least for someone who wanted to find them."

Willow shifted forward. "So you're saying this information is out there for anyone who wants it."

"Yeah, pretty much." Carrie wrinkled her nose.

"That sucks," Gabrielle said succinctly.

"Yeah, pretty much," Carrie repeated with a grin.

"All the elements aren't gathered," Prescott pointed out.

Ramirez frowned. "There's another one?"

"Water," everyone said at once.

"Great." He rubbed a hand over his neck. That was all he needed—another one coming into his city and wreaking havoc. Because these Guardians seemed to attract crime like bees to honey.

Rhys regarded Carrie. "Is that all?"

"Is that all?" Gabrielle squeaked, folding her legs under her to face him. "Isn't that enough? And why aren't you more upset? The universe is playing marionette with our lives, and all you, the biggest control freak in the room, can ask is if that's it?"

He lifted her hand and kissed the inside of her wrist. "It doesn't help to get worked up about things one can't control."

Her eyes narrowed. "Does that mean you're plotting something?"

"Would I do such a thing?"

"Yes," she said without hesitation.

A slight smile curled the corner of his lips.

Max sighed. "It's all downhill from here. They're going to start making out, and I'm going to gag."

Carrie whacked his shoulder.

"I agree." Willow stood and faced Max. "Thank you for including me in this discussion."

Max was silent a moment and then shrugged. "Fate decided by making you a Guardian. If I had my way, I'd keep you away."

Ramirez glanced at Carrie, who sighed and shook her head.

Willow didn't show any signs of taking offense, but Ramirez knew her, so he saw the stiff, defensive set of her shoulders and the way her hands flexed, as if ready to attack. To the rest, she just tipped her head and headed to the front door.

Hell. He stood to follow her, but he addressed the room first. "I'll have questions, you know."

"Of course you will, Inspector," Rhys said mildly. "Like it or not, by accepting her, you've become one of us."

Ramirez stalled and stared at the British man. He didn't know what to say to that.

Now wasn't the time to puzzle it out—he needed to catch up to Willow. He nodded at everyone, kissed Carrie on the cheek, despite Max's growl, and headed for his parked car.

Willow paced on the sidewalk next to it.

He glanced at the spot where Taylor was taken

down, offered a prayer for his partner, and went to face Willow.

She stopped when she saw him approach. He saw her swallow thickly before she said, with attitude, "Well?"

"You could have warned me."

She shrugged. "I thought the Band-Aid method was probably better."

He stuck his hands in his pockets. "You know I need time to digest this."

"Of course." Her voice was sad.

He sighed. "What do you expect, Willow? You've dropped a number of bombs on me, and I don't know how to react. This is all fantastical, a thing out of a sci-fi movie. I need time to adjust."

Her lips pinched together, but she nodded and moved to get in the car.

Taking her elbow, he spun her around and into his arms. "I'm not rejecting you. I'm just asking for a little time to get used to this."

"What if you can't?" She crossed her arms, closing herself off from him. "You said yourself you're a black-and-white kind of guy. What if this is too gray for you?"

"I'm not going to leave you," he said, cutting to the heart of the matter. "If you want me to trust you, you have to trust me, too."

"I told you I was a Guardian, didn't I?" She stepped out of his arms and slid into the car, a show of long, leather-encased legs and boots, before slamming the door.

He watched her as she sat there, looking so miserable that he wanted to take her into his arms and reassure her in every way he knew how. A week ago, he would have been worried she'd run before he could come to grips with everything she'd told him. Now he was confident she wasn't going anywhere. He had faith in her. Possibly more than she had in herself. She recognized they belonged together—she wouldn't abandon that, and she'd give him the time he needed to process.

So he went around to the driver's side and got in. He started the car, put it in gear, and took her home.

Chapter Thirty-three

Willow sat on her heels in front of the apple tree. The moon shined full and bright. Plants swayed to the night's music. The man she loved was headed toward her. All very romantic.

In theory at least. Willow couldn't appreciate any of it. Her future hung in the balance.

Sure, yesterday Rick had said that he had needed time to adjust to her being a Guardian, but what if he thought about it and realized he couldn't deal with it?

And then he'd sent her the text today, asking her to meet him. She hadn't expected that—not so soon. It couldn't be good. She watched him as he approached, trying to figure out what he was thinking, but his beautiful face was cloaked in mysterious shadows.

Well, she wouldn't let him just break it off with her. This was too important. She'd keep after him until he realized he couldn't live without her.

The two caught eyes before Ramirez knelt down in front of her. In his hands, he had what looked like a linen-wrapped plant. A consolation present as he sent her on her way?

Like hell he would. She lifted her chin. "Starsky—"

"Wait, before you say anything," he interrupted her gently, setting the package between them. "I have to tell you how beautiful you look."

"Thanks." After he'd texted her, she'd gone shopping for something special to wear, something that would bring him to his knees. She'd found this short green silk dress. It reminded her of something a wood sprite would wear. "I—"

"I need to ask you something," he said, interrupting her again.

She frowned. "What?"

"Will you show me?" He gazed at her steadily. "I had a taste of your powers when you confronted your father, but I want you to show me specifically. Do something just for me."

She blinked, shocked by the request. "Are you certain? Experiencing it means you won't be able to make excuses. You'll have to face the magic."

"I know."

Meaning he wanted to show her he accepted all of her. She wasn't dense—she got it. It didn't make her any less nervous, though. "Are you ready for this?"

Ramirez nodded, confident and sure.

"Pay close attention." One hand on the ground, her eyes never leaving his, she let *mù ch'i* flow through her arm and into the roots of the tree. She felt its warm pulse of life, its benign acceptance. She gave a bit of herself—of her light—and asked for a bit in return.

Holding up her other hand, a twig fell straight into it.

Thanking the tree, she resettled herself and held the twig up in front of her. She focused *mù ch'i,* letting it flow through her, out her fingertips and into the thin piece of wood. She felt the energy of the wood and lovingly encouraged it. Since the episode with her father, she'd felt her powers so differently. They seemed purer, more unadulterated. She'd tapped into what she always felt was missing. Elena was right—letting go of the anger had caused her to bloom. The same way the twig was now blooming.

Thin brown shoots were springing from the piece of wood, extending into delicate branches that sprouted tiny green leaves. She let her energy flow into it until it'd blossomed into a small tree. Not wanting to shock the plant, she withdrew her energy slowly.

For what seemed like forever, Ramirez stared in silence at the miniature tree in her hand. Then he held out his hand. "May I?"

Puzzled, she nodded and handed it over. He took it gently, taking care not to jostle it, as if he thought it'd be fragile or an illusion. He weighed it in his hand and rubbed the leaves. "Can this be potted?"

She frowned. "Excuse me?"

"This tree. Will it survive if it's potted?" Ramirez held it up and looked at the roots. "Or will it fade away?"

"Well, all things go at some point, but, no, it won't just die. My power doesn't create energy. It just helps it grow or die."

Ramirez nodded and set the little tree on the ground next to him. "Then we'll pot it so I can keep it on my desk at work. A living reminder of you."

Her heart expanded with warmth. "So you're really

okay with this? You don't find it weird at all that I can do this stuff?"

"No, it's definitely weird." He smiled ruefully. "But it's not like I'm a stranger to weird things. I got an early start with my grandmother."

"But isn't this"—she waved at the little tree—"more than what Elena even subjected you to?"

"Yes," he said without hesitation. "Has she ever given you her speech about fate?"

"Of course."

He nodded, taking her hand. "I've witnessed some strange things in my life, starting with Lita. But then, there was everything that's happened over the past year, with Gabrielle, and then Carrie."

Willow's gaze narrowed. "Did you really have to bring *her* into the conversation?"

He grinned. "There's nothing to be jealous of there."

"I know." She nodded reasonably, her fingers digging into the earth. "Except for her blondness, and her perkiness, and her intelligence, and—"

"There's nothing," Ramirez said with quiet force, lifting her hand and cradling it in his. "She's my friend. You're going to have to get over this irrational animosity."

Irrational—*ha*. But he was right. She'd decided to stay in San Francisco out of hope for a life with Ramirez, but also because she couldn't pass up the opportunity to learn about the other Guardians. It helped that Morgan had decided to stay there, as well. She and Weinberg had moved in together on their second date.

Willow looked down at her hand in Ramirez's. "So you're okay with my powers? And my past?"

"You have to promise you'll give up being an assassin."

"Done," she said without hesitation.

He didn't answer for a long, torturous moment. "Yes, I'm okay."

She held her breath, afraid to hope. "So...you're saying...?"

"I'm not saying this isn't difficult. I'm a pragmatic person." He held her close. "But Lita would claim that the universe was preparing me to accept you as my fate, because it's obvious everything through my life, and especially the past year, has chipped away at my disbelief."

"But my Guardianship is all that stuff on a grander scale."

"Because you're all those things on a grander scale." He tucked her hair back from her face. "I've never seen you wear your hair down. Except in bed."

She tried to think of some sassy comeback, but all she could do was blush like a schoolgirl.

She used his grip to yank him forward. "You realize you can't change your mind, right? Once you commit to me, it'll be forever. I'm not the type of woman who—"

His mouth came down on hers, shutting her up immediately. It occurred to her that she should push him back and get his answer, but it was too delicious to stop. She drank him in like it'd been years since she'd felt him, instead of twenty-four hours.

He nibbled her lips, a lick here and there. "I want forever with you, Willow."

Something in her chest melted. She rested her forehead against his. "Good, because that's what I want, too."

"I have something for you."

"I bet you do, Starsky."

He sat back, running a hand along her face, an amused smile lighting his eyes. "Something else. For the moment."

Before she could ask what, he lifted the linen-wrapped plant between them and held it out to her. The tree's energy suffused her the moment he set it in her hands. She looked up at Ramirez in question.

He nodded. "Open it."

Feeling around the base, she found the string that kept it bound, then tugged. The cloth fell away to reveal a small shrub.

A *tarata.*

"It's time you had roots." He pointed to the right. "We'll plant it right there."

She swallowed thickly, her hands gripping the plant. "We will?"

"Yes." He gazed at her levelly and spoke slowly, as though he wanted to make sure she got it. "Lita once told me you were entrusted to me, and it was the greatest challenge I'd ever know. I never back down from a challenge."

"That's what I am?" She wanted to will him to tell her what was in his heart. She needed to hear it, like a plant thirsted for water. So much so, she was tempted to send him a compulsion, even though she knew logically it wouldn't work on him. "*A challenge?*"

"Yes." His lips quirked. "But you're also a pleasure, an honor, and a joy."

"All that, huh?" she said lightly, feeling anything but.

He leaned forward, holding her firm. "You're also mine."

She melted on the inside. "You're mine, too."

"Of course I am." He stood and held out his hand. "Come on."

He led her to the spot he'd pointed out earlier. She hadn't noticed it before, but now she saw that a space had been cleared and a hole dug—the perfect spot for the *tarata*. They knelt on either side of the hole. He looked up at her, his cheekbones sharp in the moonlight. "So do we say a chant or something now?"

She laughed, feeling ridiculously light and happy all of a sudden. "Really, you're supposed to strip naked and do a little dance."

"Fantastic." He sat back on his heels. "Go ahead."

Slipping fingers under the thin straps of her dress, she shimmied the top down her torso. He stopped her, but not before the springtime air pebbled her nipples. She shivered, more from the way he looked at her than the cool San Francisco air.

"Not here." He tugged her top back up. "The neighbors will see, not to mention my grandmother is here."

"Then we better finish this fast so you can take me inside." She tipped her head. "I assume that's where you want me."

"Forever," he said, his entire being behind the word.

A feeling of warmth and comfort and belonging overcame her. A feeling she hadn't felt since her mom had been alive.

He lifted the *tarata* in his hands. "We'll do this together."

She nodded, unable to form the words for the thickness in her throat. Putting her hands on top of his, they guided it into the hole together.

"I wasn't sure it would grow in this climate," Ramirez said as they packed the dirt back into the hole.

"Then we'll make sure it thrives." Keeping her eyes on his, she took his hands and placed them on the soil. She covered them with hers and released a gentle flow of *mù ch'i* through him and into the ground to soothe the plant.

Willow felt the plant's sigh. She waited until its roots gripped firmly into the ground and its branches stretched out and up before she let *mù ch'i* trickle off and sat back.

Ramirez frowned at the plant. "I'm not sure I'll ever get used to that. What else can you do?"

"Take me inside and I'll show you."

His stunned look melted into heat. Without a word, he stood, hauled her over his shoulder, and carried her up the stairs to his home. She wanted to make a pithy remark, but she kept quiet all the way up to his room. She didn't even say anything when he stripped her, dropped her onto his bed, and crawled on top of her.

He kissed the tips of her breasts before making his way to her mouth. He looked down at her, so much emotion shining fiercely in his eyes. "I love you, Willow."

She didn't question it. She didn't fight it. Instead, for the first time in twenty years, she embraced it. Arms snaking around his neck, she held him close to her. Her voice was hoarse with emotion when she said, "I love you, too."

He kissed her, slowly and thoroughly. She was panting by the time he lifted his head. "In case it wasn't clear, this is your home from now on."

She nodded. "I think I got that."

"No arguments?"

"I'm many things, but I'm not an idiot."

"The only thing you are is mine." And then he kissed her again. And again.

And again.

THE DISH

Where authors give you the inside scoop!

From the desk of Kate Perry

In going through my desk, I found personal case notes from Rick Ramirez, the hero of TEMPTED BY FATE, Book Three in the Guardians of Destiny series...

From the files of Rick Ramirez,
Homicide Inspector,
San Francisco Police Department

There's something in the air, and it's not good.

In fact, its been stinking up the city for over a year—just about the time I first met Gabrielle Sansouci Chin, in fact. Although I was investigating a homicide at the time, so maybe I was inclined to be suspicious.

Gabrielle struck me odd, and it didn't help my image of her when she took up with Rhys Llewellyn. He may be an internationally respected businessman, but I can tell he has secrets—dark ones. So does Gabrielle, although as hard as I try I can't seem to uncover them.

As if that wasn't bad enough, my close

friend Carrie Woods got in over her head with the wrong people several months ago. Fortunately, she had her muscle-bound boyfriend Max Prescott to watch over her. That didn't stop her from getting mixed up in one of the strangest deaths I'd ever seen in my career as a homicide inspector for the SFPD.

And now this. Two dead bodies on a park bench.

It should be routine. It should be easy. But something is off—again—and I can't figure out what that is.

I hate that I can't work it out.

Worse: at the scene, I noticed a woman walking away. Or more correctly, I saw the gleam of her white-blond hair as she slipped into the night. The murderer? Highly likely. Which makes the feeling in my gut way more complicated.

Complicated? Right. Screwed up is more like it. Because I want to chase her down, and not to question her about the homicide. Let's just say when I picture putting cuffs on her, it's in less than a professional capacity.

A homicide inspector and the chief suspect in more than one murder. A match made in hell…

RR

I hope you enjoy Ramirez and TEMPTED BY FATE! Don't forget to check out the equally engaging (and hot) heroes in the other Guardians of Destiny books. And drop by www.kateperry.com to say hi—I'd love to hear from you.

Kate Perry

♥ ♥ ♥ ♥ ♥ ♥ ♥ ♥ ♥ ♥ ♥ ♥ ♥ ♥ ♥

From the desk of Laurel McKee

Dear Reader,

A while back, I read a book by Paul Collins called *Sixpence House: Lost in a Town of Books*, that stated that a writer's characters can no more take over a story than an eggplant can take over a kitchen. I had to laugh at the image of a bossy eggplant marching into my kitchen (and I sort of wish it *could* take over in there, because I'm a terrible cook), but I have to disagree about the characters.

Sometimes we're lucky enough to meet a character who comes so vividly to life in our imagination that their story *must* be told—and they insist it has to be told *their* way! One such character for me was Lady Anna Blacknall.

Anna was the sister of Eliza Blacknall, the heroine of my first "Daughters of Erin" book, COUNTESS OF SCANDAL. When I started writing that first novel, I knew Anna would have her own story, but I wasn't sure yet what it would be. Then I really "met" her, and she was so many things that I wish I could be: blond, tall, extroverted, a good card player. Even worse—she was really *nice*. She practically sat down by my desk and told me what her story would be. I just had to find the right hero for her, and he presented himself as the dark, strong, mysterious Duke of Adair. A good match for the passionate and rebellious Anna, and the two of them were more than a match for me. She told me their love story, and I just had to keep up and write it all down just as she wanted.

Writing DUCHESS OF SIN was a wild ride, and I was so sorry to say good-bye to Anna and Conlan at the end! (Luckily we'll see them again in the third book, LADY OF SEDUCTION. You can also find excerpts and historical background on the books at my website http://laurelmckee.net.)

I never could have kept up with Anna and her Duke without lots of tea and sugary desserts to see me through. Since these books are set in Ireland, writing them and picturing that country made me crave some of my grandmother's old recipes. This is one of my favorites: Sticky Toffee Pudding. It's a great inspiration!

Ingredients:

- 1 cup plus 1 tbsp all-purpose flour
- 1 tsp baking powder
- ¾ cup pitted dates
- 1 ¼ cups boiling water
- 1 tsp baking soda
- ¼ cup unsalted butter, softened
- ¾ cup sugar
- 1 large egg, lightly beaten
- 1 tsp vanilla

Toffee Sauce:

- ½ cup unsalted butter
- ½ cup heavy cream
- 1 cup packed light brown sugar
- 1 cup heavy cream, whipped

Preheat oven to 350 degrees. Butter a 10-inch round or square baking dish. Sift flour and baking powder onto a sheet of waxed paper. Chop the dates fine. Place in a small bowl and add boiling water and baking soda; set aside. Beat the butter and sugar until light and fluffy. Add egg and vanilla; beat until blended. Gradually beat in the flour mixture. Add date mixture to the batter and fold until blended with a rubber spatula. Pour into the prepared baking dish. Bake until pudding is set and firm on top, about 35 minutes. Remove from oven to a wire rack.

Sauce: Combine butter, cream, and brown sugar in a small, heavy saucepan; heat to boiling, stirring constantly. Boil gently over medium low heat until mixture is thickened, about 8 minutes. Preheat broiler. Spoon about 1/3 cup of the sauce over the pudding. Spread evenly on top. Place pudding under the broiler until the topping is bubbly, about 1 minute. Serve immediately, spooned into dessert bowls. Drizzle with remaining toffee sauce and top with a spoonful of whipped cream.

Enjoy!

Laurel McKee

Want to know more about romances at
Grand Central Publishing and Forever?
Get the scoop online!

GRAND CENTRAL PUBLISHING'S
ROMANCE HOMEPAGE

Visit us at www.hachettebookgroup.com/romance
for all the latest news, reviews, and chapter excerpts!

NEW AND UPCOMING TITLES

Each month we feature our new titles
and reader favorites.

CONTESTS AND GIVEAWAYS

We give away galleys, autographed copies,
and all kinds of fun stuff.

AUTHOR INFO

You'll find bios, articles, and links to personal
websites for all your favorite authors—and
so much more!

THE BUZZ

Sign up for our monthly romance newsletter,
and be the first to read all about it!

VISIT US ONLINE

@ WWW.HACHETTEBOOKGROUP.COM.

AT THE HACHETTE BOOK GROUP WEB SITE YOU'LL FIND:

CHAPTER EXCERPTS FROM SELECTED NEW RELEASES

•

ORIGINAL AUTHOR AND EDITOR ARTICLES

•

AUDIO EXCERPTS

•

BESTSELLER NEWS

•

ELECTRONIC NEWSLETTERS

•

AUTHOR TOUR INFORMATION

•

CONTESTS, QUIZZES, AND POLLS

•

FUN, QUIRKY RECOMMENDATION CENTER

•

PLUS MUCH MORE!

into the Hall of Justice. There was a short line of people waiting to get through the metal detector. He bypassed the line and flashed his badge.

The guard nodded at him. "Afternoon, Inspector."

Focused, he returned the nod and went down the hall to the elevators. He waited an interminable period of time before one arrived. Pressing the button, he waited impatiently for the ancient car to take him down to the basement.

Normally, he'd use the QPRL database to look up the item number for the picture, fill out the requisite request slip, and check out the piece of evidence. But he didn't want to chance running into Taylor—not with him so suspicious already. His partner would demand to know what the deal was with the photo, and Ramirez wasn't ready to field those questions. So he was going directly to the source.

Ramirez entered the property room, straight back into the restricted police-only area behind the glass door to the right. He recognized the officer on duty. They'd crossed paths a number of times, the last being when the officer nearly destroyed a crime scene he'd stumbled on. "Jenkins, so this is where they've hidden you."

When Jenkins grinned, he looked like Santa Claus, minus the long white beard. "Blew my knee out skiing. Getting old, Inspector. Should leave sports like that to you young fellows."

More than likely he'd finally screwed up one too many times. Only burnouts and screwups ended up doing time in the property room.

"What can I do for you?" the officer asked. "You need access to evidence from a case you're working on?"

"No, I have a favor to ask."

"It's yours," Max said without hesitation.

Ramirez couldn't help but smile. "You don't want to know what it is?"

"You wouldn't ask if it wasn't important. And after everything you've done for Carrie, I'd be an asshole if I didn't help you."

Ramirez had always admired Prescott. The man bucked all the stereotypes of someone born to extreme wealth and privilege. "I need help finding someone."

"Who is it?"

"I don't know." He stopped at a red light, scowling into the distance.

"Where does he work? What does he do? Do you have a license plate number for him?"

Gritting his teeth, Ramirez shook his head. "I have nothing."

"I hate to point this out, but if you can't give me any information on him at all, it'll be difficult to locate him."

"I think I can get you a picture." *Hopefully.*

"That would work. Want to meet me at my place?"

"This evening. I'll have a—" What was Willow? Lita called her *his woman*. She seemed like more, yet not even that at the same time. "I'll have a friend with me."

"Hmm."

Max's hum was loaded, but Ramirez didn't bother trying to decipher what it meant. He had other things to worry about, like finding that picture of Willow's Bad Man. "I'll call when I'm on my way over."

"See you."

Rick hung up and pulled into one of the white zones in front of the police station. Locking his car, he walked

"Yes. It's a recently opened case, early this morning." He leaned over the giant ledger sitting on the table and signed in. "I'll need everything that was brought in."

Jenkins's eyes lit as he handed over a request slip. "Oh, you mean the one with all the lingerie."

"Lingerie," he repeated flatly as he wrote down the case number on the slip.

"Yeah. Oh, boy, did I have fun checking that stuff in." He rubbed his hands together. "Wait here and I'll go get it."

Jenkins came back with a medium-sized box. He set it on the table and waved at it. "Have at it."

Ramirez nodded. One by one, he extracted the tagged items and set them aside. Laptop. Printouts of information on the three victims. The dossier Willow had on him, which made his teeth clench. A knife with flecks of what looked like wood stuck to the blade.

Still, in his gut, he knew she wasn't lying when she told him she hadn't killed those men. He had no reason to trust her—he was absolutely positive she wasn't being up-front with him about other things—but *that* he believed.

"I left the box with all the clothes in back." Jenkins chuckled. "What a thrill that was. My job isn't usually that fun."

Ramirez leveled his gaze on him.

"I've never seen underwear like that." Jenkins held his hands up like he was holding something by the edges. "Tiny froufrou stuff, like in those Frederick's of Hollywood catalogues. I never knew women actually wore stuff like that. My old lady could outfit a schooner with the panties she wears."

Ramirez clenched his jaw, trying not to think about the men in his unit handling Willow's intimate things. He was going to buy her all new underwear.

"Crazy that she had a file on you, huh?" Jenkins nudged him with a wink. "But then, if she came after me wearing froufrou panties, I might be willing to let her take me down."

The man didn't know who he was insulting. He was flirting with a black eye. How could he possibly know that the Homicide inspector in charge of the investigation had fallen for the suspect? All the same, Ramirez gave him the flat look that always cowed people into cooperation, and it worked. Jenkins smiled uncomfortably and took a step back.

"Guess I'll get back to tending the gate. Let me know if you need anything else, Inspector."

"Thank you." Ramirez waited until the man retreated to his magazine to pick up a picture.

Tattered like it'd been handled a lot, this one was of a man, most likely Willow's Bad Man. He had dark hair, light eyes, and a medium build. He wore casual clothes—expensive casual clothes—punctuated by a Rolex crusted discreetly with diamonds. His mouth was smiling, but his eyes were cold, almost snakelike. There was something there that wasn't to be trusted. He looked like he would eat his young for breakfast.

Something around the eyes looked vaguely familiar, and Ramirez took a closer look. Had he seen this guy before? If he was a criminal, the way Willow claimed, it was possible he'd seen some sort of bulletin on him.

He set the photo aside and quickly rifled through the rest of the box. He didn't find anything noteworthy, until